MIND MELTDOWN

More deadly than a radioactive cloud wafting out of Russia. More unstoppable than the fiercest forces of nature. More threatening than any weapon in the Soviet and U.S. arsenals. And more feared by both the Russians and Americans than even each other.

He's a little man with big brown eyes. Eyes that can make the most beautiful and frigid woman on earth hot to satisfy his insatiable appetite for sex. Eyes that can reduce the most powerful men in government to mere slaves to satisfy his limitless hunger for vengeance. Eyes that do not even blink when Remo and Chiun come after him—as he pits these two great warriors against each other in a struggle that only he can win and all the world will lose. . . .

___THE DESTROYER #67___

LOOK INTO MY EYES

The Destroyer

LOOK INTO MY EYES

WARREN MURPHY & RICHARD SAPIR

A SIGNET BOOK

NEW AMERICAN LIBRARY

PUBLISHER'S NOTE

This novel is a work of fiction. Names, characters, places, and incidents either are the product of the author's imagination or are used fictitiously, and any resemblance to actual persons, living or dead, events, or locales is entirely coincidental.

NAL BOOKS ARE AVAILABLE AT QUANTITY DISCOUNTS WHEN USED TO PROMOTE PRODUCTS OR SERVICES. FOR INFORMATION PLEASE WRITE TO PREMIUM MARKETING DIVISION, NEW AMERICAN LIBRARY, 1633 BROADWAY, NEW YORK, NEW YORK 10019.

SIGNET TRADEMARK REG. U.S. PAT. OFF. AND FOREIGN COUNTRIES
REGISTERED TRADEMARK—MARCA REGISTRADA
HECHO EN CHICAGO, U.S.A.

SIGNET, SIGNET CLASSIC, MENTOR, ONYX, PLUME, MERIDIAN and NAL BOOKS are published by New American Library, 1633 Broadway, New York, New York 10019

First Printing, January, 1987

1 2 3 4 5 6 7 8 9

PRINTED IN THE UNITED STATES OF AMERICA

For Martha Goodman and
her associate Donna Ahrend of The Right Word,
who do so much more than type

It was better than being in Afghanistan. In Afghanistan the bandits would shoot you from ambush, or if they captured you, they would cut you into pieces very slowly. Sometimes their women did it with their cooking tools.

Sometimes the officers would throw you under the treads of a tank if they thought you might desert. Afghanistan was where you died horribly.

And so Sergeant Yuri Gorov did not find duty in Siberia a burden, nor did he question his strange orders. He was to allow no one, under any circumstances, to leave the small town he and his division surrounded. He was to beg first and then to plead with anyone trying to leave, and if that failed, he was to call an officer, and if that did not work, he was to shoot the person, making sure the person did not leave alive.

Shooting escaping prisoners was not strange. What was strange was that supposedly no one in the village was a prisoner. Even stranger was the notion that anyone might want to escape.

Yuri and his platoon had driven into the village once to dig a sewer for one of the residents. For Siberia, it was a very nice village, and one house was particularly nice. The house was two stories high, and only one family lived in it. There were three color television sets. Wondrous American and Japanese appliances filled the kitchen. Carpets from Persia, and lamps from Germany, and wall switches that turned on the lights every time. And the rooms were the size of several apartments combined.

There was red meat in the refrigerator and fruits from all over the world, and whiskey, wine, and cognac in a little closet.

And toilets, with soft seats, that flushed every time, and ceilings that had no cracks in them. It was a marvel of a house, and every house in the village seemed to be almost as glorious.

Officers noticed the men dawdling in the house instead of just using the toilets, and ordered the house off limits. But everyone had seen the enormous luxury of this house and sensed the grandeur of this village.

It was heaven on earth. And under no circumstances were the soldiers posted outside the village to let anyone leave alive.

To this end, four soldiers were posted outside for every person inside. One of the old-timers of the division claimed the people inside did witchcraft. But a recruit pointed out he had seen high-ranking KGB officers and scientists enter. He knew they were scientists because one stopped to talk to him once. The KGB and scientists certainly would not countenance witchcraft.

But a recruit from Moscow said he thought he knew what this village did. Back home in Moscow he would sometimes meet visitors from the West who asked him about Russia's parapsychology experiments.

"What is parapsychology?" asked Yuri. He had never heard of such a thing, and neither had the others in the barracks.

"We are supposed to be famous for it, according to this American woman I met."

"Did you sleep with her?" a corporal asked of the Moscow recruit.

"Shhh," said the others.

"Let him talk," said Yuri Gorov.

"She told me," said the Moscow recruit, "that we have done more experiments in parapsychology than anyone else on earth. There are books on some of our experiments printed openly in the West, and there is a center for it here in Siberia. I think this village is the center.''

"But what is this parapsychology?" asked Yuri.

"Seeing things that aren't there. Like halos over people's heads. Or having their minds go back into past lives. Witchcraft things.''

"No wonder they would keep a thing like that secret. Assuming, of course, they were doing those things.''

"Everything with the human mind that you can imagine is done there. Mind reading, mind bending, everything.''

"I don't believe it," said Yuri. "We would not do such things.''

"I bet someone is reading your mind right now.''

"If that were so, the KGB would use it already.''

"I bet they do, but they only use it on important people,'' said the recruit.

"Nonsense," said Yuri. "Those things don't exist.''

"Have you ever had a message and known who it was from before you got it? Have you ever had a feeling that something bad was going to happen before it happened? Have you ever known you were going to win something before you won it?''

"Those are just hunches," said Yuri.

"Those are the parts of your mind that parapsychology deals with," said the Moscow recruit. "And that village we surround is filled with people who experiment in such things. I'm right.''

"I'd rather know if you slept with the American woman.''

"Of course I did," said the Moscow recruit.

"Is it true that they do strange things?" asked another. As in all barracks, sex was always a major interest.

"Yes, they enjoy it," said the Moscow recruit. Everyone laughed.

And then one night, when a gentle chill enveloped the rich land, a man in an expensive Western suit came walking up the road from the village muttering to himself. He was about five-foot-seven and walked in a splay-foot fashion, as though he couldn't care less where his feet went. He was muttering something quite furiously.

"Excuse me, sir," said Sergeant Gorov. "You can't come through here."

The man ignored him.

"Left alone. Left alone. I want to be left alone," said the man. He had soft, woeful brown eyes and a collapsed bag of a face that looked as though he was perpetually tasting something unpleasant. He wore gold-rimmed eyeglasses.

"Sir, you must stop," said Yuri. He stepped in front of the shorter man.

The man tried to walk through him, then with the physical contact realized where he was.

"You can't go any farther," said Yuri. "It's not allowed."

"Nothing is allowed," said the man. "It never is. Nothing."

"I cannot let you pass."

"You cannot. He cannot. She cannot. Everybody cannot. What is the matter?" said the man, raising his arms toward the dark Siberian sky.

"You'll have to turn around."

"And what if I told you no? The simple, beautiful, exquisite word no. That single syllable that comes off the tongue like sunshine in a winter hell."

"Look, mister. I don't want to shoot you. Please go back," said Yuri.

"Don't worry, you're not going to shoot me. Don't make such a big deal already," said the man. He put his hands in his pockets. He did not turn around.

Yuri yelled back to the little guard post.

"Sir, comrade refuses orders to turn back."

An officer drinking tea and ogling a magazine filled with seminude women yelled back:

"Tell him you'll shoot."

"I did."

"Then shoot," said the officer.

"Please," said Yuri to the man with the sad brown eyes.

The man laughed.

With trembling hands Yuri raised the Kalishnikov and put it to the man's head. No matter what was said in basic training, every soldier knew many men never fired their rifles in combat. He had always suspected he would be one of those. In combat he could maybe get away with it. But here, if he didn't fire, it would mean being sent to Afghanistan for sure. It was either this poor fellow or himself. And the man didn't seem to be stopping.

Yuri leveled the gun at the sad brown eyes.

Better you than me, he thought. He hoped he wouldn't have to look at the body. He hoped that the blood would not spray too much. He hoped that he would someday be able to forget what he had done. But if he pulled the trigger at least there would be a someday. If he went to Afghanistan, there wouldn't be. Yuri felt his finger slick with sweat against the trigger.

And then his mother was talking to him. His saintly mother was standing right in front of him, talking ever so softly and reasonably, telling him to put down his gun and not shoot her.

"Mother, what are you doing here in Siberia?"

"Don't believe everything you hear or see. I'm here. What are you going to do, shoot your own mother?"

"No, never."

"Put down the gun," said his mother.

But that was unnecessary. Yuri was already lowering the gun. And the man with the sad brown eyes was gone.

"Mama, have you seen a little guy with brown eyes?"

"He went back to the village. Go relax."

Yuri looked down the road. It stretched a mile toward the village, with no hills or bushes where anyone could hide. The little fellow had disappeared. He looked behind him, to see if the little fellow had somehow snuck by. But that road was empty also. It was quiet and empty, and the still, chill night made clouds of every breath, and the man was not there. Only his gray-haired mother, hands gnarled from arthritis, waving to him as she passed the guard post.

The officer ran out through the door and put his pistol to Yuri's mother's head. Yuri raised his rifle. This he could kill for. This he had to kill for.

He fired a dozen automatic rounds with his Kalishnikov, plastering the wooden guard post with pieces of the second lieutenant and the magazine he had been reading.

The next day at the board of inquiry, Yuri explained he couldn't help himself. He had a right to defend his mother. The lieutenant was going to kill her.

Strangely, every officer seemed to understand, even though Yuri admitted tearfully (because now he was sure he was going to be shot) that his mother had been dead for four years.

"All right. Don't worry. What did the man say to you? Remember everything," ordered the KGB commandant assigned to the village area.

"But I shot my commanding officer."

"Doesn't matter. What did Rabinowitz say?"

"His name was Rabinowitz, sir?"

"Yes. What did he say?"

"He said he wanted to be left alone."

"Anything else?"

"He said he was sure I wouldn't shoot him. He seemed happy to say the word no. He made such an awful big thing of it."

"Anything else?"

"That's all I remember. I had to shoot the lieutenant. Wouldn't you if your commander was going to kill your mother?"

"No. I'm KGB. But never mind about shooting your officer. What did your mother say?"

"She told me not to shoot."

"Anything else?"

"She said don't believe everything you see. And things like that."

"Did she say where she was going?"

"She's been dead four years," sobed Yuri.

"Never mind that. Did she say where she was going?"

"No."

"She didn't mention anything about Israel?"

"Why would she? She's not—wasn't—a Jew."

"Yes. Of course," said the KGB commandant.

There was one advantage the commandant saw. They were already at the parapsychology village and the sergeant would not have to be sent here to relive his experiences perfectly. Rabinowitz might have said something that would lead them to him again, and then it was just a matter of giving Rabinowitz whatever he wanted. Heads were going to roll for this one and it was not going to be some poor little sergeant in the regular army.

Someone had lost Vassily Rabinowitz, and there would have to be some pretty good answers all the way to the Politburo.

The picture of the sad-eyed, middle-aged man was sent to every KGB unit in the Soviet Union and especially to border countries of the Eastern bloc. The instructions were strange. No one was to try to stop Vassily Rabinowitz. They were only to report his presence to Moscow, unless Rabinowitz was spotted near any border to the West. Then without talking to the man, without looking into his eyes, they were to shoot him.

The secret police of East Germany, Poland, Albania, and Rumania found the next message totally confusing. They were to report to Moscow the sighting by any guard at any post of anyone strange, such as a relative who had been dead for many years, or a close friend.

"Appearing where?" the satellite police asked.

"Anywhere they shouldn't," answered the Moscow KGB.

There were questions, too, about how the dead could appear.

And the answer was that they really didn't but the guards would be sure they had.

In Moscow, a Rabinowitz desk was set up. It had three functions. First to get him back, and second to find out who had failed to give him what he wanted. The third objective was to get him what he wanted.

Even as it tracked Rabinowitz's route away from the parapsychology village, the inquiry revealed a problem that should have been worked out.

The officer assigned personally to Rabinowitz, who knew his life was at stake, explained it.

"When he wanted women, we gave him women. We gave him blond women and dark-eyed women. We gave him African women and South American women. We gave him women from the Middle East and women from the Middle West. Kurds and Koreans did we supply," came the statement.

"And what was his reaction?"

"He said we never came up with the right one."

"And who was the right one?"

"The one we hadn't come up with."

Rabinowitz had been given a catalog from Neiman-Marcus, a great American department store, and told to mark off the items he wanted and they would be delivered. Exotic foodstuffs, hams and smoked salmon and tropical fruits by the barrel, rotted in his basement. Military priority for any item destined for Rabinowitz had been declared in four major defense command zones. In a world of luxury, Rabinowitz had lived in the highest luxury.

Every morning, noon, and evening someone from the KGB command came to his home or laboratory to ask him what he wanted. And when they weren't doing that, generals and commissars were phoning him personally to ask if they could do favors for him. He had lots of friends in high places, people who needed him and would not take his loss lightly.

Even though the KGB commandant of that village could prove beyond any doubt he had given Rabinowitz everything a human being could want, someone was going to have to pay. And the price would be death.

In growing horror, Moscow command tracked the route of the strange incidents, from east to west.

A conductor on a train headed west through Kazan, south of Moscow, was demanding a traveling pass when he realized he was talking to his pet dog. He reported this strange incident when he got home to Kuybyshev because there he found his pet had been at home all the time. Therefore he was suffering some form of mental breakdown; therefore he was due a vacation. The conductor was surprised that it was not the hospital board that examined him but the KGB.

In Kiev, an Aeroflot stewardess confessed she had allowed her favorite uncle onto the airplane without a ticket. She confessed her deed because she was sure she was going crazy; she had seated the favorite uncle twice on the same flight, both in the luxurious rear cabin and in the crammed front seats. She had walked back and forth three times to confirm that he was sitting in both seats.

The uncle who got off in Warsaw was the one she would have bet was the real one. But when the one she thought was the impostor went to bed with her aunt, she was sure she was going crazy.

And then from a bus in Prague, the Rabinowitz desk got their first breakthrough.

A passenger was asking questions about Berlin. This was not unusual, except a fight occurred on the bus where several people tried to take care of him, thinking he was a close relative. Then the bus driver suffered a migraine headache. He told all the passengers they would have to wait half an hour or so while he wished he were dead; then the migraine would pass.

But the passenger with the multiple family ties went to the front of the bus, spoke to the driver, and the driver drove off singing, his headache gone. Of course the driver changed his route to drive further west, closer to Berlin. But no one minded. After all, who would deny such a small thing to his closest relative?

By the time Rabinowitz reached Berlin, the city with the wall to keep in all the people of the East who might want to leave the liberated and progressive countries for the decadent West, fourteen specially selected KGB units were waiting for him. The East German guards were dismissed from their posts and Russians stood five deep, guns at the ready.

But these were not just any Russians or any KGB officers. Every one of them had been carefully selected to be willing to shoot his closest relative if that relative tried to make it to the West.

"Let us warn you, you will only think you are shooting your mother and your brother and your favorite pet. Your mind will not be your own. Don't trust it. What you will shoot is the greatest danger that could befall Russia. Of course, if that greatest danger chooses to go back home, give him anything he wants. Anything. If he wants to ride on your back all the way to Moscow, get on your hands and knees."

"Hello, Vassily," said the deputy commander of the KGB at the access point the Americans called Checkpoint Charlie. A tired man of five-foot-seven with sad brown eyes trudged wearily to the last gate to the West. Backing up the deputy commander were enough ruthless, vicious men to clean out half of Berlin. He didn't know if they frightened Rabinowitz but they certainly terrified him.

The deputy commander, Krimenko, was in his seventies and had risen so high not because of ruthlessness, usually a requirement for the policemen of a police state, but because of his exceptional judgment. Krimenko had been given this job personally by the premier.

"I want him back. And if we don't get him back, no one else can have him. He's got to be with us, or dead."

"I understand. I've used him myself."

"I am not talking about personal things. I am talking about international things. I am talking about our survival as a nation. We cannot let the West get its hands on him."

"I understand that too," Krimenko had said.

And what he wanted now most of all at this bridge between East and West, where exchanges of spies took place, was a little reasoning talk with Vassily Rabinowitz.

And he did something quite shrewd. He pretended a greater weakness than he really had. Because Rabinowitz had no way of knowing his special talents and powers might be of no use at this bridge, that even if he succeeded in what he did so well, he would still be dead if he tried to leave.

"Look, my friend," said Krimenko. "I know I can't stop you. And since I can't stop you, maybe you will tell me something before you leave."

"Will you people never leave me alone?" said Rabinowitz.

"Certainly. Just tell me, Vassily, if we are ready to give you everything, anything you want, why on earth do you have to leave? What is there to leave for?"

"Do you really want to know?"

"I am not here with an army at my back for my health," said Krimenko. He was careful to show Rabinowitz he was making no threatening moves. He knew Rabinowitz operated so quickly the average human mind could not keep up with him.

He had first met this wizard of the mind when he had a vicious toothache and was complaining that he did not want to undergo the pain of Russian dentistry so late in his life. A Politburo member had told him about Vassily Rabinowitz. He had flown to the special village in Siberia and had gotten an immediate appointment along with a warning not to bother the hypnotist with questions.

"Is he just a hypnotist? I have been to hypnotists. They don't work with me," Krimenko had said.

"Just go in, state your problem, and leave."

"I am sorry I came so far just for a hypnotist," Krimenko had said.

Rabinowitz was sitting in an armchair by the window, reading a prohibited American magazine. It was one famous for its artistic photographs of nude women. Rabinowitz had a large black crayon. He was checking off the women. He hardly looked up.

"Yes," he called out.

"I have a bad tooth. Incredible pain. It's abscessed and rotting."

"Okay, and I'd like the redhead first, an Oriental maybe at the end of the month. Sometimes I like to stay with the redheads." He handed the magazine to Kimenko and went back to his window.

"What am I supposed to do with this?"

"Hand it to the man at the door. Those are who I want today."

"But what about my toothache?" asked Krimenko.

"What toothache?" asked Rabinowitz. He was smiling. Krimenko reached for his jaw. Blessedly, it was free of pain. Just like that.

"How did you do it?"

"That's why I'm here. The redhead first, please."

"This is wonderful," said Krimenko.

"You can eat candy on it right away. Won't hurt you. But I'd have it pulled if I were you. The abscess can kill you. Don't worry about Russian dentists. No pain. You won't feel a thing. If you want, I can make you have an orgasm while the dentist is butchering your mouth. Some people like that," Rabinowitz had said.

He had looked so fresh there in that room, and so tired now coming to the bridge. Krimenko actually felt sorry for him.

"You want to know what I want? I want you people to get out of the way."

"I would do that, but these men won't. Come, let us just talk somewhere. Let us find a café, and we will talk. Just a bit. Then you can leave."

Shots rang out in Krimenko's ears. The men behind him were firing. Ugly sharp bits of pavement ricocheted up from where Rabinowitz was standing. Rabinowitz fell and his body continued to be riddled by automatic fire, bullets shredding it like a Chinese cleaver. And then another Rabinowitz appeared and he too was shot down, and Krimenko felt the sharp, hot, burning slug hit his back and throw him to the pavement, where he became so much shredded meat on the bridge where East and West trade spies.

Less than a day later, in New York City's Kennedy Airport, a customs officer saw the strangest man standing at his counter.

Here was a Russian-sounding fellow without a passport, unshaved and looking very seedy, and smiling at Luke Sanders as though he were going to let him through.

"You don't have a passport. You don't have identification and you're a Russian to boot. So I'm going to have to hold you, fella."

"Nonsense, son. Here's my passport. You know me," said the man, and sure enough, Luke knew him. He was his brother. He asked his brother what he was doing coming in on a German flight, when Luke thought he was back home in Amarillo, Texas.

"I've come to get a bialy and maybe a shmear of cream cheese," said Luke's brother.

"What's a bialy?" asked Luke.

"It's a Jewish roll. And I want one."

"Then you've come to the right city," said Luke, who tried to find out where his brother was staying in New York because he sure as shootin' wanted to meet him that night. He passed him through with a handshake, a laugh, and a hug.

"Not so tight on the hug, already," said Luke's brother.

In Moscow Krimenko's death was not the disaster. Nor were the deaths of twenty-two other KGB officers. The real disaster was that none of the bodies picked up on the bridge was Vassily Rabinowitz.

The question that haunted everyone was, what if the Americans should get hold of him? There was even talk of launching a first nuclear strike immediately. Better to take a chance on survival than to be sure of losing.

But cooler heads prevailed. First, Russia had not been able to conquer the world using Vassily, although he was incredibly useful in training people for so many special missions.

Nor was there any guarantee that the Americans would be able to capture him and use him.

The only, and therefore the best, solution was to alert every agent in America to be on the lookout for him. Every mole, every counterintelligence operator, every secret police operative was to divert all efforts to the finding of that man.

And most important of all, America was not to know what might be within its borders. No one who looked for Vassily Rabinowitz, late of the Soviet Union, would know why he was looking.

Someone mentioned the risk of such a blatant, all-out effort. The Americans were sure to spot the activity. How many agents would be risked? How many moles who had worked so hard to penetrate into the belly of the American beast might expose themselves to capture? Just what was Moscow willing to pay to stop America from getting Rabinowitz?

And the men who had seen him work answered, "Everything."

2

His name was Remo and he couldn't count the number of men he had killed, nor did he want to start. Counting was for people who thought numbers meant something. Counting was for pepole who didn't understand what they were doing so they needed numbers to reassure themselves they were doing well.

Counting was for people who wouldn't know which side won if there wasn't a score. In Remo's game he always knew who won.

He was going to kill three men who could count. They could count transistors and microchips and all the electronic devices that kept them invulnerable to surveillance. They could count on their lawyers who had made them invulnerable to conviction. They could count on all the people they bought along their way, and they could count on the American drug users to make them rich.

Perhaps the only thing they couldn't count was all the money they had made, hundreds of millions of dollars. They controlled two or three South American governments where coca leaves grew and were made into the white crystals Americans liked to suck into their noses to rot out what was left of their brains after all the other chemicals had gotten to them.

Remo wasn't counting. He sensed the strong cold of the damp clouds and the harsh wind pressing his body against the metal. He could smell the special chemicals used to polish the metal he pressed his body into, could feel the metal carry the vibrations of the engine, and was prepared for the only real danger. If the pilot should dive suddenly and Remo allowed an air current between him and the roof of the plane, he would be sheared off like confetti and plunge thirteen thousand feet to the jungle floor below the luxury Lear jet.

The scant oxygen at those heights was more than enough for him, although if he needed to he could always put a hole in the airtight skin of the jet, forcing the pilot to dive lower, where his passengers could breathe without the use of oxygen masks.

That wasn't necessary. There was more than enough oxygen at these heights if the body used it properly, but people tended to use it like drunks, burning vast quantities in uncontrolled gulps. People did not know their bodies, did not understand the powers they were capable of but refused to allow to develop.

It was this loss of balanced use of oxygen that made people pant from running, come up after only a minute underwater, three at the most, and hold their breath when frightened.

Scientists had yet to discover that holding of the breath when frightened was a weak attempt to energize the body for flight. It didn't work because the only breathing that unlocked the power of humans was controlled breathing, giving the process up to the rhythms of the universe and in so doing becoming part of all its powers. One didn't fight gravity or wind or weight, one worked with them, like a piece pressured into the roof of the cabin of a Lear jet at thirteen thousand feet, closer than the paint that had only been sprayed on, closer than the wax that had only been spread on. The controlled body made itself one with the alloyed metal of the jet, and if Remo did not allow any air to disrupt the bond, he would remain attached tighter than a rivet.

It was the only way to break into the protected realm of Guenther Largos Diaz of Peru, Colombia, and Palm Beach.

Guenther had done wonderful things for himself with the profits from the coca plant. He had made friends everywhere, this man who could count. He helped supply the communist guerrillas, and in exchange they guarded his fields. He helped finance retirement programs for government troops and now they acted as his stevedores.

And in those American centers where cocaine was distributed, Guenther Largos Diaz had played havoc just as easily with the policemen earning twenty-five thousand dollars a year as he did with policemen earning five thousand dollars in pesos.

This handsome South American with a German mother and a Spanish father knew how to bribe, knew, as they said south of the border, how to reach a man's soul. He had every man's price, and so, after he had met the prices of many men, it was decided that it was no use losing more good men to Guenther Largos Diaz. He was so good, so competent, that he would have to die.

Remo felt the plane change pitch. It was going to land. It came down out of the sticky, wet, cold clouds into the sharp air of the Andes and continued to descend. At this height he could not tell what country was below them. He saw a river sparkling like tinsel under the sun off to the east, but he had no idea what river it was.

He didn't care. Of course, if he didn't know where he was, there might be a problem getting back. But he was sure someone in the plane would know. The trick was not to kill that person. Remo didn't want to be left with a bunch of peasants who thought wherever they were was the center of the world and knew only vaguely how to get outside. Also, he didn't want to walk through hundreds of miles of jungle.

He had to remind himself not to lose concentration, because the moment his mind and body separated, so would he, from the plane.

The airstrip was surprisingly modern for such a backward-looking area. There were no major roads leading to this strip, just small tree-lined single-lane asphalt strips. And yet the runway could accommodate big jets, and when the wheels touched down in that screaming burst of rubber, Remo could see sensors implanted into the strip every ten yards. Moreover, the runway was dyed a color that most human eyes would not recognize as asphalt from above, a dark color that sparkled in the sun so the landing strip looked like part of a river that began nowhere and ended in a bunch of trees. The control tower looked like a pile of rocks.

Remo did not know how upstairs knew this was head-quarters. He didn't understand how computers worked or how the minds of people who understood computers worked.

But when someone went to the trouble of disguising the place, someone who was vastly shrewd, then the place had to be his real home.

As it was said in the histories of Sinanju, home is where a person feels safe, and a man like Guenther Largos Diaz could never feel safe in one of his exposed mansions.

From the disguised control tower, people came running, pointing guns and yelling. The door to the jet swung open and someone beneath Remo waved the guards back.

"What's going on?" came a voice from inside the cabin.

"I don't know, they're crazy. They've been radioing that someone is on top of the plane."

"Are they using the product? If they are, we've got to stop it now."

"There's no product allowed in here, sir."

"Then why do they claim they see someone on top of the plane? We just landed. We were flying at thirteen thousand feet."

"They're aiming their guns, sir."

"Cut them down," came the calm voice from inside the cabin, and suddenly bright yellow flames danced from the door of the plane. Remo saw the light first, heard the shots second, felt the slight impact of the backfire third, and finally saw each bullet land on its target on the runway, sending shiny bursts of reflective coloration dancing along the landing material designed to imitate a river to nowhere.

On the open landing strip, the men from the tower were easy game. The slugs dropped them like laundry sacks. Apparently the marksmen inside were competent because there was not the wild, continuous fire one saw in soldiers who would use a machine gun when a slap would do, and artillery when a gun would do, and a bomb when artillery would do until they earned a reputation as a professional army.

"Has someone taken over?" came a voice from inside.

"They're reporting everything is all right," answered another voice. "They say there really is a man on the top of the cabin."

"That can't be."

"They're saying it's so, sir."

"Tell them to get us a visual, but don't trust it entirely. This could be some trick."

"By whom? They're all our men."

"Anyone can be bought," came the voice.

"But we are the experts. We would have spotted something. No one knows better how to buy people than you, sir."

"Still, check the visuals. Have them give us a camera angle."

"Or we could just look," said the man at the open door.

"No. Shut the door."

The door clanked shut with such force that the jet trembled on its rubber tires.

Remo could still hear them talk.

"If someone is really up there, we will take off again and do maneuvers."

"'But if he lasted the flight, how are we sure the maneuvers will shake him off?"

"Because we flew smooth before. It certainly is worth a try, wouldn't you say?"

"Yes, Mr. Diaz."

So Diaz was aboard. Remo hadn't known that. He was

just told that since a large amount of money was being transported, Diaz had to be close by. That was how counters worked. They counted where people would be.

Remo had climbed on the roof just before takeoff. He had dressed as a ground mechanic, and then as soon as the blocks were removed from the wheels, he had slipped onto the roof at the tail, carefully compressing himself so the sudden weight wouldn't shake the plane and alert those inside. During the takeoff he hid himself on the far side of the plane's skin. Out of sight of the control tower. He had known the money was inside, but not that Diaz was. Until now.

That was really all he needed. As the people inside the plane worked the electronics to receive the television signal from the tower, Remo pressed the fingerpads of his right hand into the alloy skin of the plane. The metal, still cold from the flight at thirteen thousand feet, became sticky and warm under the increasing pressure from Remo's fingerpads. Pressure that flowed with the very atoms of the metal itself in rhythms with the electrons moving around the nuclei, collecting the metal within itself until the skin of the plane melted like ice cream on a hot day. As the hole enlarged, vaporized metal rose into the air in a cloud.

Remo peered down into the airplane.

"Hi, I'm up here. Don't settle for the replay. I'm live from America."

"Who are you?" said one of the bodies ducking away from the hole, as others scrambled to the cabin or aft. Remo tore off a bigger piece of the cabin and slid down, removing a firing automatic along with the wrist that fired it. He threw the garbage out of the plane as the bodyguard collapsed from shock.

"Would you believe the spirit of Christmas Past?" asked Remo. Which one was Guenther Largos Diaz? You couldn't tell the millionaries nowadays because they dressed in jeans and leather jackets like teenagers.

In fact, it was very hard to tell who was who, although Remo did assume that the man behind the instruments was the pilot. He was going to have to save him. That might be difficult because there were lots of bullets going off now from all directions. Apparently Christmas Past was not the answer these people wanted.

Remo saw the source of each bullet flash while he used other bodies as sandbags. It might have been more confusing if he didn't see everything so slowly, if he had not slowed the world and all its actions to a drowsy universe by slowing himself. The secret of speed, as athletes knew, was being able to slow down the perceptions of the world. A flash could be seen and recognized much faster than the bullet, signaling that the bullet was on its way, announcing it as a matter of fact, and then the bullet would be there.

Of course, one did not duck, because that was the easist way to put the body into a receiving position for death. One had to let the body understand its role, and to do that, one moved alongside one slug while deflecting another with lesser bodies. Those were the bodyguards.

Someone was screaming "Stop" long before the trigger-happies stopped, or, to be more precise, before Remo stopped them.

The cabin was filthy with blood and torn metal.

One man in a once-white suit stood proudly at the cockpit door, unyielding.

"Excuse me, Christmas Past, but my men panicked. I assume you are of sterner stuff. Sit down."

"Where?" asked Remo. "This place is a mess."

"It would have been much neater if you hadn't torn your way inside and dismembered my employees."

"I didn't know they were your employees. I was looking for you."

"Well, you've found me. How can I be of service?"

"Actually, Mr. Diaz, you don't have to do a thing. I do everything. I kill you. No work on your part whatsoever."

Diaz was cool to the marrow.

"Before I die, may I ask why?"

"I think it's drugs and buying people. Or something,"

said Remo. "Whatever it is, nobody else can get to you, so here I am."

"My most reasonable young man, may I ask what your name is, and why you would not care to reason with me a bit before I die? I could make you very wealthy, just for a few moments of talking with me. A bank account would be set up for you, and for, say, one minute of talk, provide you with a million dollars. I am not even buying my life, mind you. You can do your duty as you see fit. But for one minute of conversation, you will get one million dollars and of course remove this scourge you believe me to be. What do you say?"

"Nah. I don't need a million."

"You are rich then?"

"Nah," said Remo.

"A man who does not want money. What a rarity. Are you some kind of saint?"

"Nah. I just don't need money. I don't have a real home. I don't have anything."

"Ah, then you must want something."

"I'd like transportation out of here after I kill you. I don't know how well this plane will work with its roof torn off and bullets peppered into the cabin."

"Agreed," said Diaz with a smile of arrogant grace. The man certainly knew how to give up his life.

"Okay, you've got twenty seconds left."

"I thought I would get a minute."

"I've given you talking time. I mean, if I'm getting paid at the rate of a million dollars a minute I'm not throwing away hundreds of thousands of dollars. You've got fifteen seconds left."

"Fifteen?"

"Twelve," said Remo.

"Then of course all I can do is say good-bye and express my felicitations."

Guenther Largos Diaz nodded and clicked his heels, folding his arms together and waiting for his death as others would for a glass of champagne. Remo was impressed by this dark-haired man of calm and grace.

"Where's my plane out?" he asked. "You certainly don't look like the type who would bother to lie."

"But my time is up, sir. I don't even have the pleasure of your name."

"Remo. How many minutes do you want for the plane?"

"A lifetime," answered Diaz. The pilot peered around from behind him and then quickly looked back to the controls when he saw the thin man with the thick wrists smiling back at him. What was so chilling to the pilot was not the dark-haired, high-cheekboned handsomeness of the man standing in so much blood, it was the casual, almost friendly way the man looked at him with those dark eyes that seemed oblivious of the carnage.

And especially the answer he gave when Mr. Diaz asked for a lifetime.

"Don't worry. Whenever you give me that plane and pilot out of here, it will be your lifetime."

Diaz laughed. The pilot looked to his copilot. Men worked for this ruler of an illegal empire out of respect almost as much as money. But this was more than Mr. Diaz's legendary courage. This was sheer folly. The pilot cringed when he thought of the strange way the bodies had been strewn around the cabin. He looked straight ahead at the landing strip, as his stomach screamed for him to run and his legs sent up signals that they would refuse to move in such a dangerous situation.

And Mr. Diaz was still laughing.

"I like the way you do things. I will tell you what, my friend. We will talk while I arrange another plane. We must bring one in. I never allow two of my planes to be in the same airport at the same time."

"Why's that?" asked Remo. "In case someone rides in on the top of one, tears it up, and needs another to get out?"

Diaz laughed.

"No. You see, one way to ensure the loyalty of your

people is to keep them out of contact with others. Contact creates danger. Come, we will get out of this bloody mess and get some fresh air, a shower, dinner while the plane is on its way from another base of mine. And then, if you must, kill away. Agreed?''

Remo shrugged. It was better than walking through jungles. Diaz was a lion among his sheep. While his soldiers and bodyguards and ground personnel cringed or kept sweaty palms near their weapons, Diaz coolly ordered another jet into the airport.

And then he ordered a repast set before them, great shiny mounds of delicacies set on white Irish linen in the still, pure air at the foot of the Andes.

Amid shellfish, meats, and champagne, Remo ate only a few grains of rice.

"Are you afraid of being poisoned?" asked Diaz.

"All of that's poison," said Remo. "You eat that junk and you need to burn up oxygen just to get it into your system, and then your system closes down."

"Ah, so you have special eating techniques."

"No. I just don't kill myself with my mouth. How long is that jet going to take?"

"Shortly, shortly," said Diaz. He lifted a glass of champagne and savored it a moment. "You work for the government, I take it, the American government. That is why you want to stop an evil man like myself."

"You got it, Diaz."

"Call me Guenther, Remo," said Diaz with a gentle gesture of a palm. The smile never left his eyes, as though he was as amused by his death as threatened by it. "You know I am not the big shot who escapes. I am more a very rich middleman."

"Yeah? Who're the big shots?"

"Certain very rich and established banks. They are the ones who make my dollars usable."

"You mean certain banks in Miami?"

"Small-time. I mean a very big bank in Boston, owned by an old, establishment family which regularly allows us

to bring the money back into America and buy very safe
American property, and very safe American stocks, and
very safe American havens for the American dollar. And
yet, who ever hears of them?''

"Your water's good, too.''

"I take it you don't care about that?''

"Matter of fact, I do. Very much. It's in my bones. I
hate to see the big shots get away with it.''

"I thought that might be the case," Diaz raised a finger.
The smile now disappeared from his eyes. His voice was
low and intense. He spoke slowly. "I will make you this
deal. I will give you the big shots.''

"And let you go?''"

"Would you?''

"Probably not.''

"Then considering that life is but one day after another,
why don't I offer you this. Let me live as long as I give
you the big shots in your own country. Unless of course
you are here just to kill Latinos. In which case, I will
finish my champagne, and you may finish me. The plane
will be over the mountains shortly.''

Remo thought about the deal. Somehow, this cool, cunning man had found the one price Remo might accept.

"Can you get me a phone link-up to the States?''

"Of course, I have everything your Central Intelligence
Agency has in the way of electronics.''

"It's a very private call, so you'll have to keep your
distance.''

"Any call can be listened to without standing nearby,
you know,'' said Diaz.

"Yeah I know,'' said Remo. "But it's form.''

The telephone Diaz gave him was hardly bigger than a
coffee cup. It was shiny aluminum and had a speaker at
the bottom and a receiver at the top, and a dial pad.

"That is about as safe as you can get, but I wouldn't
guarantee anything,'' said Diaz. "No matter how it is
scrambled, someone will pick up the message.''

"Will they be able to read it?''

"Probably not. But they will know it has been sent."

"That's good enough," said Remo.

"It may not be for your organization."

"I don't know what is good enough for them," said Remo. He called for another glass of water as he dialed. There was no such thing as pure water. All water really carried elements of something else. But when you got it from the runoffs of the snows of the Andes you did not get the chemical wastes of poisonous factories which was known as pollution.

As soon as the phone rang, another strange ringing occurred. And a computer voice said:

"This is an open line. Use another. Use another. Use another."

"No," said Remo.

"This is an open line. Disconnect. Disconnect immediately," came the computer voice.

"C'mon, willya, Smitty, just talk for a minute."

And then a screeching interruption. And the voice of Harold W. Smith himself.

"Remo, hang up and reach me on another line."

"I don't have one."

"This is important."

"It's always important."

"There is a national emergency regarding Russia. Now will you get to another phone before someone gets a fix on us?"

"Can we get another line?" Remo called out to Diaz, who was, out of courtesy, standing away from the table, leaning against an elegant carved stone railing looking at his mountains.

"I think so," said Diaz. "Yes, I see the problem. They're picking up certain waves. Yes, I could have assured you there would be a problem."

"You did," said Remo.

"Who is that?" asked Smith. The voice was horrified.

"Diaz," said Remo, hanging up.

"I think your commander will not like the fact that I heard things."

"Yeah. He'll hate it," said Remo, smiling.

Diaz called an aide and was very specific about the type of telephone he wanted. This one would use a different transmission system, which Remo did not understand in the least.

He did understand Smith, however. Smitty's normal, taciturn, dry behavior had turned hysterical. He spent three minutes explaining the dangers of letting the organization be compromised. Even more important than the success of any mission, Remo had been made to understand, was that the organization never be made known to the public.

For its purpose was to do outside the law what America could not do inside. It was to carry out the survival missions of the nation that the nation could no longer perform. It was an admission in its basest form that America did not work within the Constitution.

"All right. All right. I understand, Smitty. But first, I'll be killing Diaz, so that information, whatever it is, will die with him, and second, he has a wonderful idea. I like it."

"Remo, do you understand that Diaz is so dangerous precisely because he offers people wonderful ideas? That's how he ruined the narcotics squads of three police departments."

"Yeah, but we're missing the big guys. There's this bank in Boston that—"

"Remo, neither the bank nor Mr. Diaz matters. There is something coming in from Russia that may be the most dangerous threat to our country ever."

Remo put a hand over the receiver.

"I think you've been dropped to second place, Diaz," said Remo.

"In these circumstances it might be welcome," said Diaz, toasting Remo again.

Remo took his hand off the speaker.

"You're already having conversations with Guenther

Largos Diaz that you're not sharing with me. If that doesn't
tell you something, Remo, nothing will.''

"What is this big deal from Russia?"

"We don't know. But something big is happening."

"When you find out, let me know, Smitty. In the
meantime, Guenther and I are going to Boston,'' said
Remo, and he hung up.

"Shall we take a slow boat?'' asked Diaz.

"Nah. You bought yourself a day at most,'' said Remo.

"Then to a wonderful last day,'' said Diaz.

The flight to Boston in the Diaz jet was luxurious. The
747 had beautiful women and movies and couches and
deep pile rugs.

But Diaz found Remo more interesting than these plea-
sures. He sent the women to the rear of the plane while he
talked with the thin man with the thick wrists. So well
appointed was the plane that it carried its own tailor and
Diaz offered Remo new clothes instead of his bloodied
dark T-shirt, gray slacks, and loafers. Remo asked for a
new dark T-shirt and a new pair of gray slacks.

"You will have it by the time we reach Boston. I gather
your agency is not listed in the line of command in
Washington.''

"Right.''

"I would gather very few know of it, less than a handful.''

Remo nodded.

"But let me take another guess,'' said Diaz. "Because I
have quite an extensive knowledge of what I thought were
all of your country's law-enforcement structures.''

Remo nodded for Diaz to guess away.

"An agency could not remain secret using many personnel, least of all those who kill like you.''

Remo nodded.

"So I would estimate that there are fewer than three of
you in the entire organization, three who are licensed to
kill.''

"I never knew someone needed a license.''

"Governments give them to agents. The only way your

organization could have escaped detection was with a very small enforcement arm."

"Are you trying to find out that if you kill me, there won't be someone else coming after you?"

"No, as a matter of fact. I've given that up. I don't think I'll have to. I am more valuable to your people alive than dead. And I think you people and I can make a deal. I would like to meet this Smitty."

"No deal. He'd have a heart attack."

The boardroom of the Boston Institutional Bank and Trust Company of America seemed unchanged from the nineteenth century. The walls were paneled in dark mahogany. The painted portraits showed rigid, moral New Englanders casting their gazes down as if considering whether the viewer were good enough to be in the room.

These were the framers of the American Constitution, and the arbiters of America's moral standards. These were the men who, when they decided slavery must go, helped finance the Civil War. Of course, these same men had built their family fortunes on buying slaves in Africa, selling them for molasses in the Caribbean, and turning that molasses into rum in New England, which they sold for slaves in Africa. It was called the golden triangle. And it made them and their descendants rich beyond imagination.

But only after the slaves were bought and paid for did New England provide the strong impetus to abolish slavery. As one Southerner had said:

"If we were smart enough to have bought our nigras on time instead of paying outright, there never would have been a Civil War."

The descendants of these righteous souls now sat beneath the portraits of their ancestors in the boardroom, keeping to the strictest morality in their banking. They would accept no cash of uncertain origin.

However, when one talked hundreds of millions of dollars, one was not talking cash, one was talking wealth. With that amount, there were no questions asked; so when their biggest depositor, Señor Guenther Largos Diaz, insisted on a meeting that day, they were more than happy to talk with him.

And this despite the presence of the man in the very casual black T-shirt and gray slacks, which were such a contrast to the elegant white suit of Señor Diaz.

"Tell me, young man, where do your people come from?" asked the chairman of the board.

"I don't know. I'm an orphan," said Remo. "I'm just here with Mr. Diaz to see if what he says is so. That he does business with you. And I see by this meeting that he does."

"We find him above reproach."

"Guenther here runs cocaine and suborns police departments. Is that above reproach?"

"I know nothing of that," said the chairman of the prestigious bank.

"Well, you do now," said Remo.

"I only know what you say, and I am not going to jump to hasty conclusions to defame the character of an upright businessman," said the chairman of the board. The other board members nodded.

"Well, I'm sorry to say, fellas, this isn't exactly a fair trial."

And there in the stuffy boardroom of the Boston Institutional Bank and Trust Company of America, the chairman of the board watched a thin man go from chair to chair, and as though flicking a finger, send head after head crashing to the table. Some members tried to run, but they were caught, their eyes going wide and stupid as their brains fluttered out under the shrapnel of their shattered skulls.

Their best depositor only stood by as though waiting for the beginning of a show. The chairman of the board was about to use his imposing moral presence when the intellectual signals for that presence scattered with the rest of his nervous system around the prestigious boardroom of the Boston International Bank and Trust Company of America.

''Thank you for your lead, but I really am sorry, Guenther, to tell you you've had your day.''

''But, my dear Remo,'' said Diaz. ''These are only the small fry.''

South of Boston in Rye, New York, on Long Island Sound, a computer gave Harold W. Smith some of the most frightening information to come in during CURE's history. Through its actions, Russia was telling the organization's computers that it was after something far more formidable even than atomic weapons. And there was no way to reach the killer arm. He was off somewhere disposing of bankers.

3

The President was calling, and for the first time in his life, Harold W. Smith did not answer his commander in chief when he should have.

He watched the blinking light signal that the President was on the line and he let the light blink off. He knew what the President wanted, and he knew he couldn't help him.

The network that had made this one organization so powerful was revealing two things. First, Russian internal activity was extraordinary in volume. Anyone could spot it. There was no great mystery to intelligence operations. When one nation prepared to attack another nation, you could see the armies massing for months and miles.

Something very important was happening. What Smith didn't know, and he was sure the FBI had to be just as aware of this, and just as worried. They had to have contacted the President. He could imagine the FBI mobilizing its magnificent staff; the organization that had momentarily faltered with a loss of its strong leader was now better than ever. It was the great secret of international politics that the FBI was perhaps the finest counterintelligence agency in the world. So, if the President was phoning Smith, it had to be for the use of CURE's special techniques, namely Remo, and hopefully not his trainer, Chiun.

The second piece of news coming into the headquarters

hidden within Folcroft Sanitarium on Long Island Sound was a multiple murder in Boston. Six directors of a prestigious bank had been killed when, according to the best police reports, someone using a powerful device had crushed six skulls.

The coroners had determined that only a hydraulic machine could have done such damage to a skull, and since there were no marks of such a multi-ton machine within the boardroom itself, it was therefore concluded that all six were killed elsewhere and brought to the boardroom. The papers were rife with speculation.

But Smith knew who had done it, and he was furious.

The organization only existed to handle that which the government couldn't. And now Remo was off somewhere keeping Diaz alive in order for Remo to vent his own delusions of a crusade. He had forgotten what they were about. He had forgotten their purpose. He had become lost in the killing and couldn't tell what the war was about anymore.

Maybe it was too much to expect Remo to keep his head after so many years. All the man had wanted was a home and a place in the world, and these were the last things he could have. He had to remain the man who didn't exist, serving the organization that didn't exist. And so it was hotel room to hotel room, for years now. And how much had his mind changed under the tutelage of Chiun, the Master of Sinanju?

That one was stranger still. Smith toyed with the Phi Beta Kappa key from Dartmouth stuck into his gray vest. He looked out the one-way windows of his office on the darkening clouds over Long Island Sound.

The President's line was ringing again. What could he tell him?

Perhaps he could tell him that it was time to close down the killer arm of CURE, that it had become too unreliable. And that was the reason he had not been answering the telephone. Because the moment the President asked for their services, Harold W. Smith, sixty-seven, was honor-bound to tell him the truth. The organization now had to be considered unreliable.

Harold W. Smith picked up the telephone, knowing that all his years of service might now be over. What was it about time? It seemed like yesterday when a now dead President had commissioned CURE for an interim job, just to help the country through the crisis ahead, and then disband. It was supposed to be a five-year assignment. And it had become decades. And now the decades might be coming to an end.

"Sir," said Smith, picking up the red phone in the right-hand drawer of his wooden desk.

"Is everything all right? You're usually there at this time," said the President. "I phoned before."

"I know," said Smith. "No sir, everything is not all right. I regret to inform you that I believe the organization is out of control and it has to be shut down now."

"Doesn't matter. The whole shooting match may be out of control now. What do you have left?"

"We only have one in the enforcement area. The other is his trainer."

"His trainer is even better than he is. And he's older, too. Older than me. Not too many people can make that statement in this government. He's wonderful."

"Sir, the Master of Sinanju is not exactly the congenial sort of fellow he makes himself out to be."

"I know that. They're an ancient house of assassins. The glorious House of Sinanju. I know all the talk Chiun makes is just buttering up clients. I wasn't born yesterday. But we need him or his pupil now. The whole Russian spy system is going crazy. Joint Chiefs, CIA, NSA, they all say Russia is activating its whole network. We are seeing activity from moles who would only be called on in case of war."

"So are they getting into position for a war? What about their missiles and submarines?"

"No. That's just it. It may not be a war, but the KGB is acting as though there is a war."

"Just what can we do that isn't being done already?"

"About time you asked it, Smith," said the President. On television talking to the nation, he appeared to be a sweet, reasonable man. But underneath he was all cold logic and finely honed executive skills, a lot harder than most reporters could perceive. But reporters rarely knew what was going on. They only knew what appeared to be going on.

"We want," said the President, "to stop the unstoppable."

"And what is that?"

"That," said the President, "is a special-force team from the Soviet Union. And they're headed toward America to get something. Now our FBI can handle everything else within our borders. But they can't handle this team of men."

"Can they get Army backup?"

"They have, and did. Twice. And twice that team came into our borders and got out again. Once they managed to take a missile warhead with them."

"So I heard. The CIA seems to be trying to work through a few solutions, but I don't think they'll come up with anything," said Smith.

"You're not alone. We only found out about these boys after they got out of the country. They could have been in here three or four times for all we know. We know we've had them at least twice."

"How do you know they're coming in again?"

"Because Russia is sending in everything. We can handle all the other stuff. Can your people handle their special team?"

"We'll have to," said Smith. "What else do you know about them? Any identification? The big thing is going to be finding them."

"We'll have the CIA feed you."

"That's all right. I'd rather tap into their lines. Any idea if it's something we have that they are afraid we'll use to start a war?"

"Doubtful. All we know is that it has a code name, Rabinowitz."

"Strange code name. Sounds like a person."

"I would have thought so too. But can you imagine any single person who is so valuable as to put Russia's entire spy network on virtual war alert?"

"No, sir. I can't. We'll do what we can."

In a time of crisis, Smith, perhaps the most perfect organizer ever to come out of the old OSS, always got a pad and pencil. For some reason a computer was not good for flat-out reasoning. The pencil and paper somehow made it real. And within a few lines he set a parameter. If Remo did not check in by noon that day, he would enlist Chiun. He had time. The CIA still did not know who had to be stopped as Russia searched for this code name Rabinowitz.

And Smith did not want to deal with Chiun now if he did not have to.

Remo checked in by eleven A.M. and he was gleeful.

"Guess where I am, Smitty."

"Remo, your country needs you."

"And it's getting me. I'm here at the Chicago Board of Trade, and guess who is not going to be able to use narcotics money anymore to manipulate the grain market."

"I could tell you in five minutes, if we had five minutes. Remo, this is a national emergency."

"So is a bunch of farmers going bankrupt."

"Has Mr. Diaz convinced you that you're saving farmers by eliminating a corrupt broker?"

"At least I know I'm getting the bad guys."

"Who made you a judge?"

"All those judges who let these bastards off."

"Remo," said Smith, looking at the instruments attached to the line in use, "this is not a secure line. I have very important information. Get to any land line phone. Stop using that damned gadget Diaz must have given you."

"Smitty, there's always a crisis. And you know what

comes after one crisis? Another crisis. At least I know now I'm doing some good. And I'll tell you something. I've never felt better in my life."

"Good, because you're in the wrong place, idiot, if you want to help farmers. Their problem is that oil prices have made food more expensive while their own technical ability to produce more drives down prices. They've been caught in the middle. It has nothing to do with the Chicago Board of Trade one way or the other."

"Never felt better in my life, Smitty," said Remo, and the phone went dead. There was no choice but to contact the Master of Sinanju. If Remo was an unguided missile, Chiun, his mentor, was an explosion. This latest Master of the most deadly house of assassins in all history would do absolutely unfathomable things. Even if he had an assignment from Smith, which he usually did, he might end up at the other end of the world eliminating an entire royal court for some reason entirely his own.

Using Chiun always had the element of throwing a bomb into a crowded theater hoping the person you had to get might be inside. But Smith had no choice. The deadly killer had to be ready to be unleashed. He dialed.

In New Hope, Pennsylvania, among the apple blossoms of spring and the gentle green hills of Bucks County, a ringing telephone interrupted the placid perfection of what had to be the most gentle mind at a gentle time of year.

So kind and perfect was this mind, so innocent in its love of simple beauty, that to interrupt its serenity had to be a crime worthy of immediate and final punishment.

Thus when the jarring noise of the telephone cruelly abused the tranquillity of the innocent one, the innocent one looked about for some help for the frail, gentle soul that wished above all only peace for the entire world.

And in so doing, his gaze rested upon a repairman for a television company, and in simple supplication did Chiun, Master of Sinanju, ask that the phone be taken from the wall.

"Hey, buddy, I ain't gettin' paid to tear up phone-company property," answered the repairman.

What would a gentle soul with a spirit of such placidity do when abused by one who denied that soul the quiet it so desperately sought? He begged again. Of course the repairman did not understand the simple three-word pleading. He took offense at:

"Do it now."

And the repairman began an answer with the letter F. Fortunately the forces of peace and tranquillity did not let him complete the hard consonants CK at the end of the word.

Chiun walked over the body and quieted the noise of the phone by enveloping it in his fingers. Altering the rhythm of the molecules of the plastic, soon caused it to disappear into steam.

He glanced back at the body. He hoped Remo would be home within a day, before the body began to give off foul odors. And yet, for this gentleman in the bright kimono with a wispy beard, long fingernails, and calm countenance wrapped in parchment-yellow skin, the day might prove regrettable. Remo might not come, and even if he did come, he would, as he always did, make a fuss about who would remove the body. Even after all Chiun had given him. And to support his sloth and ingratitude, he probably would accuse Chiun of murder without cause, an accusation against the perfect and pure reputation of the House of Sinanju itself.

Thus was Chiun's day ruined, but this was to be expected. The world had a nasty habit of abusing the gentle souls. He would have to be less accommodating in the future. His only problem was, as it had always been, that he was too nice a guy.

In Moscow, an American mole secreted in the higher echelons of the KGB since the Second World War received his message the way he had been given instructions for the last forty years: by reading a famous American newspaper's front page. On the front page, for no reason the paper ever cared to explain, were classified ads. Since it was such a prestigious newspaper, everyone assumed it was a traditional quirk. The ads were small, usually less than three lines each, and filled the bottom of the page.

But they had been absolutely vital in the intelligence agency's efforts to reach people throughout the world. After all, no intelligence agent would be suspect for reading the front page of this most prestigious newspaper. It probably would be part of his job anyhow.

And thus, reading the paper over three days gave the colonel an entire message. Decoded, it revealed a request to know what Rabinowitz stood for and when the special force would be dispatched to get it.

As with all good intelligence agencies, no one was allowed to know anything he did not need to know. Though the colonel was in electronic surveillance, and sent messages through this same surveillance equipment, as he always had, he did not know what a Rabinowitz was and had never heard of the special force.

But unlike all the other times, this time he was pressed to risk exposing himself to find out. And so he opened computer files he was forbidden to open and got answers that were not complete, but they were better than nothing.

The special force Russia used within America was marvelously protected until it was used, and only then it would be vulnerable. Its commander was the youngest general in the KGB, Boris Matesev, a man with a licentiate from the Sorbonne in France.

Rabinowitz was not a code name, but the name of a person assigned to the parapsychology village. There had been a botched attempt to keep him within Russia. And he was considered extraordinarily dangerous—the most dangerous single human being on the face of the earth.

The CIA knew the information was correct, because the mole had paid for it with his life.

Smith's tap on the CIA lines picked up the name Matesev, and he sent out under CIA auspices an urgent request for more information on this man, what he looked like and, most important, where he was. The request cost three lives.

On the day this costly information arrived, Smith got another phone call from Remo, this time in Denver. He was punishing a bookmaker. And the report on Chiun's phone was that the service had been disconnected for equipment failure.

There was nothing for Smith to do but go himself to New Hope, Pennsylvania, and try to reason with Chiun face-to-face. For some reason the phones that he had ordered installed never quite worked, and the phone company refused to send any more men into that area because repairmen and installers kept disappearing.

Smith arrived in a plain economy car, and if he were not so tired he would have sensed the silence in the area. Even the birds were quiet. Two telephone trucks and a TV repair vehicle were parked in the driveway.

Inside the unmistakable odor of death permeated the walls. The door was open. But blocking the entrance were four brightly colored steamer trunks.

"Quickly, pack them in the car," came Chiun's high, squeaky voice.

"What's happened?"

"Viciousness and discord have run rampant. We must move quickly lest the sheriff come with all his white viciousness. You are, after all, a racist country."

"I don't know if I could lift the trunks," said Smith.

"You must. You don't expect a Master of Sinanju to carry them himself, do you? What will the world think of you hiring an assassin who carries his own baggage? Quick. Quick. I will help, but don't let the world see."

The help Smith got was an occasional long fingernail balancing a trunk on Smith's shoulders. The chests filled the back seat of the car and the car trunk itself. Smith could hardly see well enough to back out of the driveway.

"What happened in there?"

"Someone kept trying to phone me," said Chiun, smoothing out his gray traveling kimono.

"What does that have to do with killing? How can a phone call create rotting bodies?"

"Ah, that is Remo's fault," said Chiun.

"Remo's returned?" asked Smith, feeling a wild sense of panic creep up on him with every bizarre and inexplicable answer from the Master of Sinanju.

"No. That is why Remo is responsible. If he were here it would be his job to take care of the bodies. But he is not here. And why?"

"Well, I think he has some problems. He has gone off on his own."

"Eeahhh," wailed the Master of Sinanju.

"What's the matter?"

"The Master's disease. It happens every fifteenth generation."

"But that's for Koreans, isn't it?"

"Remo has become Korean in his soul, even though he may not respect that fact," said Chiun. "And now the Master's disease."

"What is it?"

"I should have known. Does he think now that he alone provides justice for the world?"

"Something like that, yes," said Smith, making sure he kept the proper speed limit on the narrow winding road through the beautiful countryside of Bucks County. Behind him he heard the wail of police sirens. He had gotten to Chiun just in time. They couldn't afford the attention if an entire police department were wiped out. That would be too much to cover up, even for CURE.

"This is a very crucial time. Remo must be allowed rest. Above all he needs rest, and he needs me. He needs me most of all."

"Is there any way we can use him for a mission at this time? It's vital."

"Ah, a vital mission. They are the most important, but Sinanju, which has served you so well and faithfully, must reorient its basic unity with the cosmos. Remo must meditate. He must breathe properly. He must rethink himself, and then, after the visitation, stronger, we will come back to carry the standards of Emperor Smith to final and ultimate victory.''

The long fingernails fluttered as Chiun spoke.

"We need someone now. Can we use you?"

"I am always of service, ready to bring your glory to its ultimate brilliance at your every whim."

"Good. Then I think you should know we have a target who will be coming to America, we suspect possibly in the vicinity of New York. I want you placed in New York City now—"

"It would be the wrong time to leap to your very whim. We must get Remo well again before we go on."

"How long will that take?" asked Smith, who remembered he had a back problem that doctors had pronounced incurable until Chiun, with less than three seconds of manipulation, blessedly cured it forever.

"A rapid fifteen years," said Chiun.

"We don't have fifteen years. What can we give you to get your services, services I might remind you we are this very moment paying for in gold tribute to the village of Sinanju, gold that is delivered on time when you want it."

"And we are here for you. Forever to sing your praises. Only in your service has Remo's mind been injured. Yet we humbly accept that harm as part of our service to you."

"Remo is now gallivanting around the countryside with a man I ordered executed—"

"One you have certainly paid to have executed," said Chiun. "And it should be given you."

"And Remo is eliminating people we have not asked him to."

"For nothing?" asked Chiun, in horror.

"Yes. Remo doesn't care about money. You know that."

"It has come to this. He has taken the wisdom and skill

of Sinanju and become an amateur. Oh, how the world has cruelly vented its scorn upon this lowly head in your gracious service, O Emperor Smith.''

"Well, I am glad that for the first time we have agreed on something, Chiun," said Smith. "In this disaster, at least that is a blessing.''

He wondered if the sheriff's car would be following them. He wondered how many other reasonless killings this aged Oriental had committed, only to have them hidden by Remo.

He wondered if he could keep things together enough to save America one last time. He felt tired. His body and mind were telling him to toss it all in, maybe drive off the road into the river along which the road ran. Let the water come in cold and dark and final and give him some peace at last.

And then without even being aware, Harold W. Smith felt as bright as a summer morning, fresh as his orange juice, and more chipper than anytime since the morning of his tenth birthday.

He saw Chiun remove his long fingernails from behind his neck, and Smith's neck was still tingling.

"You were letting the tiredness of your body make your decisions," said Chiun. "Now how does the world look?''

"Difficult.''

"For the great emperors it is always difficult.''

"'I don't suppose it would do any good to tell you I'm not an emperor. I guess not. There is a difficult problem. And I can't reach Remo.''

"All problems are the same. They just have different faces and times," said Chiun.

"You mean you may have run up against something like this in the histories of Sinanju?''

"I guarantee we ran up against it in our history. The question is, will I recognize it? You see, our histories are our strength. That is what Remo must learn. He would know what he is experiencing now if he had properly revered our histories.''

"He didn't like that part of the training, I take it," said Smith.

"He called it an ugly name," said Chiun.

"I'm sorry," said Smith.

"Now we are all paying for it," said Chiun. "Ah well, he will be back soon. I will tell him you are angry also."

"How do you know he's coming back?"

"He always comes back to me after he completes a service for you."

"But I thought you said he suffered from the Master's disease."

"And he does, most gracious Emperor Smith. He will wreak acts of vengeance upon mankind. It is an old Hindu curse interpreted by them as a duty imposed by one of their gods."

"But if he is wreaking vengeance, his own personal vengeance, how will he do what he is supposed to do for me?"

"You mean your assignment?"

"Yes. This man he was supposed to eliminate," said Smith.

"Oh, that," said Chiun, dismissing the worry as trivial. "That's business. The man is dead."

"Guenther Largos Diaz is perhaps the most cunning briber in the world. He should have been dead days ago."

"Yes, I admit, Remo may be late, but there is no question. Mr. Diaz may think he is saving his life, but Remo will come to his senses because the disease fevers the brain in waves, not in a constant barrage. Don't worry. Remo is Remo."

"Yes," said Smith wearily, "but who that is, I don't know."

"You read the souls of all men, O most gracious Emperor," said Chiun, who thought that it would take a white to deal with someone for twenty years and then come out with a statement as stupid as that. If he didn't know Remo by now, he never would.

*   *   *

Guenther Largos Diaz had understood immediately there was a quality to this man called Remo that he had never seen before. And even though he had learned many things about him in the last few days, he did make the disastrously impulsive judgment that he knew Remo.

He had seen him kill at the foot of the Andes, seen his work in Boston and now in Denver, seen the flippant grace that made awesome deeds seem no more than the simple manipulation of the hand, like swatting away a fly.

It was this very simplicity that made it all seem so natural, which in Diaz's understanding made it all the more magnificent. He could feed this force victims and thus prolong his own life, but life was too valuable to live it poorly, to constantly be running around America one step from death.

There had to be a significant move along the way when Remo would make that switch to working for Diaz instead of Diaz working for Remo. The more subtly it was made, the more possible it would become. What Guenther Largos Diaz wanted was for their goals, his and Remo's, to become indistinguishable, and then once that had been established, to slowly substitute Diaz's real goals.

For in this one man Diaz would have an army of killers.

To this end, he questioned Remo. They were aboard the private jet on their way to Atlanta, where Diaz had assured Remo a major builder was also using Diaz cocaine money.

"We are really getting the big shots, Remo."

"You seem happy about it, Diaz."

"I am happy to be alive," said Diaz. He examined a tray of truffles brought to him by the steward aboard his jet, and dismissed them as inadequate. They could always fly to France for the best truffles. Life was so short, why settle?

"You didn't seem to be too frightened," said Remo.

"Why be frightened even though life is dear? But I am thinking, why not get the true masters of crime. We have dealt with bankers and bookies and commodities dealers, and now we seek a builder. Let us get the great criminals of the world.''

''These are big enough for me,'' said Remo.

''Do you know how much a country steals every day? What does one communist government steal when it has everyone within its borders providing cheap labor? What does the American government steal when it taxes? Cocaine smugglers are pipsqueaks, and so are bankers. Are you willing to go for the really big boys, Remo?''

''No,'' said Remo. ''As a matter of fact I should be getting home. I'm late.''

''I thought you didn't have a home.''

''I don't really. It's my teacher I live with.''

''And he teaches you these powers.''

''Yeah. In a way,'' said Remo. He liked the plush white cushions on the plane. He wondered what it would be like to live this way, to have many homes. Guenther Largos Diaz had many homes. If he worked for Diaz, so would he.

''In what way, Remo?''

''I'd tell you but I don't have time.''

''We have all the time in the world,'' said Guenther Largos Diaz, making a broad gesture with his hands.

''No you don't,'' said Remo, and he did not throw Diaz's body out of the plane because they were over America and it might hit someone.

4

Vladimir Rabinowitz was free. He was in the land where people ate meat all they wanted. No one stood over your shoulder. No one told you what to think. No one bombarded you with the correct view of the world.

Those were the good parts. The bad part was nobody cared what you thought. Nobody cared where you slept or whether you ate at all. You had no set place in the world. Living in Russia was like wearing a truss around your soul. It smothered the spirit, but when the truss was removed, you felt as though the spirit was now dangerously without support.

For the first time in his twenty-eight years of life Vladimir Rabinowitz had no place to go, no place to be, no one to have to talk to, and it was not exhilarating. It was terrifying. He looked over his shoulder for the police. He looked around for some official, and then with a deep sigh he told himself this was what he had wanted all his life and he should enjoy it.

He watched the people rush through Kennedy Airport until one glanced at his eyes. She was young, but apparently wealthy because she wore a fur coat. Her eyes were ice blue, and he caught them in his own gaze.

The trick was to get behind the eyes into the mind. Human eyes were really set like those of predators, not victims. Antelopes and deer had their eyes in the sides of their heads to spot anything sneaking up on them. They were runners for their lives. Lions and wolves had their eyes set in the front of their heads. They were hunters for their food.

When people glanced for the first time at anything, their eyes were really searching for weaknesses or strengths. If one knew the eyes, one knew that. The second glance was sexual. And only after these two stages were over did people get to talking. But it was in these stages that Vassily Rabinowitz worked.

The woman's eyes said no danger, and then said no to sexual partnership. But by that instant he had locked her pupils with his and smiled, and what he did here with people rushing around them and distracting them, with overhead speakers blaring in English, with the scent of harsh cleaners still on the floor and the air stuffy from so many people using it, was to let her eyes see through his that she was safe. The message was friendship. She no longer had to worry about safety.

"I am telling you what you know," said Vassily in his best English, "better than what you know."

His voice was not soft, but held that note of confidence beyond confidence. It was someone speaking the truth. The people never remembered he had said this afterward, in fact sometimes they didn't remember direct suggestions at all. As he had explained to the scientist who was assigned to him back at the village:

"Most of the decisions for immediate action and recognition are not decided in the conscious part of the brain. That's too slow. It's an instantaneous thing. It's there immediately. What I do is lock in at the first stage."

"But all hypnotism requires relaxation, comrade," the fellow scientist at the village had said.

"The mind is never relaxed. You're thinking of pre-sleep," Vassily had said, and the scientist had liked that. He liked the description of the levels of the mind. He liked the stages of recognition through the eyes. He liked all of it, and Vassily, being rather creative, kept on expanding. Of course the scientists could never reproduce what Vassily

Rabinowitz did, because Vassily didn't know how he did it. Never did. Nor did he know why everyone else in his village could do it to those born outside the village.

All he knew was that when he went to the outside world, which at the time was the special village in Siberia, he promised the elders of the village never to tell anyone about them.

And here in America the woman with the ice-blue eyes said:

"Darling, I didn't know you were in New York!"

"I'm here. Don't hang on me. I want something to eat already," said Vassily.

"You're always so thoughtful. Never thinking of yourself, Hal. Always me first. Of course we'll get something to eat."

"Right," said Vassily.

"I love you too, precious," said the woman. Her name was Liona. Her mind had taken over the job of telling herself what she wanted to believe. This Hal she was in love with apparently had a nice way with words.

Vassily never had a way with words, least of all English words. So he told her what he wanted, and she heard what she wanted, and they got along fine all the way into the biggest, busiest, dirtiest city he had ever seen. New York. And she bought him lunch. And took him to her apartment. And made violent love to him, screaming, "Hal, Hal. Hal."

"So long," said Vassily.

"You're wonderful, Hal."

"Sometimes. Sometimes I'm this guy Morris, who is awful," said Vassily, but he knew she didn't hear that. He had been three Morrises in his life; none of them had ever been good lovers. Once he was a Byron. Byron was terrific. He liked being Byron.

Vassily, untrained in war and the strategies of war, could not imagine he would ever be a danger to anyone. When you had the powers of his home village of Dulsk you really didn't have to worry about dangers from the outside.

But as he left the apartment, something bad happened. The worst fears of Russian planners were realized, though not in a way they might have expected.

In this fine country, in this land where store windows were filled with plenty, Vassily Rabinowitz was mugged.

They were three teenagers. They were of the oppressed black race. Vassily, whose only knowledge of American racial matters was the historic injustice done to these people and the daily persecutions they suffered, felt an immediate sense of brotherly compassion.

In the midst of his compassion he suffered contusions about the eyes, lacerations of the head, a broken left wrist, and a damaged kidney. When he got out of the hospital he was told to check his urine for blood.

This could never happen in Moscow. A drunk might take a loose swing at someone, but never would anyone so blatantly assault another.

Coming out of the hospital, Vassily Rabinowitz knew he was going to have to take care of himself. In every aching part of his body, in every accidental brush against a wound, he knew he was never going to allow this to happen to him again. He would create a fortress Vassily. He would trust no one to take care of him. He would do everything for himself. He would protect himself, he would set up a business for himself, and foremost, he would never again expose himself to the vicissitudes of brotherly love. He was going to get his own police force, to substitute for the people dressed in blue who called themselves police, whom he had never seen hit anyone on the head with a nightstick. He was going to get himself the strongest, deadliest, most powerful protection available in this new country.

Rabinowitz wasn't quite sure what that was, but he knew how to find out. And so he began protecting himself.

He talked with a policeman. The policeman thought he was talking to his father.

"Dad," said the policeman, "the toughest man in the city, the one I would hate to be left alone with, the one I would walk miles to avoid, has got to be Johnny 'The Bang' Bangossa.''

''Is a strongy, huh?'' asked Vassily.

''Pop, that man has been breaking bones for a living since he was twelve. I heard he beat up four patrolmen by himself when he was sixteen. By the time he was twenty he had made his bones.''

''What is this making of bones?'' asked Vassily.

''Dad, how long have you been on the police force, that you don't know what making your bones is?''

''Talk to your father already,'' said Vassily. They were in a luncheonette. Some of the food Vassily recognized from Russia. The rest he wanted to eat.

People were looking strangely at them. Vassily could sense that. He didn't care. The man had red hair, blue eyes, and was six feet tall, almost a half-foot taller than Vassily. He was also by any reasonable estimation a good ten years older than Vassily.

''Pop, making your bones is killing someone for money.''

''So where does this Bangossa fellow live?''

''Queens. He's been under surveillance for a month. And he knows it. Word on the street is he's going crazy 'cause he hasn't busted anyone's skull in a hell of a long time. Everyone's waitin' for him to break.''

Vassily got the address of the stakeout, took a large sugary roll from the counter, told the counterman his son would pay for it, and headed out for Queens, New York, and the address of the stakeout.

When the wife of Johnny ''The Bang'' Bangossa saw a little fellow with sad brown eyes come up the walkway to their brick house in Queens, she wanted to warn him to stay away. If he did not stay away, Johnny would mangle him, the police stakeout that everyone knew was in force would close in, and Johnny would be incarcerated, using the remnants of the sad-eyed little fellow as evidence, probably for a lifetime, leaving Maria Venicio Bangossa virtually a widow. A woman without a man. A woman who could not marry again because in the eyes of the Church she would still be married.

Maria Bangossa opened the door.

"C'mon in," she said. "Have you come for Johnny Bangossa?"

"Indeed I have," said Vassily Rabinowitz. He was amazed at how much red brick was used in this house. Someone would think this was a bunker. The windows were small and narrow. The roof was low, and nothing but brick reinforced by brick was used in the exterior.

Inside, furniture glistened with a sheen he hadn't seen anywhere else in America except on luncheonette counters.

Suddenly Maria Bangossa realized she was talking to her mother.

"Ma, he's in a lousy mood. I just leave some pasta by his door three times a day. I don't go in. You gotta get outta here."

Maria saw her mother shrug.

"Don't worry already. We'll be all right, and everything will work out. Just show me where the animal is."

"I'm fine, Ma, and Johnny's in his room. But he's sleeping. He's even worse when he wakes up. I rush out of bed because I don't want to be near him when he opens his eyes."

"It's all right, Maria. Your mother will be fine," said Vassily.

The carpeting was a deep maroon and looked like bad imitation fur. The lamps were porcelain figurines holding facsimiles of fruit. The stair banister was made of chrome. Airports were better decorated than the home of this Johnny Bangossa.

When Vassily got to the room, he knocked on the door and called out.

"Hey, Johnny Bangossa, I want you should talk with me awhile."

Johnny Bangossa heard the foreign accent. He heard it in his house. He heard it outside his room. He heard it while he was asleep and when he awakened from that sleep. The first thing he did was swing wildly, hoping someone was near him and would be crushed by the blow. But his fist met only a piece of the wall, shattering plaster.

The voice had come from the door. Johnny grabbed the corners of the door and ripped it away. Standing there in front of him was a little man with sad brown eyes, probably a Jew.

Johnny reached for the Jew. His anger almost blinded him.

Vassily Rabinowitz saw the big, hairy hands come down toward him. Johnny Bangossa filled the doorway. He wore an undershirt. His massive shoulders were covered with hair. His face was hairy. His nose was hairy. Even his teeth and fingernails seemed to be hairy. He had small black eyes that looked like coal nuggets, and a wide face that underneath the hair was very red.

Vassily sensed he was going to die very soon. And then he locked eyes with the massive man.

The hulk paused, then cringed.

"Hey, Carli, leave me alone. C'mon, Carli," whined Johnny Bangossa, covering his head and retreating into the room.

"I'm not going to hit you. I need you," said Vassily.

"Don't hit," said the large man, and he winced as though he was being struck on the head.

"I need you for protection," said Vassily. "You will be my bodyguard.'

"Sure, Carli, but don't hit."

Vassily shrugged. He knew his bodyguard would be actually feeling the slaps and cuffs used by the person who raised him.

It was a bit unsettling to walk downstairs with a hulk of a man wincing, ducking, and covering his head.

Maria Bangossa stood in shocked amazement as the two of them left the house. It was as though her beloved husband was reacting to his older brother Carl who had raised him. Johnny had said Carl had raised him strictly, in

the old-fashioned way. Nowadays, with the advent of
social workers, this was considered child abuse.

Carl Bangossa had been proud of the way he raised his
younger brother Johnny to follow in the family footsteps.
Unfortunately, Carl never saw Johnny reach manhood because Carl too followed in the Bangossa family footsteps.

He was buried at the bottom of the East River in a tub of
cement. It was the Bangossa way of death. A great-
grandfather was the only one to have died in bed. That
was the place he was stabbed to death.

"Hey, Carli, there's a stakeout here," said Johnny as
they reached the sidewalk.

"What is stakeout?" asked Vassily.

"You don't know what a stakeout is?" asked Johnny,
and then ducked, expecting a hit in the head for asking that
kind of question.

"You tell me," said Vassily.

The large hairy man talked a foot over Vassily's head.
This Carli had to be big also. A stakeout, he said, was
when the police were watching you.

Why were they watching him? Vassily asked.

" 'Cause they hate Italians. You know, you got a vowel
at the end of your name and they think they got a right to
lean on you."

"All Italians?"

"No way. Some of the paisans are the worst cops and
prosecutors. You got a vowel at the end of your name,
they lean on you harder."

"And a paisan is?"

"Carli. You crazy? . . . Sorry, Carli. Sorry. Don't hit.
Don't hit. All right."

It was very difficult dealing with someone who had been
raised with violence as a teaching tool, but Vassily came
to understand that the policemen in the stakeout were
sitting in a car across the street.

"You stay here, Johnny. I'll take care of them."

"Not in front of my house. They'll get us for sure. You

can't kill a cop in front of your house. We'll never get away with it.''

Johnny Bangossa felt the slaps and the hits on his head, heard Carli tell him not to worry about it, and then to his amazement saw his older brother walk over to the car, and not kill anyone. Nor did he have money in his hands. He only spoke to them and they drove away.

That was even more amazing than Carli being alive. Johnny could have sworn Carli had been put in the East River for good.

"Hey, Carli, word had it you was sleeping with the fishes,'' said Johnny.

"Don't believe everything you hear,'' said Vassily Rabinowitz.

He now had his bodyguard, but of course one had to be able to feed a bodyguard, and probably pay him too.

Vassily needed a business. He could go into a bank and probably withdraw money, but sooner or later, numbers, which did not lock eyes with people, would show something was wrong and eventually people would come looking for him. Besides, he had looked in one of the banks and there were cameras on the walls. They would probably get his picture anyhow. He could have become the lover of a wealthy woman or the lost child of a wealthy man. But he had not come this far to be cosseted with some stranger who needed to be intimate. He wanted freedom. And to have this freedom he knew he had to start his own business.

And what better business than what he did better than anyone else in the world? He would set up an office to supply hypnotism. He was, after all, the best hypnotist in the world.

Johnny Bangossa would stay near him all the time, and act as doorman to his little office. He would act as chauffeur when Vassily got a car. He would do everything for Vassily while making sure no one ever laid a finger on his beloved Carli. Otherwise his beloved Carli would punish Johnny Bangossa.

But business was not easy at first. Not even for Vassily.

His first customer refused to pay him. He was a chronic smoker.

"Why should I pay you for quitting smoking? I never smoked in my life and I don't smoke now," said the customer.

"Then what are the cigarettes doing in your pocket? Why are your fingers stained with nicotine?" asked Vassily.

"My Lord. You're right. What have you done to me, you bastard?" said the man, who had come in with a cigarette in his mouth, hacking away, explaining how he had tried everything and couldn't quit. Johnny had to quiet him down, but Vassily learned it wasn't what you did for a person but what they thought you did for them.

For the next patient the first thing he did was to convince the obese woman she was going through an exotic experience of hypnotism. And this time, the important message was not that she would no longer overeat. Not that she did not want to overeat, but that she was getting her money's worth.

"This is the best hypnotic experience of your life and you will come to me twice a week for the next fifteen years," said Vassily. "And you will pay me ninety dollars for a mere fifty minutes of my time even though you will have to imagine any improvement in your life, because there's going to be none."

The woman left and recommended fifteen friends, all of whom agreed Vassily was just as good as their psychiatrists. In fact he functioned just like one.

And Vassily had another trick up his sleeve. He learned to give fifty minutes in thirty seconds' time. All they had to do was believe they were getting that much time.

The line stretched out of his office right to the elevator every day. He was making fortunes. But he was spending fortunes, too. There were the lawyers he had to hire because Johnny Bangossa defended him a little too well.

There were tax advisers he had to get because he was making so much money. And he realized Johnny could not do it all. Johnny had to sleep from time to time. So

Vassily had to get other bodyguards and of course he got the toughest men that money and great hypnotism could buy.

And he had to have somebody to order them around. So in came a second in command. Within a very short time, Vassily Rabinowitz, formerly of Dulsk, Russia, formerly of the parapsychology village in Siberia, was running one of the most powerful crime families in the country, but he couldn't support them all with just hypnotism. No matter how profitable that was, he had to let them earn their money at what they knew—narcotics, extortion, hijacking, and sundry other things.

It was a horror, except something began to stir in the heart of Vassily Rabinowitz, and it would ultimately threaten the entire world.

A portion of his mind that had never been used was being called on now. He had to organize his deadly people, and he found he liked it. It was much better than hypnotism, which he could do with no effort at all: this was a challenge.

And so what had started as a way to be safe from muggers now became a game of war. And it was just the nightmare that Russian planners had always feared. Because here was a man who, once he looked in someone's eyes, owned that person, could get him to do virtually anything. What would happen, asked the Russian strategic planners, if he got into the game of international conflicts? He could go from one small state to another, and all he had to do was have one meeting with an enemy or one with a general. He could turn the whole world around.

That was the real reason they had never used him against enemies. They never wanted him to get a taste of war.

There was nothing closer to war than the manipulation of racketeer armies.

But Russia did not yet know this had happened. They were only out to find out where he was. And they found out only by accident, an accident that accomplished what their entire alerted espionage network failed to do, pinpoint exactly where Vassily Rabinowitz was.

Natasha Krupskaya, the wife of a Russian consul who had been assigned to America for the last ten years, decided at last that weighing 192 pounds might be a fine thing in Minsk, Pinsk, or Podolsk, but not on Fifth Avenue. Americans had started to make fun of Russian figures on television. And since she also had a face like the back end of a tractor, she decided she had to do something to avoid ridicule. But dieting was hard. She would find herself at the end of the day craving a roll slathered with butter. Dieting in America was impossible. Not only was there wonderful food, but it was for everyone. And not only was it for everyone, but television advertisements created by geniuses enticed everyone to eat. In Russia the best minds went into making missiles hit targets; in America the finest minds went into making people buy things. And when they made you want to eat food, no one from Minsk, Pinsk, or Podolsk could resist.

Natasha needed help, and when she heard of the greatest hypnotist in the world, she decided to try him. She waited in line, hearing people come out saying the strangest things, like:

"That was the best fifty minutes I ever spent in my life."

"That fifty minutes went like three seconds."

"That fifty minutes was grueling."

What was strange about all this was that they had been inside the office for less than thirty seconds.

A big hairy man sat in front of the inner office. He made sure a younger man got the money. The younger man had very curly hair and the wife of the consul could see he carried a gun. The receptionist, a very pretty blond, called him Rocco.

The woman found herself pushed through into the inner office and there she saw an old friend. She was about to say hello when she was out of the office feeling drained from fifty hard minutes working on her weight problem.

But in her case, she recognized someone she had seen just the year before in a visit to Russia. She had been privileged to use Vassily Rabinowitz in the parapsychology village where he had solved a sexual problem for her.

Natasha had been having difficulty enjoying an orgasm. More specifically, she couldn't get one at all. Her husband had the nasty habit of being a world-record premature ejaculator. If she smiled lasciviously he was through. And so was she.

Ordinarily the man would have sought treatment. But he was a ranking member of the Communist party and she was not. Therefore it was her problem, not his, and therefore she went to see this wonderful man who had cured another wife of the same problem. He had helped her to understand that she could have an instant orgasm as soon as her husband wanted to make love.

It worked beautifully. Natasha could even honestly tell her husband he was a great lover.

"Next time, wait until I take off my pants," he had said proudly.

But here in New York she had recognized Vassily Rabinowitz and she wanted to ask what he was doing there. Unfortunately, no one was going to get through those thugs. So she mentioned this strange occurrence to her husband, seeing a Russian citizen do business in America.

"Has he become a spy for us?" she asked.

"Vassily?" said her husband.

"I saw him today. Practicing on Fifth Avenue. I went to lose weight."

"Vassily!"

"Yes. I remember him from the parapsychology village."

"This is fantastic!" said her husband. He notified the head KGB officer in the consulate, who practically fell out of his chair. He refused to let the consul leave, demanded that Natasha come into his office immediately, and grilled her for twenty minutes before he sent an urgent message back to Moscow. The man Moscow was looking for was right here in New York City on Fifth Avenue and they had the address.

The response was even more urgent.

"Do nothing."

In Moscow, there was jubilation. This time, though, they would not be sending some KGB officer, or KGB troops.

This time Boris Matesev himself would go into America, as he had before, and with his special force snatch Vassily Rabinowitz and bring him back to Russia where he belonged. Maybe kill him just to be safe. It didn't matter. The nightmare was coming to a close.

Matesev was a thin man by Russian standards, more German-looking, with an aquiline nose and blond hair. He was also very neat. He had been waiting for word to go back into America for many days now.

When an officer arrived with the message, he merely smiled and packed a grooming kit with a brush, a comb, a razor, and a toothbrush. Then in a fine English tailored suit he boarded a plane to take him to Sweden, where he would catch another plane to America.

The officer, worried about Rabinowitz' legendary abilities, asked the young General Matesev where his special-force troops were. Wouldn't it be dangerous to send them in separately? An axiom in a surprise raid was to have the highest-ranking officer with the troops themselves.

To this General Matesev only smiled.

"I am asking because I know how important this is."

"You are asking because you want to know my secret of getting a large number of men in and out of America without being discovered until we are gone. That is what you want to know," said Matesev.

"I would never reveal it to anyone."

"I know you won't," said Matesev, "because I am not telling you. Just let me know if they want this Rabinowitz alive or dead."

"Alive if possible, but definitely dead if not."

5

The CIA, alerted to his coming, spotted Matesev almost immediately. His handsome face had been logged and posted, and the minute he got on a plane bound for New York City from Sweden, the man with the Norwegian passport and name of Svenson was recognized immediately as the Russian commander of the special force that had entered America twice without being spotted, which was known to exist only after it had sucessfully gotten out of the country twice.

Two strange things happened almost immediately. First, although everyone knew that the special Russian force was coming in again, Matesev arrived in Kennedy Airport alone. Not one other Russian was logged coming in with him. Both FBI and CIA coordinating teams began an alert for any large body of men arriving together or even many men arriving singly from one location.

And shortly thereafter, intercepted in communications to Moscow from New York, was an unmistakable Matesev message:

"Force assembled. Preparing to strike within twenty-four hours."

For the third time General Boris Matesev had smuggled in no less than 150 men without being detected, something the President had been assured would be impossible for a third time.

And stranger still was the order from the White House.

"Stand down. Matesev and force will be handled elsewhere."

None of them knew what the elsewhere was.

And if they knew what the elsewhere was, they would have been far more worried than they were now, seeing this danger enter America's bosom with no apparent defense.

Once Harold W. Smith got the contact call from Remo, he told the President that CURE would be capable of handling this Russian mystery man who could move 150 men invisibly into America three times. Handle Matesev with ease. In fact, Smith's people were expert at movement without being seen. They knew all the tricks of thousands of years of the House of Sinanju.

And Remo was back. He had, as Chiun had assured Smith, performed his services. As Chiun had proclaimed, no Master of Sinanju had ever failed a service. Of course Remo had implied the histories of Sinanju were a bit suspect when it came to the service of the House of Sinanju. In other words, if Sinanju ever failed a commitment, Smith was never going to hear about it from Chiun.

And yet Chiun was right. Remo was back. And the mission was too complex and important to trust communication by sound alone, no matter how secure the most modern electronics could make it. Smith had to have a face-to-face conversation with Remo.

Smith would not have been so happy if he knew what was happening the very moment his plane took off for Remo's and Chiun's new safe house just outside Epcot Center in Orlando, Florida. Smith had secured a condominium for them at Vistana Views, where visits of a week or a month or even a year would not be particularly noticeable.

After the New Hope incident he needed a place for Remo and Chiun where their neighbors were transients also. It was much safer.

But for Remo this two-room condominium with a view of an elaborate fountain, televisions in almost every room, and Jacuzzi, was just another place he was not going to stay very long.

He arrived at the condo glad to see Chiun and not knowing if he could share the sadness he felt now. Surprisingly, Chiun was solicitous. He did not have some peeve to work out on Remo. He did not stress the fact that Remo was ungrateful for the wisdom of Sinanju, that Remo thought more of his country than he did of Chiun, when Chiun had given him everything and his country had given him nothing.

None of these things did Chiun mention when Remo entered without saying hello. Remo sat down in the pastel living room and stared at the television set for an hour. It wasn't turned on.

"You know," said Remo finally, "I don't own this place. And if I did, I wouldn't want it. I don't have a home."

Chiun nodded, his wispy beard almost unmoving in the gentleness of the old man's affirmation.

"I don't own anything. I don't have a wife and family. I don't have a place."

"These things that you don't own, what are they?" asked Chiun.

"I just told you," said Remo.

"You told me what you don't know, but you did not, my son, tell me what you do know. Show me a house that has lasted thousands of years."

'The pyramids,' said Remo.

"They were tombs and they were broken into almost immediately, within a few centuries," said Chiun. "This country you so love, how old is it? A few hundred years?"

"I know what you're getting at, little father," said Remo. "Sinanju is five thousand years old, older than Egypt, older than the Chinese dynasties, older than buildings. I know that."

"You know, and you don't know. You don't know what is alive today at Epcot Center."

"Mickey Mouse? You tell me," said Remo. He knew

the Master of Sinanju liked Walt Disney, along with one
other American institution, and that was just about it for
whites and America.

"What endures today more unchanged than the very
rocks of the earth? What is more unchanged than precious
jewels that time wears away in infinitesimal amounts?
What is more unchanged than great empires that come and
go? What is that which defies time, not just delays it for a
few millennia?"

"You playing games with me, little father?" He looked
at the dark television screen. No wonder he wasn't bothered by what was showing.

"If life is a game, I am playing games with you.
Something is going on in this room, this very room, more
lasting than anything you have seen."

Remo cocked an eyebrow. Whatever Chiun was getting
at, it was the truth. Unfortunately it was opaque as the
rocks he'd been talking about, and Remo knew that the
harder he tried, the less he would understand it. That was
one of the secrets of Sinanju, that effort and strain really
worked against a person's powers.

One had to learn to respect them and allow them to
work. All the great geniuses of mankind understood that.
Mozart could no more tell where a symphony came from
than Rembrandt could his miraculously inspiring lighting.

The average human had powers he had ignored since the
day he started to rely on tools. Spear or guided missile,
every dependency on a tool caused the death of those
powers. So today when someone discovered little parts of
it, they called it extrasensory perception, or some extraordinary act of strength like a mother being able to lift a car
by herself when her baby was underneath it.

The truth was, she always had that power, and so did
everyone else, except they did not know how to gain
access to it, except in extraordinary situations when the
body took over.

Sinanju was the way to the full use of man's power.
Remo was no more extraordinary than anyone else. He

simply knew how not to let his mind interfere with his intelligence.

Ordinarily.

When Chiun was not staring at him.

When Remo was not so depressed.

On other days, and at other times.

"I give up. I don't have the foggiest what's going on in this room."

"Perhaps it is not going on now," said Chiun. "Now that you have given up."

"What are you talking about? Just tell me," said Remo.

"Are you breathing in gulps of air, without thinking? Are you letting your nervousness and body decide how to breathe instead of your essence? Are you gulping air?"

"No. Of course not."

"Then just as perfectly known as it was to the first Masters of Sinanju, beyond the pitiful recorded histories of the world, so it is known to you undiminished. No one time will wear away your excellence. No little war will end your skills as some empires have ended. No thieves can enter as they have in the pyramids. You have the only thing that will last all the days of your life. The skills that I have given you."

Remo looked at his hands. They were thinner than they were when he began, decades ago. But they had knowledge now and sensitivity he could not have even imagined before.

"You're right, little father," said Remo.

"So let us leave this temporary country you happened to be born in, and once, just once, serve Sinanju, whose treasures you lost."

"I didn't lose them, little father. They were stolen," said Remo. Chiun headed for the door.

"We're missing Sea World and Future World while you deny guilt," said Chiun.

"There was this thing that could have melted the polar ice cap. I am sorry that the collected treasures of Sinanju were stolen, but I didn't steal them. That Korean intelligence guy stole them. Not my fault someone killed him before he told you where he put them. It was his trick to get you to work for North Korea.''

"Exactly. Your fault,'' said Chiun.

"How is it my fault?'' asked Remo.

"If you had been willing to serve other countries, North Korea never would have had to steal our treasures to get our services.''

"That's like blaming the people who won't give in to the terrorists for what the terrorists do. It's nonsense.''

"We have never recovered the treasure. Five thousand years of treasure. Gone. Your fault.''

"You didn't spend it anyhow, little father. It sat there for five thousand years. Tribute from Alexander and the Mings. How many thousands of mint-condition Roman coins lay in that house? And stuff that isn't even valuable nowadays. A chunk of aluminum from 1000 B.C., when it was a rare metal; hell, a case of soda would be worth more today.''

Remo was feeling good again. And so was Chiun, seeing Remo come back with his usual ingratitude. He was healthy again. As they walked out to the road that would take them to Epcot Center, Chiun told Remo of the wonders of the world and emperors yet to be served, of treasures they could exact, of tricks they could use to manipulate the wisest leaders. There was a great new day waiting out there for the services of Sinanju, but first, Chiun wanted to see Future World.

Smith arrived at the condo and found Remo and Chiun were out. He had to wait until evening. When he noticed the unmistakable smooth movement of Remo and Chiun's walk, it was getting dark.

"I'm glad you're back, Remo. We don't have much time,'' said Smith.

"Yeah, I want to talk to you about that, Smitty. I'm afraid this is the end of the line.''

"Stop joking, Remo. America has been penetrated by a

Russian no one's been able to stop. The world's going to end.''

"That's what you said when the treasure of Sinanju was stolen. Five thousand years of Sinanju tributes stolen, and almost none of it recovered,'' said Remo.

Chiun was so pleased he almost cried. Of course, Remo was breaking the basic rule in dealing with an emperor. One never told an emperor the truth. One allowed an emperor to find the truth one presented. An emperor was never wrong or to blame. An emperor was the person who could take the right course when that course was laid out clearly for him.

Remo should have learned the proper good-byes. Chiun would show him. Remo would need them now that they would be servicing many clients. The long years of serving the mad emperor Smith, who had never used Sinanju to seize the American throne called the presidency, were over now.

Chiun chose the most florid of laudations to lay at the feet of Harold W. Smith, who had already gone down in the histories of Sinanju as the mad white emperor in the land discovered by Chiun.

It took twenty minutes to deliver them, and at the end, Smith thanked Chiun, and then said to Remo:

"What are you waiting for? We've got to start the briefing. This is a complicated matter.''

"Smitty, when Chiun told you the glorious name of Harold W. Smith would live on in the histories of Sinanju, eclipsing Alexander, Augustus of Rome, and the great pharaohs, he meant good-bye. It's good-bye for me, too.''

"But you can't. Not now.''

"Now's as good a time as any, Smitty. I think I've done my job for America. Good-bye.''

Smith followed the two of them into their condominium. It was on the ground floor and had a small screened porch facing the water fountain. The spray masked sounds more effectively than any electronic device.

"Which country are you going to serve? You can tell

me that at least," said Smith. The problem here was that
in his heart, Smith knew Remo was right. Remo had done
more for the country than any single man ever had. He had
done it year after year after year. He never flagged and he
never failed. And what had America given him? There had
to be a time when it all stopped, even for a patriot.

Remo answered that he did not know which country
they were going to.

"I may not even work for anyone. I may just rest and
look at palm trees and pyramids. I don't know. I'm tired.
I'm more than tired. I was tired years ago. It's over,
Smitty. Good-bye. And good luck."

"So it isn't determined yet who you will work for?"

"No," said Remo.

"Let me speak to Chiun a moment, if I may."

"You won't understand him."

"Let me try," said Smith.

Remo went into the main bedroom, where Chiun was
packing his kimonos.

"He wants to talk to you," said Remo.

"Aha. Now you will see him bid for our services. You
should come and watch. Now you will see as I have
always suspected that the tributes of gold brought by American submarines to the village of Sinanju might only have
been a pittance."

"I'd rather not see," said Remo. He knew Chiun would
never understand that Smith served a country he believed
in and it was not his private gold but the property of the
taxpayers of America. It was a country Remo still felt for.
He would always be an American, and he didn't want to
be there while his country was twisted by a thousand-year-
old manipulation.

Remo was going because he was going, and that was it.

Smith did not hear Chiun enter the porch, but then he
never heard Chiun. He was gazing at the fountains when
he noticed Chiun was there, totally composed as always,
and looking not one day older than he had when first they

met and he was told this was the man who would train the one enforcement arm for CURE.

"It's been a long time, Chiun. I want to say thank you, for America is honored to have had the magnificent services of the House of Sinanju."

"Sinanju is honored, most gracious one," said Chiun. Just when they were leaving, Mad Harold of America was learning how to speak to his assassin.

"I hear you are going to bid out your services," said Smith.

"We can never find one as gracious, O Emperor," said Chiun.

"May we bid also?"

"We will always consider the offer of the gracious Harold."

"We have shipped gold regularly in amounts that are now twenty times the size of what they were the first year. How can we improve?"

"If it were just gold, O wise one, we would never leave your sublime service. But as you know, the treasure of the House of Sinanju is missing. Five thousand years of collected tribute is gone."

"Gone is gone, Master. We can help replenish it."

"Can you replace the obols of Alexander, the marks of Demetrius, the tolons of the Ming? Where are the bracelets from the great African tribes, or the statues from Athens? Where are the boxes of coins with the visage of Divine Augustus therein stamped?"

"I'll make you an offer. What we cannot find for you, we will replace. We will never stop until we replace it. There is no country as capable of this as we are."

"You will undertake to replace fifty centuries of tribute to the House of Sinanju?"

"Yes," said Smith. "We will do that."

Chiun thought a moment. This was awesome. America was going to match what all the previous civilizations in the world had contributed. Ordinarily an offer like this from a king or emperor would be suspect. But Chiun had seen America, had visited its cities and factories, villages and farms. He had seen its great electronics and land so rich that crops grew in a profusion never before seen in the world.

As he had always thought, there was plenty of money here. Now Sinanju was going to get a real piece of it. America just might be able to do what Mad Harold had promised. This could mean only one thing. Smith had to do the sane and reasonable thing for the employer of Sinanju. He was going to have Sinanju do what Sinanju did best. Replace the current president and put Smith on the throne. There could be no other reason for such an awesome sum.

"Agreed. It is our true honor."

"I'd like to speak to Remo, please," said Smith.

"Of course. A fine selection. Let Remo hear it from your lips himself."

Remo had packed his one small suitcase when Chiun entered the bedroom, chortling.

"We have one last mission for Wise Harold," said Chiun.

"Why is he no longer Mad Harold? And I thought we were tired of this place."

"Remo, if you do this one thing for Wise Harold, then I will forgive you forever for the loss of the treasure of Sinanju. It will make up for your chasing around the world on foolishness while our treasures remained unfound. Smith has agreed to replace the treasures. I must prepare the list. It is very long."

"He must be desperate. What does he want?"

"Not desperate. He realizes the time has come. I have agreed on your behalf to kill the President of the United States so that Wise Harold might bring order and decency to a ravaged land."

"I don't believe it," said Remo.

"We have promised. There is no greater sin than for an assassin to break his promise."

"I'll handle one more, little father. But I am sure it is not doing in the President."

"What else could it be?" asked Chiun.

"Something extraordinarily big that only we can do."

Chiun had barely begun on the list when Remo returned, asking him if there was nothing in the history of Sinanju showing how a man could enter a country two times with more than 150 men and not be even noticed until he was gone.

General Matesev knew the moment he had lost his tail. That was the first part of his invasion of the United States, that he had pulled off twice before and had no reason to believe he could not do again, at least once more.

He moved through the giant and busy New York City for two hours, testing to see if by some miracle a tail could stay with him. When he was assured it did not, he went into an American bank and pushed a five dollar bill through the window.

"Ten quarters, please," he said.

The teller shuffled out the coins quickly. Without knowing it, she had just given General Matesev the tools he needed to bring about another successful invasion of America.

He took the ten quarters and went to a phone both. Within three hours, 150 select Russian commandos would be operating within America itself. The special force would have invaded again without a trace.

With the ten quarters he made ten phone calls. With each phone call, he said:

"Good afternoon. The sky seems a bit yellow today, don't you think?"

And with each phone call he got back a statement:

"More blue, I think. But who knows. Life is so strange, yes?"

And to that answer he said ten times:

"Riker's Island Stadium."

*　　*　　*

Joe Wilson's wife saw him pick up the phone. She had been sure he was having an affair until she listened in to one of the conversations. There was never another woman on the end of the line.

Joe didn't work. He didn't play much, other than exercising by running around the backyard five miles every day in a simple circle, and doing jumping jacks and other routines that reminded some neighbors of basic training.

Yet he didn't need money. He had income from a Swiss bank account his father gave him and the checks were deposited in his Queens bank account with more regularity than his mother received her social security.

In fact, the only way Joe's wife had ever gotten him to marry her was to agree to have the wedding at the house. And why not? That's how they met. That's how they dated. And that's how he insisted on living. Well, that wasn't so bad. Lots of people had the disease called agoraphobia that kept them chained to their homes all the time.

Yet this was entirely different. She had picked up the phone for him in the other room because he was outside exercising. When she said it was a man talking about the sky he practically ran through the door. She listened in.

"Good afternoon. The sky seems a bit yellow today, don't you think?" asked the man on the other end.

"More blue, I think. But who knows? Life is so strange, yes?" answered her husband, Joe.

"Riker's Island Stadium," said the man.

Joe hung up and began dialing other numbers. And giving orders. She had never heard him give orders before. He made fourteen phone calls and told every person at the other end the same thing.

"Riker's Island."

And then for the first time since she knew him, Joe Wilson, her husband, left their home. He kissed her lovingly good-bye and said something that terrified her.

"Look. I wasn't supposed to marry you in the first place. And you're a good kid. You've put up with a lot.

An awful lot. You've let me stay at home all this time. But I want you to know that no matter what happens, it doesn't mean I don't love you.''

''Are you leaving me, Joe? Are you leaving?''

''I love you,'' he said, and he was gone. The house seemed woefully empty without him in it. He had never left before, and the way he left so quickly and so easily told Mrs. Joseph Wilson he had never suffered agoraphobia at all.

The man called Joe Wilson took a New York bus to Riker's Island. The bus was unusually crowded that day, crowded with men, all going to Riker's Island, all in their late twenties and early thirties, all quite fit.

Riker's Island Stadium was not being used that day, and their footsteps echoed through the tunnels out onto the field. They all took seats at the fifty-yard line, looking every bit like some large team getting ready for a game.

But the man who came out of the tunnel was not a coach. No coach ever got this sort of respect.

He snapped his fingers and said, ''Group captains,'' and ten men left the stands where the other 140 sat, and walked out onto the running track to speak to General Matesev, in his fine English suit.

''We are going to be out of America in two days maximum. If we can't leave on a plane peacefully we will shoot our way out at any point I select along the Canadian border. Any of you have men who you think are unreliable?''

All ten shook their heads.

''I didn't think so. You were all well selected,'' said Matesev with a little smile. The joke was that he had selected every one of them individually, men who could keep in training and wait for that one phone call.

Because the method he had devised to invade America at will with 150 men was as simple as good logic could make it. No 150 men could invade in a single body without being seen. But 150 separate men coming into a country one at a time over the course of a year would never be noticed, 150 men who would only have to wait for a single phone call to become a unified force again. One hundred and fifty men each trained to speak American English fluently, each trained as part of a team years before in Russia, now becoming that team again.

Matesev had pulled this off twice before so that the only time America knew he had been around was after he had left, after it had seen the force leave.

It had cost the services of three hundred men, because none of them could be used again. Each operation used one deep-planted force. Expensive in training and time, but during a crisis like this so definitely worth the cost.

"We have a special problem," he said. "We have to do a snatch on someone who might be unsnatchable."

"Explain, sir," said one of his captains.

"He is an escapee from the parapsychology village in Siberia. He has special powers. He can hypnotize others instantly. A KGB unit failed to stop him at Berlin. He got out of the best protection in the village. I don't think he's stoppable. I think the minute he knows someone is going to try to snatch him, he will use his powers."

"So we are going to kill him?"

"Wrong. We are going to make sure we kill him."

"How?"

"Give me a little flexibility on that. I want to see what he's got. I'd rather spend forty-seven hours of the forty-eight hours we have to do our job in planning and preparing, than forty-seven hours of shooting up a building and one hour figuring out what went wrong. We'll get this little hypnotist good."

"What about drugging him?"

"How do you know someone is drugged? You could be hypnotized to think he was, when he wasn't."

"You could be hypnotized to believe he is dead."

"That is why we are going to work in waves. He is not going to get all one hundred and fifty of us hearing and seeing the same things. First, we stake him out. He has an office on Fifth Avenue."

"A typical capitalist address," said one captain, glad to be using the language of communism again.

"Our consulate is just off Fifth Avenue, you idiot."

Matesev assigned one unit to the stakeout, a second unit to back them up, and to the other eight units he gave the mission of procuring the proper weapons.

With the first two units, he isolated the building by intercepting all communication lines and putting them through his own command center. Vassily Rabinowitz did not know the day a new neighbor moved in downstairs that now Hypnotic Services of Fifth Avenue Inc. was located directly above a headquarters of the most effective commando squad in Soviet history.

In Washington, the President of the United States heard the one thing he never thought he would hear from the organization called CURE. When it had been organized, the need to keep its budget secret was just as great as keeping the organization itself a secret. So it was allowed to covertly tap into budgets of other departments. This avoided a hearing on its costs that would in turn, reveal its nature.

CURE could have run an entire country with its budget without anyone knowing where the cash went. Of course, Harold Smith was a man of the greatest probity. That was why he had been chosen to run this organization with an unlimited budget.

What the President had to deal with that day, besides the still mysterious danger from Russia, was the startling news from the man with the limitless budget.

"Sir," said Harold W. Smith, "I'm afraid we're going to need more funds."

To save America, CURE was going to have to pay the accumulated fortunes of five millennia of Sinanju Masters.

6

On the day before the world was supposed to fall on him, Vassily Rabinowitz heard a terrifying story from Johnny Bangossa.

"They gonna do the job on you," said Johnny, wincing.

Vassily had tried to make Johnny believe his brother never used to hit him. This, of course, the master hypnotist did easily. The wincing and ducking bothered Vassily. However, the moment Johnny Bangossa didn't believe that his older brother Carli (in the form of Vassily) would abuse him anymore, he became downright disrespectful, and even dangerous. Vassily had to get him to believe again that his brother Carli was a brutal, insensitive, and cruel dolt.

This fact having been reestablished, Johnny Bangossa returned to his form of loyalty.

"What is this thing 'doing the job'?" asked Vassily. "I have heard you mention the same phrase in regards to romance."

It had amazed Vassily with what hostility his men talked about the women they seduced. It was like a war. They talked of doing the job on this woman or that, of really "giving it to her," a phrase they would also use for beating up someone.

"Doing the job, Carli, is they're gonna kill you. Waste you. Off you. Give it to you."

"And how did you find out this information?"

"They tried to bribe me to set you up."

"I see," said Vassily. "How boring."

"Why is that boring?"

"Because they also did it with Rocco, Carlo, Vito, and Guido. This is the fifth plan to kill me. Why?"

"Carli, you know that you're cuttin' into their territory. They gotta make the move on you."

"The move. Didn't you make the move on the secretary?"

"No, that's a different move."

"How am I cutting into their territory? I just run a weight-loss, quit-smoking, sexual-problem clinic. That's all I do. I only try to protect myself."

"Well, you know the guys do a little stuff on the side. Rocco's got some narcotics, Carlo's got some prostitution, Vito does a little extortion, and Guido breaks people's legs."

"That's a business? That's a territorial territory?" asked Vassily, panicked at what America would consider a profit-making enterprise. He had heard capitalism had evils but had always assumed most of it was propaganda from the Kremlin.

"That's what they're in, and you should be taking your cut. It's good business, especially the narcotics."

"I don't want to be in narcotics, prostitution, extortion, and breaking people's legs, Johnny," said Vassily. What had gone wrong? All he wanted was to live in freedom and then after he was mugged all he wanted was to live in safety. Now he had to deal constantly with these hairy animals, and people were always trying to kill him.

"We got to do the job on them first. We gotta lay it on them. We got to really bang them hard," said Johnny Bangossa.

"I suppose we will have to fornicate them," said Vassily, trying to get into the spirit of it all. But it didn't seem to work. There were a full half-dozen men he was supposed to kill. Considering his powers, he thought, there had to be a better way.

"I'll meet with them," said Vassily.

"They'll kill you on the way to the meeting," said Johnny Bangossa.

"I'll tell Vito, Carlo, Guido, and Rocco to stop."

"Vito, Carlo, Guido, and Rocco will start workin' with the others. And we'll be done for."

"Is there any way I can get out of committing murder?"

"What for, Carli? We can have the whole thing. If we win."

While Vassily did not see breaking legs as winning something, there definitely was a major advantage to living through the day. But he had seen these men work for him. Their collective IQ was insufficient to build an outhouse.

He had also seen that reason was not something that appealed to them. They had two emotions, greed and fear. Usually they showed these two emotions in a combined form, which was anger. They were angry all the time.

The moment any one of them realized Vassily was not the man they thought him to be, he would be dead. He thought of running again. He even thought momentarily of running back to Russia. But in Russia, once he got back, they might think of a way to keep him there forever.

Something about the size of a fingernail decided Vassily's course of action that day. It was not an especially imposing thing, being a dull gray, and was rather soft for a metal. It was an ugly little piece of lead. What made it such an important piece was how quickly it was moving, faster than the speed of sound. And even more important, it was moving very close to Vassily's head. Three inches. He felt the wind of it in his hair as he got into the rear seat of his limousine. It cracked through a large plate-glass window on Fifth Avenue, and Guido and Rocco had their pistols out almost instantly.

The man who fired the rifle was now speeding away in the rear seat of a car.

Vassily picked himself up out of the gutter and wiped the dirt off his expensive new blue suit. He was more frightened than he had ever been in his life. Always before in danger he could catch the eye of his attacker. But here he could be killed without ever seeing the man.

Like most people captured by fear, Vassily lost all sense of balance and proportion. He was yelling when he got his boys together. He wanted to know everything about his enemies. What were their habits, what were their routines?

And in that state of mine, he devised a simple plan that could be put into effect that very night. He took three leaders of his opposition and targeted them for death, even as he told them he wanted to make peace with them. He hated himself as he did this, but fear almost always wins over self-respect.

Slimy was the way he felt about himself, but he had no choice. He had one shotgunned to death inside an elevator where the man couldn't move. Fat Guido took care of that one. Another was machine-gunned in bed with his woman, and the woman was killed also. But the most vile part of it all was having one of his men, Carlo, pose as a policeman and shoot one of his targets on the steps of Saint Patrick's Cathedral, a house of worship, a place where people prayed.

By midnight, as the reports came in of one horrid deed after another, he found he couldn't look at himself in the mirror. Outside the plush living room of his Park Avenue apartment, Vassily heard noise. It was his men. He could always hypnotize them to believe they hadn't done these horrible deeds. He could have them know in their bones that this horrible day did not happen, but he would know. And one day, he might be so overcome with remorse that he would slip and fail to keep one of these men in a hypnotic state.

The noise increased outside his living room. Were they in a state of rebellion, revolted by the horrors they were forced to commit, horrors that even for gangsters had to wrench their souls?

Suddenly the door burst open and there were Johnny Bangossa, Vito, Guido, Rocco, and Carlo, and they were all coming at him. Johnny was the first to grab his right hand. So stricken was he by his guilt that Vassily failed to make eye contact and convince Johnny he had never done such a horrible thing as to machine-gun a man in bed with his lover.

Vassily closed his eyes and waited for the first horrible sensation of death. He felt something wet on his right hand. Then he felt something wet on his left hand. He couldn't pull his hands away. Was this some form of liquid poison?

He waited for it to penetrate the skin. But there was only more wetness. He heard a strange sound at one hand.

All right, he thought. Poison is not the worst thing. There are worse ways to die. Being shotgunned in an elevator is a worse way to die. Being machine-gunned while making love is a worse way to die. Being surprised by a man posing as a police officer shooting you on the steps of a house of worship is a worse way to die. Perhaps poison is too good for me.

But he was not dead. He could not free his hands, but he was not dead. He heard the noise of kissing coming from the ends of his arms. Smelled the horrible oils his boys used on their hair. And felt lips caressing the back of his palms. He opened his eyes.

Vito, Guido, Rocco, and Carlo were bumping heads trying to be the first to kiss his hands.

It was a form of honor, he knew.

"You really did it, Carli. You're wonderful. You're a power now. You got respect. You always had our love, brother. Now you got our respect. And the respect of New York City," said Johnny "The Bang" Bangossa to the man he thought was Carli Bangossa.

"We're a major family now," said Guido, who allowed as how for his wonderful services that day, he should be made a *caporegime*. And so did Johnny, Vito, Rocco, and Carlo.

"Certainly," said Vassily. Only later was he informed that he had just given these five thugs the right to recruit and organize their own crime families under his general command.

The bodies were still warm when the New York media began analyzing the results. Dealing with the brutal killings like some ball game, they announced a new player making a brilliant move. None of the inside sources knew for sure who this new Mafia don was, but he had shown himself to be a brilliant strategist. In one master stroke he had immobilized the other families who were now suing for peace. And an informed source indicated this organizational genius was collecting the remnants of the other temporarily demoralized crime families.

Vassily Rabinowitz realized now he was some kind of hero. What he had considered a form of degradation was genius here. Who knew, maybe he would even like breaking legs for a living, if they broke cleanly and did not create too much pain and blood.

He wished his mother could see him now. She would have to agree he was not the most reckless boy in town as he had been called back in Dulsk, before he allowed himself to go to that village in Siberia, before all this, when he was just a simple ordinary lad. He wondered if he could get his mother out of Russia, perhaps set her up here. Maybe as the mother of a don, as he understood the head of a "family" to be called, she would be called a donna. There were women here of that name. He would be Don Vassily and his mother would be Donna Mirriam.

When General Matesev's first unit hit the Rabinowitz office of Fifth Avenue the following morning, they made their way through a long line of customers, pushing aside the secretary, and opening the door to the inner office, using an old technique for city warfare. You didn't rush into a room. You threw a hand grenade into the room first. They you looked to see if anyone was in there.

When the first unit had determined there had been a kill in the office Vassily Rabinowitz had been using every day for the last few weeks, the second unit quickly followed with bags, suction equipment, and various specimen-collecting devices. Quickly the remnants of what had been a person would be whisked out of that office into a truck that was really a laboratory. What they wanted from the remnants of a person was blood type, cell type, and fingerprints if they were lucky. If they got a whole face, so much the better.

But General Matesev was not going to risk anyone talking to this man who could turn even the most hardened minds of the finest KGB officers. Kill first, identify second, return to Moscow third, the mission accomplished. One had to keep things simple.

Unfortunately the first wave found only shattered furniture and windows. No one had been in the office.

"Mr. Rabinowitz is not seeing anyone," said a secretary, getting up from behind a desk. People were now scattering in the hallways and screaming.

"Where is he?" demanded the unit leader of the fourteen men of the lead squad of the Matesev force.

"Won't do you any good. You can't get an appointment."

"Where is he?"

"I think he's moved to Long Island. He's got a big house and a wife with a mustache, I think. I don't know. He's not coming in anymore. He phoned this morning. No more appointments. I've been telling that to everyone."

Remo approached the large brick house on Long Island, walking between the moving vans that were unloading dark lacquered furniture, pink lamps, and sequined chairs. It was a collection of furniture that any merchant would have been glad to pawn off on a drunken aborigine.

General Matesev had come to America looking for Vassily Rabinowitz. Rabinowitz' Fifth Avenue office had been blown up that morning by hand grenades. Fifteen men working in unison had demolished the place. The police came. The newsmen came. Then the newsmen started asking if this were another hit in the new Mafia war. Remo mingled among them. He had found out Rabinowitz had an apartment on this fashionable street. He rushed to the apartment. He didn't want Matesev getting this Rabinowitz and getting out of the country before Remo had a chance at him.

Smith had also had another requirement: he wanted to know what Matesev was after. Remo had said that was simple. Rabinowitz.

"But why does he want Rabinowitz? No one can figure that out. A simple Russian citizen is not worth all this."

So there were two things to do that morning. Matesev first, Rabinowitz second, get them both before one did in the other.

At Rabinowitz' apartment, he saw workmen carrying out furniture.

He asked where it was going. The workmen refused to say anything and warned him that if he knew what was good for him, he would keep his mouth shut and his eyes closed.

Remo said that was an unkind way to respond to a simple question. The movers said if Remo knew what was good for him, he wouldn't ask those kinds of questions. Besides, they didn't have to answer. There was nothing that could force them.

So Remo offered to help them with the moving. He moved a large couch by grabbing one leg, and held it perfectly level with complete ease. Then he used the other end of the couch to play with the movers.

"Tickle tickle," said Remo, coaxing a large mover's rib with the far end of the stuffed white couch. He coaxed the mover up into the truck. Then he coaxed him to the front of the truck. Then he coaxed him against the front of the truck. Remo was about to coax the mover through the front of the truck when the mover had something very important to say to Remo.

"Great Neck, Long Island. Baffin Road. He's got an estate there. But don't mess with him."

"Why not? I like to mess."

"Yeah. You don't see how we're haulin' this furniture? You don't see it?"

"No, I don't see a scratch on it," said Remo, dropping the couch and giving the load its first scratch. With a crash.

"Yeah, well, when you see movers not even getting a

scratch on furniture, you gotta know it's for racketeers. No one who can't break your arms and legs is going to get furniture moved this nice. Mafia.''

"Rabinowitz. That doesn't sound Italian. I always thought you had to be Italian.''

"Yeah, well, that ain't what I just heard. This guy's got more funny names than anyone I know. One guy calls him Carli, one calls him Billy, and another calls him Papa. And I wouldn't want to be alone in an alley with any of those guys. So you tell me. Is he Mafia or is he not Mafia? I don't care if the guy's got a name like Winthrop Winthrop Jones the Eighth. If you got the thugs around you like he's got, you're Mafia.''

And so Remo had gotten the new address of Vassily Rabinowitz, and went out to the Long Island estate to await the attack of General Matesev's men. It was a large estate with high brick walls and a big iron fence at which two very tough-looking men stood guard.

"I'm looking for work,'' said Remo.

"Get outta here,'' said one of the guards. He had a big lead pipe on his lap, and under his jacket he had a .38. He allowed the bulge of the gun to show, no doubt considering it an effective deterrent. He had the sort of pushed-in face that let you know he would happily use either weapon.

"You don't understand. I want work and I want a specific job. I want yours.''

The man laughed and tightened his ham fists around the lead pipe. He started to push it at Remo's chest. He hardly saw the thin man's hands move, but suddenly the pipe was doubled in half.

"Sometimes I wrap it around necks,'' said Remo, and since the man looked on with some incredulity, he showed him how. Remo bent the gray lead pipe around the man's thick neck like a collar, leaving a little bit extra for a handle.

The other man went for his gun, and Remo put him quickly to sleep by glancing a blow off his skull, causing reverberations that would not allow the brain to function.

He tugged the pipe along with him, down the long brick path to the elegant main house with the gables and dormers, and guns sticking out of them.

He tugged the guard a good quarter-mile to the door of the main house. Yellow and red tulips, the flowers in full blossom, made a bright pattern against the red brick. Newly trimmed grass gave a rich earthy smell to this walled haven on Long Island. The door opened and was filled with a hairy man.

"I want his job," said Remo, nodding at the guard whose neck was still encased in the lead pipe.

"You do that?" asked the man.

Remo nodded.

"He do that?" asked the man.

The guard nodded.

"You're hired. You're in my regime. My name's Johnny Bangossa. My brother Carli runs this family. There's no one more important after Carli than me."

"And what about Rabinowitz?"

"Who is that Jew?" asked Johnny. "I keep hearing about him everywhere."

"I heard he owned this place," said Remo.

"Maybe he was the one what sold it to us," said Johnny Bangossa.

"But his name's on the furniture and address here."

"That guy gets around," said Johnny. "But my brother Carli says he's all right. He says nobody should hurt him for nothing."

"I see," said Remo. But he didn't.

The entire first unit had failed. The second unit was useless, and the third did not know where to go.

General Matesev smiled slightly and took a sip of coffee. The men had to see he was not panicked. The worst thing a commander could do to men behind enemy lines was to let them succumb to fear. They had enough tension already. Many of them had been living with it for years. Perhaps much of it had dissipated after awhile, but now they all knew they were going to have to fight their way home and something had gone wrong.

What Matesev would do now would earn him the awe of his men. Ordinarily when something went wrong a Russian commander would punish someone. Nothing bad could happen without someone being at fault.

Matesev merely looked at his coffee intently and asked what kind it was. He was in the back of what looked like a large refrigerator truck that was really his headquarters. It could easily hold thirty men and all the equipment they would need. It had been waiting for him with one of his units.

"I don't know, sir," said one of the men hastily.

"Very good. Very good. But we now have a very serious problem. Very serious."

The men nodded gravely.

"How do we get enough of this wonderful coffee back to Russia to last us a lifetime?"

Everyone in the back of the sealed truck suddenly burst into laughter.

"All right," he said. "Back to our problem. Unit One didn't fail. Neither did Unit Two. Our friend Vassily Rabinowitz failed. He failed to be there. Now, we have a day and a half to find out where he is. That should be no problem. But what I want you good fellows to think of is how we can get this coffee back with us."

Matesev knew Moscow would not accept such levity, but Moscow was helpless. They wouldn't have wasted this last group on this mission if they could have done it with anyone else. The problem with secreting entire units within America was that once the unit was used, it could never be used again.

But Matesev did not tell his men how alarmingly bad the news got. His reports came in that Rabinowitz had somehow gotten himself involved with local criminals and now was beginning some sort of an empire. This was the Kremlin's worst fear. No one cared whether Rabinowitz controlled all the narcotics in America, or the world for that matter. That was not what frightened those at the parapsychology village who knew his power.

Their worry was where he would stop, because once he had a taste of criminal power, he most certainly would want more and more and no one would be capable even of delaying him. The time to get him was when he was alone, before he used his powers to create followers.

But that point had already passed.

Matesev decided to ignore it. Instead, he made a calculated gamble. He was sure no criminals in the world could match 150 of the best Russian commandos. Criminals were never that good in a group. The attack this time would not be by small units but one massive assault with everyone thrown into it. There might be one or two or at most three effective men with weapons among that group Rabinowitz had surrounded himself with, but no more than that. Let them taste a full-scale assault.

And of course this time he was going to make sure Vassily was home.

When it was determined that he was secluded in an estate in Great Neck, Long Island, Matesev drew a large loose ring around the estate, leaving his men in little groups at every road, far enough away so that the gangsters would not think Rabinowitz' estate was being surrounded. Sure now that Rabinowitz could not escape by road, Matesev waited until the first night, and then sent in two of his most agile men, not to kill, and most assuredly not to look into Rabinowitz' eyes, but to place extremely accurate sensors in the building itself.

This time, Matesev would only attack when he was sure Rabinowitz was there. And this time it would work. He himself insisted on constant access to the eavesdropping devices. They provided him with many strange bits of information and an insight into American life he never had before.

Rabinowitz, as could be expected, had all his top lieutenants believing he was someone else, so that if Matesev wanted to be sure where Rabinowitz was he had to understand that a man named Johnny Bangossa thought Rabinowitz was Carli and a man called Carlo referred to Rabinowitz as "Papa."

Even more interesting was how well this organization seemed to work because everyone thought he was related to the boss.

Matesev began to appreciate how truly dangerous Rabinowitz could become if he were going to survive another day. The Kremlin, as was their occasional wont, was most right in this matter. The fact that Rabinowitz' voice print could be picked up and verified from the equipment on the truck was reassuring.

In the morning, Matesev's men spotted the police chief's car headed into the Rabinowitz estate. Was Rabinowitz getting police protection? Was he getting arrested?

The sensors verified neither. There was no arrest and no talk of protection. In fact, the lieutenants of the mob greeted the policemen most cordially.

And then the police officers, Monahan, Minehan, and Moran, were heard talking to Rabinowitz. And since none of them started talking to relatives, Matesev had to assume Rabinowitz had not hypnotized them yet.

"Look here. You move into town with all this criminal element, Mr. Rabinowitz, and you could give this pretty little village a bad name. There could be shootings. There could be gangsterism. And we're worried about that," said Captain Monahan's voice.

"We got to look out for this community," said Lieutenant Minehan's voice.

"There's decency and a clean spirit here," said Lieutenant Moran's voice.

"I have three very fat white envelopes for you boy-chicks," said Rabinowitz' voice. "Johnny Bangossa, Rocco, Vito, and Guido said that's what you wanted. That's how business is done here in America."

"Always glad to receive an upstanding new member of the community," said the voices of Monahan, Minehan, and Moran in unison.

When the police car was outside the gate, new words came from Monahan, Minehan, and Moran. The words were "kike" and "wop." They were having difficulty distinguishing which one Rabinowitz was. The only thing Minehan, Monahan, and Moran could agree on was that "they" were all alike. Unfortunately, with Vassily Rabinowitz and his brother Johnny "The Bang" Bangossa, Minehan, Monahan, and Moran couldn't exactly decide which "they" they were talking about.

It was 9:35 A.M. Rabinowitz had been in the main drawing room. He was probably still there. The key fact of this meeting was that when it came to police, Rabinowitz was not using his special powers.

Matesev saw now not only exactly how he could kill Rabinowitz with certainty, but also how he might even attain the harder goal, capturing Rabinowitz alive.

Not until this very moment had he dared even to consider this harder plan. But there was just a chance. The question was how to make the most of that chance and still make sure that, at worst, Rabinowitz would be dead.

It was ten A.M. when three of his strongest men, each dressed as a policeman, entered the gates of the Rabinowitz estate asking to speak to Mr. Rabinowitz. They said they were bringing information from their commanding officers, Monahan, Minehan, and Moran.

They were allowed into the house. So far so good. Matesev heard the voice of Rabinowitz. Better yet. There was a scuffle, and then silence. No voices, just some scraping. Then a loud thud.

Now all Matesev's other units had left their road posts and were ready to converge on the estate. It was a full-scale assault one way or another. Dead or alive, win or lose, there was no better time than now.

"He's taped on the mouth and eyes. We got him," came the voice.

"All right," said Matesev. "Hold there as long as you can. If you're about to lose him, kill him. Good work."

And then the order went out: "Attack now, full speed. Everyone hits. We've got him."

The assault forces poured out of their cars and over the wall. One unit broke through the main gate and headed straight up the driveway. It was a charge to shame the greatest Cossack legions.

Inside the Rabinowitz house, the forces of the great new don ducked under chairs and tables and looked for ways out. They knew instantly those animals on the lawn meant business and were no friends of theirs. Treachery and sellouts would do no good. When a few shots hit some of the advancing men, and the rest kept coming anyway, all resistance ceased. For a while.

In the confusion no one saw a thick-wristed man grab one soldier by the neck, speak to him briefly, and then head the other way. After all, why notice one more gangster trying to save his life? Except this "gangster" had just found out where General Matesev was.

Matesev listened to the reports as his precise plan worked to the letter. The group that had seized Rabinowitz had linked with the main assault force, with a loss of fewer than three men, and were now headed back toward the escape points for their flight out of America. Only when they were out of the country would America know they had been there. But by then General Matesev's special force would have performed its third successful mission.

Now Matesev contacted the Kremlin for the first time. Now he would let them say whatever they wanted.

It was all over but the shouting. The message he wired home was that they had gotten what they came for and were bringing it home alive.

He had a big grin on his face when he heard someone knocking on the steel doors of the back of the refrigerator truck.

"Hey, c'mon, sweetheart. I don't have all day here."

7

Remo saw into the darkest corners of the refrigerator truck. The equipment was set into the walls so it could travel and still work. It was a command post and the blond man with the shocked face seemed to fit the description of Matesev. Considering this was where his man said he would be, it was almost a positive identification.

"General Matesev, welcome to America," said Remo. The man still did not move. Sometimes things like that happened when the rear doors of trucks were taken off and a person was counting on it for protection. Perhaps it was the fact that the steel door was still in Remo's hand, held off to the side, catching the wind like a heavy wing on an aircraft, and that Remo just peered in like a child who had ripped the top off a box of ants.

"No. No Matesev here," said the man. "We are an electronics firm. Would you be so kind as to put down the door?"

"C'mon, buddy. I got work and I'm tired. You're Matesev."

"I've never heard of a Matesev," said Matesev with perfect control. His first instinct was to ease a pistol into firing position and let off a clip. But that was a steel door he saw held out behind the man. He was sure this thing that looked like a man had done the ripping. If he could do that, what else could he do? A bullet at this distance might not work.

Besides, the units with Rabinowitz would be converging on the truck any moment now. Better more than 140 men than one man.

This one certainly was different. He didn't climb into the truck, he moved into it with what would have been a jump, except there was no effort. No more effort than a cat sitting down and he was in the truck and at Matesev's back where suddenly the man was pouring molten metal down Matesev's shirt.

Matesev screamed as the metal tore through his rib cage, obliterating his intestines and reproductive organs on its way through his chair.

And then it was gone. No smoke. No burning flesh. No burns. Not even pain as the man removed his fingers from Matesev's chest. Matesev was still quivering as he examined himself and was surprised nothing stuck to his hand. Not even his shirt was damaged.

"I can do it again," said Remo. "It's a trick, you know. Do you know when I stop doing it?"

Matesev shook his head. He was afraid if he spoke his tongue would fall out. Even if his body had recovered instantaneously, his mind had not. He was being held in a vat of molten metal even though the metal did not exist anymore. And never had. It was all in the manipulation of this strange man's hands.

"I stop doing it when you tell me who you are. Now I think you're Matesev, General Matesev, and I've got to talk to you."

"Yes. I am. I am he." Matesev glanced out of the rear of the truck. The men would be there any moment. The trick was to let the men know this man had to be killed without letting the man know he was doing it.

"Good. Now who or what is Vassily Rabinowitz?"

"A Soviet citizen."

"There are a few hundred million of them. Why are you people so excited about that one?"

"I am just an ordinary soldier. I was assigned to capture him."

The molten metal was burning Matesev's chest, and this time he was sure he could smell the burning, that it was not a manipulation, that somehow this man of great powers had actually melted the metal to wound Matesev. Only when it stopped did the general realize that if it really were molten metal it would have burned right through and it would have killed him. The pain was so intense his mind had snapped into thinking the flesh was actually burning.

"I am Matesev. I am in charge of the special force. Rabinowitz is the greatest hypnotist in the world."

"So?" said Remo.

"Don't you understand what that means? He can hypnotize anyone instantly. Instantly. Anyone."

"Yeah?" said Remo.

"Well, if he can hypnotize anyone instantly, what happens when he tells one general to do this and another to do that?"

"He joins the Defense Department. I don't know," said Remo. "Lots of people tell generals to do this and that. That's what you have generals for."

"You don't understand," said Matesev. How could a man with such powers be so dense?"

"Right," said Remo.

"He could take over any government in the world."

"So?" said Remo.

"We couldn't allow that to happen."

"Why?"

"Don't you understand the international implications?"

"Better than you, Russky. There's always going to be another country every few hundred years. Five hundred years from now you'll probably have the czar again. I don't know what we'll be. Whole thing doesn't matter, jerk," said Remo.

Matesev had always been taught that Americans never really planned ahead. That if you were to ask them where they would be in fifty years they would say that was the business of some astrologer instead of a government planner. American foreign policy ran from one four-year election to another. That was its trouble.

But here was a man, obviously American, obviously thinking in terms not of fifty years or even a century, but in millennia.

And it all didn't matter. Matesev saw the units come down the street, almost like a mob, not marching of course, but walking in a pack.

They had a trussed bundle with them, its eyes and mouth taped. Rabinowitz.

"We've got company," said Matesev, nodding to his own men. The man turned.

"What's in the bundle?" he asked.

He kept looking at the unit advancing on the truck. The back of his head was within reach. It was too good a target for General Matesev to pass up. The small handgun was within an instant's grasp.

Matesev took it smoothly, put it to the dark hairs in the back of the man's head, and fired.

The bullet hit the roof of the truck. And the head was still there. He fired again, this time aiming at a specific hair. The bullet hit the roof again.

"Don't do that," said the man softly.

Matesev emptied the chamber, and missed with all the rest of the slugs, but in so doing, in firing rapidly, he was able to get a glimpse of the head moving back and forth as it dodged the shells.

"All right. You happy? You had your thrill?" asked Remo.

"I'll call my men off," gasped the stunned Matesev.

"Who cares?" said Remo. "You are General Matesev, though. I mean, is that determined? There is no question about that?"

"Yes."

"Thanks," said Remo, who rattled the man's brains into jelly by shaking the skull like a soda jerk mixing a milk shake.

Then he was out of the truck and amidst the startled

Russians, bouncing many, killing some, and getting the trussed bundle out of their hands. He took it behind a house, over a fence, and to a road about a mile away, where he untaped the eyes and mouth and hands of Vassily Rabinowitz.

"You okay?" asked Remo.

Rabinowitz blinked in the harsh sunlight. He was still trembling. He didn't know where he was. He had released his bladder in panic. The man could barely stand. Remo got to the spinal column, and with the pads of his fingers set the rhythms of peace into Rabinowitz's body structure. With a little cry, Rabinowitz recovered, brushed himself off, and noticed the wetness in his pants.

"The bastards," he said.

"Is there anything I can do for you?" asked Remo. Rabinowitz looked shaky.

"No. I'll be all right."

"Your countrymen say you're the world's greatest hypnotist. Is that true?"

"To them anything is true. I can do things," said Rabinowitz. "How did Russian soldiers get into the country?"

"I don't know. Maybe they posed as Mexicans," said Remo. "You sure you're going to be all right?"

"Yes. I think so. Do you know what happened to Johnny Bangossa, Guido, Rocco, Vito, and Carlo?"

"I think they ran."

"Some crime family," said Rabinowitz. They could see the beginning of the main street of the town down the road and walked to it. Back near the truck there was gunfire. Apparently the Russian soldiers, without the genius of General Matesev to plan their escape, resorted to what soldiers naturally did. They dug in and shot at everyone who wasn't their kind. Now they were zeroing light mortars on the Long Island Expressway and planning to fight to the death.

Remo found a coffee shop.

"You are the first person who has been kind to me since

I have come here to America. You are my first friend,''
said Vassily.

"If I'm your friend, buddy, you're in trouble."

"Is what I am saying. I am in trouble," said Vassily. "I
don't have a friend. I don't have my crime family. I had
one of the best crime families in America. See? I'll show
you."

As the large sugary Danish pastry arrived with the heavily creamed coffee, Vassily came back to the table with a
handful of New York City newspapers. He went right to
the stories. Apparently he had read them before.

Proudly he pushed them across the Formica table for
Remo to read.

"You know, sugar's a drug," said Remo, glancing at
the glistening layer of chemically colored goo enveloping
the sugar-and-flour concoction. If Remo had one bite, his
highly tuned nervous system would malfunction, and he
would probably pass out.

"I like it," said Vassily.

"They say that about cocaine and heroin, too," said
Remo, wincing as Vassily took a big bite.

"Is good," said Vassily. "Read, read. Look at the part
about the 'cunning mastermind.' Is me."

Remo read about shotgunning in elevators, machine-
gunning in bedrooms, and shooting in the back of the steps
of a church.

"Pretty brutal," said Remo.

"Thank you," said Vassily. "Those were my bones, as
they call them. Have you made your bones?"

"You mean do a service?"

"Yes. Most assuredly. Do service."

"Yeah," said Remo.

"Would you like to join my new crime family?"

"No. I'm going overseas somewhere."

"Where?"

"I don't know."

"Crime families are not what they're cracked up to be,"
said Vassily. "They all ran. What is this with them? I

made them *caporegimes,* too. And then they ran. What are crime families coming to nowadays? That is what I ask. I hear so much about America deteriorating. Is this true of the crime families?''

"I dunno," said Remo. "I got my own problems. Once I find out what you do, then I'm done. More than twenty years and I'm through here. Well, okay, good enough. What should I tell my boss you do? I mean exactly. I mean, would a country invade another country just to get back a hypnotist? I thought he might have been lying.''

"Was not lying. Russians are crazy. Crazy people. They invaded, you say?''

National Guard helicopters buzzed overhead. In the distance, small-arms fire could be heard. Many people had rushed out of the luncheonette and were being warned by policemen to stay back. Somehow the Russians had invaded America, but the word was, not too many of them.

A bunch of Russians was trapped, someone yelled.

"And in one of the best neighborhoods, to boot,'' said another.

"They sent soldiers,'' said Vassily, covering his eyes with his hands. "What am I going to do? I can't fight a whole country. Not a whole country. You've got to be my friend.''

Vassily now decided that if this man would not be his friend voluntarily, he would do it the other way. It was always better to have a sincere real friend, but when one couldn't, one had to make do with what one had.

Just like with women. One would prefer that a woman would undrape herself with honest passion, but when one did not have honest passion available, the next best thing was dishonest passion. It certainly was better than no passion at all. He would give the man who introduced himself as Remo one last chance.

"Be my friend,'' he said.

"I got a friend,'' said Remo. "And he's a pain in the ass.''

"Then hello,'' said Vassily, taking his hands away from

his eyes to make contact with Remo, who was going to be his best friend whether he liked it or not.

Unfortunately the man moved faster than anything Vassily had ever seen, and he did it so gracefully it hardly looked as though he were moving, except that he was out the door and into the street in an instant.

The reports out of Washington buzzed with relief. The President had nothing but praise for CURE. Smith, however, felt uncomfortable with praise. As Miss Ashford used to say in the Putney Day School back in Vermont:

"One should never do a job for praise, but because it should be done. And it should be done well. One should never be praised for doing what one should, because all jobs should be done well."

This parsimonious attitude was not peculiar to Miss Ashford. It was what the Smiths believed, and the Coakleys, and the Winthrops, and the Manchesters. Harold W. Smith had been raised in an atmosphere that was as rigidly uniform as in any of the courts of China. Everything had changed since then but the memories of the older folk, of which Harold W. Smith at age sixty-seven legitimately counted himself.

And so when the President told Smith he had come through in the hardest times, Smith answered:

"Is there anything else, sir?"

"We easily captured that special Russian group, and do you know how they got in every time without us finding them? They were planted ahead of time. All set to go. Bang. All they needed was their commander to tell them to go. And your man got him, and the rest of them are useless. And we know now how to take precautions against any other attempts at this. These are tough times and it feels damned good to win one for a change," said the President.

"Sir, what can we do for you?"

"Take a damned compliment for once," said the President.

"I do not not believe, sir, we were commissioned to win medals and such. If I ever mentioned a medal to either of our two active people, they would laugh at me."

"Well, dammit, thank you anyhow. You should know that the Russians have denied any involvement with their own soldiers, publicly declaring it a capitalist imperialist Zionist plot. Privately they threw up their hands and apologized. I think this thing is turning everything around. Their espionage system is exposed as it never has been before, their special group will never exist again, and we have them on the run. They've pulled back into their shell and word is they are running scared. Scared."

"Except we don't know why they risked so much yet."

"Did you find out?"

"Not yet, but I suspect when one of our active people calls in, I will."

"Let us know," said the President, and again he surrendered to bubbling enthusiasm. "These are great days to be an American, Harold W. Smith. I don't care how expensive that laundry list of treasure is to get. It's worth it."

"It might be a strain on the budget, sir."

"What budget? Nobody knows how this thing works. Besides, what's another few billion more if it's worth it? We lost a few billion just in accounting."

"Yessir," said Smith, hanging up.

Down at Vistana Views, Remo looked around the condominium to see if he had left anything. He was leaving America for good now. He had completed his last mission. Smith would be here soon for the last debriefing.

He felt sad, but he didn't know why he felt sad. He told himself it was fitting that he was leaving from Epcot Center, a Walt Disney production. His whole life might have been Mickey Mouse all along.

Was America any better for the work he had done? Was he any better? The only thing that made him better was his training. Chiun tried to cheer him by talking about the glories of the courts of kings, how one could play games with dictators and tyrants as employers, how Smith was inexplicable and treated his assassins poorly, ashamed of them, hiding their deeds, even hiding himself. But in the land of the true tyrant, an assassin was flaunted, an assassin was honored, an assassin was boasted about.

"Yeah, good," said Remo. And still he felt like yesterday's old potatoes, somehow being thrown out with the rest of his life.

"Do you feel bad, Remo. The Great Wang understood these things. It happens to all Masters, even the great ones."

"Did it happen to you, little father?" asked Remo.

"No. It never happened to me."

"Why not?"

"Well, you have to feel that somehow you have done something wrong. All I had to do was look at my life. As the Great Wang said: 'Do not judge a life by how it ends, as do those of the West, but judge it by the whole.' If I did nothing but fail for the rest of my life, I would still be wonderful."

"That's you, not me. I feel like the world has fallen out from underneath me and I don't know why."

"As the Great Wang said: 'Before perfection is that awareness of not being perfect, so that you feel your worst before you achieve your new level.' You are only getting better, Remo. And we should be grateful for that, because you certainly needed it."

"Great Wang. Great Wang. Great Wang. There are lots of Masters. I studied them. Why is he so damned great? I don't see it."

"Because you're not good enough to see it."

"Maybe you're better than the Great Wang. How do I know?"

"You are not to know, I am to know. Hurry, all the good tyrants seem to be falling."

"How do you know the Great Wang was so great? Was he greater than your father?"

"No. I was greater than my father."

"Then how do you know?"

"When you reach a certain level, you see the Great Wang."

"Is he alive? Does his spirit still exist in this world?"

"No. It exists in the greatness of Sinanju. And when you achieve that, that next level, you will see him."

"What does he look like?"

"A bit overweight, as a matter of fact, but he told me I was thin, so on his advice I gained an ounce and a half."

"You actually talked to him?"

"You can when you make the passage. What you are feeling now is the beginning of your passage."

"So what is the big deal about passing into a better level? I'm already more than good enough for what I need."

"How cruel the stab of one's own son, nurtured like a natural son, reverting to his white attitudes again. It is the reason that the white race will never be great."

"Anytime you want to call it quits with me, little father," said Remo, "say so."

"Testy today, aren't we?" said Chiun with a smile.

The Master of Sinanju knew he had won. No matter what Remo said, he was on his way to his new level. It was not that he would seek it. Indeed, if he didn't try so hard sometimes, he would be there already. But the truth about Remo's new level was that it was not taking hold of him. And soon he would see the Great Wang for himself and hear the advice given only to the great Masters of Sinanju, whatever that advice would be. It would be right. The Great Wang was always right. Never was there a time when he was not right. This was recorded in the histories of Sinanju, this was reality. Every time Remo could move up a wall vertically and understand it was only the fear of falling that was his enemy, every time he breathed in concordance with the great forces of the cosmos, the Great Wang lived. And now he was only waiting to say hello to Remo at the right time.

This Chiun knew, and this Remo could not know until it happened.

Mad Emperor Smith arrived, a half-hour late. The one thing the lunatic had had in his favor was punctuality and now that was gone. Good riddance, said Chiun in Korean.

The translation for Smith into English lost something, however.

"Oh, gracious benignity," intoned Chiun as he opened the door for the head of CURE. "In our last day of perfect service, glorifying your name, the tears of our parting rend the hearts of your faithful assassins, knowing there will be no equal to your glory."

Even Smith, color-blind, recognized the red kimono with the gold dragons. That was the kimono Chiun had worn the first day they had met, and never worn since. They were actually leaving at last, thought Smith. It was good-bye. Well, at least they had saved the country. That force that had invaded America with impunity not only had been destroyed, but Russia had been thoroughly embarrassed and was really whipped on all fronts as the President had said. The two sides were no longer teetering toward a world-ending conflict. Russia was in retreat. They had given America the breathing space it needed to avoid launching missiles that could never be called back. Now all Smith had to do was find out why Russia had sent in the Matesev group.

Remo offered his hand.

"I guess this is the end," he said.

"I guess it is," said Smith.

"Yeah. Well, who knows," said Remo.

"Sit down. Let's talk about Matesev's mission."

"Don't have to sit, Smitty. They were after a hypnotist. Supposed to be a great hypnotist."

"They have lots of hypnotists," said Smith. "The Russians are famous for doing experiments with the human mind. Why would they be after this one?"

"Supposedly he could do it with everyone instantly. I

mean when I found him, Matesev's people had his eyes taped and his mouth taped. They were scared of him.''

"Of course, they should be. If he is what they say he is, someone like that could control the world. I could see how he would escape Russia easily. Escape anywhere easily. This man could walk into the Department of Defense and start a war. No wonder they wanted to keep him under wraps. I'm surprised they didn't kill him when they found out he could do those things.''

"Why not use him to their advantage?" asked Remo.

"Who would be using whom when he could hypnotize anyone into believing anything? He was like an atomic warhead, but with a mind of his own. They must have been on tenterhooks all the time they had him.''

"Maybe," said Remo. "In any case, Smitty, good luck and good-bye.''

"Wait a minute. What did he look like?''

"About five-foot-seven. Kind of sad brown eyes. Nice guy. Lonely.''

"You spoke with him?''

"Sure," said Remo.

"You let him go?" asked Smith. The lemony face suddenly turned red as horror set in. "You let him go? How on earth could you let him go, knowing what he was? How could you do such a thing?''

"That wasn't my job. You said do Matesev. I did Matesev. All right? You said find out what he wanted. I found out what he wanted. Case closed.''

"You could have thought. We have to get Rabinowitz. There's no way we can let that man roam around this country. For both our sakes. Those damned stupid Russians. Why didn't they tell us? We could have worked together.''

"Good-bye, Smitty.''

"You can't leave, Remo. You can recognize him.''

"Recognize him, hell. He wanted to be my friend.''

"You have too many friends, Remo," said Chiun. He was waiting for Remo to lift the trunks. It would not be seemly for a Master of his stature to carry the luggage. He would have Smith do it, but like most Westerners Smith only became more feeble as he grew old.

This was not a way for a Master of Sinanju to leave an emperor, carrying his own bags.

"I have one too many," said Remo. Chiun was too happy to be leaving the Mad Emperor Smith to quibble about such minor slights.

"Remo, do you understand why we have to get Vassily Rabinowitz, and do to him what the Russians did? Do you understand?"

"Understand?" sighed Remo. "I don't even want to think about it. C'mon, little father. I'll carry your steamer trunks out to the car."

"If you wish," said Chiun. Life was becoming good already. He didn't even have to work on Remo to make him do what he should have done out of the love in his heart, instead of forcing Chiun to practically beg for it. If one had to ask, one was demeaned. This might not be the absolute truth, but it sounded good, so Chiun decided to use it sometime when he had an opportunity.

"Chiun, tell him the job isn't over," said Smith.

"How can I reason with one who has served you so well? Only your words, O Emperor, are inviolate, and once spoken must be followed forever. You said he should eliminate this evil one Matesev. Is Matesev alive?"

"Well, no, but—"

"You said he should find out about this Rabinowitz. Did Remo not personally speak to Vassily Rabinowitz himself, even to the discussion of friendship?"

"Yes, but—"

"Then we leave with glad hearts knowing we followed to the absolute letter your magnificent commands."

"Name your price," said Smith.

"We are still waiting for the last tributes," said Chiun. "Not that we are crass servers of gold. But we understand as you understand that America's credit is its most price-less possession. And you most of all wish to keep your name and your credit at the highest levels of history. This when all the treasure of Sinanju is restored according to our agreements, then we would be more than happy to serve you again."

"But it will take years to search out that list you sent us. There are artifacts in there that haven't been around for centuries."

"A great nation faces a great task," said Chiun, and in Korean to Remo:

"Get the blue trunk first."

Remo answered in the language that had over the years become like his first language.

"Pretty neat, little father. I never could have gotten out that clean."

"It's only time. You'll learn it. When you know you're not working for some patriotic cause but realize you are in the family business, then you'll see. It is the easiest part of things. Emperors are all stupid because they can be made to believe we actually think they are somehow better than we just because of the accident of their births."

"What are you two talking about?" asked Smith in English.

"Good-bye," said Remo.

"I will match what any other country, tyrant, or emperor offers you, Chiun."

"Put back the trunk," said Chiun to Remo in Korean.

"I thought we were leaving," said Remo.

"Not when we have a bidding situation. It is the first rule of bargaining. Never walk away from a bidding situation; you will regret it forever."

"I don't know about you, little father," said Remo. "But I am through with Smith and CURE. Get your own trunk."

Smith saw the blue steamer trunk fall to the ground, and watched Chiun look aghast at such disrespect.

"So long," said Remo to both of them. "I'm going to play with the real Mickey Mouse instead of you two guys."

When Remo was gone, Smith asked Chiun what he knew about hypnotism.

"Everything," answered Chiun. "I used to own five hypnotists."

If Smith knew what Rabinowitz was doing at that moment, he would have run after Remo on his hands and knees and begged him to be the sad Russian's friend.

8

Two men, each with different keys, were needed to launch an American nuclear missile. Each missile was pretargeted. In other words, those who fired it did not decide where it would land. They only followed orders. There was a strict procedure. First, the airmen had to make sure the missiles absolutely did not go off accidentally, and second, when they did, it would be only on properly validated orders from Strategic Air Command.

"And where does the Strategic Air Command get its orders?"

"From the President, Ma. Why are you asking me all these questions?"

Captain Wilfred Boggs of Strategic Air Command, Omaha, did not like coffee shops, and especially meeting his mother in one. And what really bothered him was that his mother had been asking around town about where the big missiles were, the ones that were aimed at Russia.

Captain Boggs, on security duty, had been assigned to interrogate the person. Boggs thought he was to interrogate a Russian immigrant, something so ludicrous as to make him laugh when he first heard it.

"You mean to tell me that there's a Russian going around looking for our biggest in Omaha?"

"Says he was told the missile bases was out here," answered the local police liaison officer. "But don't be too mean to him. Fella's real nice. Wants to see you, anyone from SAC. I told him, you wanna see someone from SAC, you go around this city asking for the biggest missile and you'll see someone real fast.''

But the local police had made the biggest mistake of their lives. It was Wilfred's mother whom they had arrested.

"You want to speak to me, Ma, phone me."

"I'm here, so tell me. How do you fire a missile at Russia?" And that was how his mother began the questions of who controlled what and where in the Strategic Air Command. Of course he got her out of jail immediately and went to a more suitable place to talk, a coffee shop she insisted on because she liked pastries. He was lucky to get her out of jail, but the policemen seemed unusually willing to break a few rules for a person every one of them found very special.

The question Ma wanted answered most of all was:

"You couldn't fire one for your mother?"

"Ma, it takes two."

"Let me speak to the other one."

"Ma, I don't have a key. I'm in security now. I don't fire them."

"All of a sudden you can't fire a little missile? This is what you're telling your mother?"

"I never could fire a missile even when I had a key. It takes two and then we have to have the proper orders. Even if two of us decided we were going to fire one of these things, we'd have to have the proper command sequence wired in to our station."

"Hold on. Just a minute already. We're into a lot of things I didn't suspect," said his mother, and she took out a little notebook and a pencil and said:

"All right, give it to me from the very beginning."

"Will you put away that pad and pencil? I can't be seen telling you the SAC structure with you taking notes. And why are you taking notes?"

"Because I'm trying to find out why a red-blooded American boy who will fire a missile if some machine says fire, won't fire one for his flesh and blood. That's why.

One missile and you're making a big deal already. One little missile. How many missiles do you have? Hundreds, right?''

"It could start a war, Ma."

"It won't start a war," said his mother in a strange singsong, dismissing such an idea with a touch of her hand and a low sad nod. "Russia will learn not to bother innocent people. They respect that sort of thing.''

"I don't know that the missiles at our base are aimed at Russia. It could be Eastern Europe. Asia. We don't know.''

"You mean, you'd fire a missile and not know where it landed?''

"It helps. We don't want to know who we'd be killing. We might read books about those places and refuse at the last minute.''

"So I've come all the way out to Omaha in Nebraska for nothing?''

"Not nothing, Ma. We haven't seen each other since Christmas. Boy is it good to see you. How're Cathy, Bill, and Joe? You've got to fill me in.''

"They're fine. Everyone's fine. Everyone loves you, good-bye. Are you going to finish your Danish?''

"I don't like pastry, Ma. Come to think of it, neither do you.''

And his mother left without kissing him good-bye. Stranger still, when he confessed to the local police that he had released the subject they had put into his custody, the one who had been asking about missiles, his mother, all they said was, "Thanks. We owe you a lot. And we'll never forget it.''

Spring in Omaha was like spring in Siberia. It was warmish nothing, as opposed to winter, which was frozen nothing.

Vassily Rabinowitz stood on the street corner with one single Danish pastry in his hand and the entire Soviet Union as his enemy.

Missiles were out. He had nothing against Russia, never had. All he wanted was to be left alone. All he wanted was to be able to walk around awhile without having people come up to him asking questions. He had thought America would be like that. Yes, one could walk around, but not for long. Muggers could get you before you could get them into a proper frame of mind.

So he had gotten himself a crime family, and from the newspaper reports, he was pretty good at it. He had become a criminal mastermind. And one single Russian commando unit had shown him that his crime family, his tough desperate criminals, were about as tough as a dozen cannoli in a paper box.

They had deserted him, and Vassily had been bound sightless and soundless and carried, terrified, over a long distance until the only family person he met in this country rescued him and then left. The man had been definitely friendly even without Vassily's influence.

But Vassily had been scared out of his wits. He knew the Russian government. A nice word to the government meant you were weak. Peace was weakness. How many times had he heard Russian generals comment, on hearing of a peace overture, that the country offering it was weak? Peace was weakness. Of course, when the other country armed itself, then it was aggressive.

"Why," Vassily had once asked a field marshal who had come to the parapsychology village for treatment of a headache, "are we not weak when we make a peace overture? These things have puzzled me."

"Because when we make a peace overture, we want the other side to disarm. That will make us stronger."

"Why do we want to be stronger?"

"If we are not stronger they will destroy us."

"And if we are stronger?"

"We will destroy them," said the field marshal happily.

"And then where will we get all those wonderful Western goods if we destroy them?"

"I'm not in charge of politics," said the field marshal.

"Would you really want to cook your bread in a Russian toaster?"

"Don't bother me with politics."

"Have you ever had Russian Scotch?"

"You're being subversive," said the field marshal.

It had really been just another incident to prove to him what he already knew. What the Russians understood was absolute force. Kill, and they would talk fairly and decently with you. Show you could not kill, and they wouldn't even answer your mail.

Vassily Rabinowitz understood that if he could get a missile shot off at some place in Russia, he would be able to embrace his newfound American comrades as allies even before the nuclear dust settled. Only after he showed everyone he was a major danger did he have the slightest chance of being left alone.

Communist Russia had always been like this. It was they, not the West, who had signed the nonaggression treaty with Nazi Germany. It was they, not the West, who had collided with the Nazis to take Poland. It was they, not the West, who had waited happily for the Nazis to destroy Europe, giving them whatever raw materials they might need, including materials to build gas ovens.

In the end, of course, the Nazis invaded Russia, and then the propaganda machines went to work. It became Russia and the West against fascism, and then at the end of the war, when the West disbanded its armies, Russia kept its forces at full level and put up the Iron Curtain.

And if the West had not rearmed, there would have been a red flag flying over Washington.

To know anything about history was to know this about Russia. Vassily Rabinowitz, whether he liked it or not, would have to go into the army business.

He had gotten over his revulsion at his crimes in New York. The initial shame had turned to pride. If he could kill gang leaders, he could easily kill Russians. And probably outsmart them to boot, although one fact the West always seemed to ignore was that the Russians were very shrewd.

It would be quite a test. Unfortunately, as he finished

his pastry on the street corner, he understood he didn't even have one missile yet. And his problem, he realized, was that he was starting at the bottom.

The lights went out, and the shooting started. They could see only gun flashes, and they shot at the flashes. But as they shot, their own guns gave off flashes, and they were hit. The room filled with the groans of dying, cursing men, and when the lights went on, the blood had made the floor slippery, so slippery that Anna Chutesov sent in a man to see if everyone of them was dead.

He came back with blood all over his shirt. He had slipped three times.

"Blood is more slippery than oil," he said.

"Are they dead?" she asked.

"No. Not all. Some are dying."

"That's fine," she said to the soldier. Men, she thought. I knew they would react like that.

But she did not say this to the young lieutenant who had gone into the room for her. Even now soldiers were running up stairways and down hallways with guns, looking for the source of the firing.

Men, thought Anna Chutesov. They are so stupid. Why are they running? What will they figure out faster by running? Most of them don't even know where the gunfire was coming from. But they run. They run because another man told them it was a good way to get someplace faster. Actually, walking had gotten Anna Chutesov farther in Soviet Russia than any man her age.

She was twenty-six years old, and despite her youth she had more influence in more places than anyone from the Berlin wall to Vladivostok.

And she did not get it because of her great beauty. She was blond. Soft honey-colored hair caressed her magnificent high cheekbones and her smile flashed with such perfect whiteness that some men gasped.

Of course, men would always gasp at beauty without ever figuring out how it got there. The real beauty of Anna

Chutesov was in her presence. It was cool, friendly, and only hinted of sexuality.

Anna knew that average men became absolutely useless when in heat. A man in heat was like a telephone pole on wheels, virtually uncontrollable and completely dysfunctional.

She walked calmly through the running men, and by the time she reached command headquarters, fifteen stories down into the earth, sheltered from any possible American attack, she had been asked no less than ten times what had happened on the first floor among the special mission commanders.

Each time she answered that she did not know, and each time she thought how stupid the question was. No one gave out information freely in this command headquarters designed for the last struggle against capitalism in case of an American invasion.

It was a wonderful headquarters and the result of typical male thinking. It was here they could direct the remnants of Russian forces if America should be successful in penetrating Russian borders.

What no one bothered to ask was why America would penetrate Russian borders. There was only one reason: if there was a war in which America had to fight for its life.

One would be perfectly safe if everyone respected the status quo. But America looked on every rebellion in every stinkwater backward third-world country as a threat, and Russia, thinking it was weakening America, supported every one of those backward third-world garbage pits called countries.

America knew those countries weren't worth the sewage they couldn't get rid of, and so did Russia. But the men kept on building weapons and scaring themselves. And so, like the room upstairs where men trying to survive had gotten themselves killed or wounded, the leaders of Anna's country built silly defense networks like this one that went fifteen stories underground.

Whether there would still be something around to command after an atomic war was doubtful. But they had to play their games.

At the bottom floor, she entered a room with a long white table that reflected a harsh fluorescent light in the ceiling. The walls were concrete. They could have been fine porcelain. Fifteen stories down into bedrock, they weren't going to need any greater support.

"Anna, we heard there was a horrible disaster on the first level. Someone got in and shot up a room full of special-missions commanders."

"No," said Anna Chutesov. "The only people who got in were in already."

"What happened? You always knew everything," said the heavy man with gold-braided epaulets big enough for toy planes to use as aircraft carriers.

"No, I only seem to know everything," said Anna. The implication for anyone using a brain was that she appeared to know everything because no one around her ever seemed to know anything.

She received smiles of approval from the men she had just insulted. There was one other woman in this higher command. She was the one with the heavy mustache. Anna knew that person was a woman because she wore the colors of the female army corps. They played up her massive biceps very well.

"What happened?"

"What happened was that you are going to have to send me after Vassily Rabinowitz. There is no one else. The others have all just killed or wounded themselves."

"That's awful. Do you know General Matesev himself was killed trying to get Rabinowitz back to the country?"

"Yes," said Anna. "I believe we also lost the special force, and any chance of using similar techniques to penetrate America. I know it all, gentlemen. I know that Vassily Rabinowitz was wrapped like a bundle with tape and carried back to Matesev, where some other force rescued him."

"We're doomed. If they have him, we are doomed."

"We are doomed to the extent that he believes he is surrounded by a malicious world. I have gone through his dossier. All this man wanted for the years he was in the parapsychology village was to be left alone. Do you know what our response was? We sent in round-the-clock teams to find out why he wanted to be left alone. So he left. Now he is in America, and we don't know what on earth he is doing. If he is frightened, as he may well be, he could be planning to set off a missile right now. This very moment a nuclear warhead could be coming at our country. And do you know why? So he would not have to feel defenseless. And against whom? The people who would send a Matesev to bring him back. Shoot, kill, capture, and run. Lunacy."

"It was a good decision," said a KGB general. This did not tell Anna about how good the decision was, but that it had come from the KGB.

"A good decision, comrade, except the results were bad, yes?"

"Yes," said the KGB representative.

"Well, that's possible," said Anna. "We all can't be expected to know how everything will turn out. Except I will take that onerous burden. I will guarantee the results of my taking over. I take full and absolute responsibility."

"How can you guarantee the results?" asked the KGB representative. He did not trust her. He did not trust any women in important roles. A woman could be put in a post, paraded in a post, but a man had to be behind her.

"Because I will do it."

"If the likes of General Matesev could not succeed, how can someone like you guarantee you will succeed?"

"The same way I could guarantee that I would get this mission after the special commanders killed themselves." Anna smiled.

"But you asked for this meeting yesterday. They only killed themselves just now."

"About ten minutes ago, five minutes after I told each of them someone was planning to kill them, I turned out the lights and threw in a firecracker. They acted the way I knew they would.''

"You killed them! Do you think we will send you out on the mission after you connived to deprive us of our best special-missions commanders?''

"Yes. Of course. Deprived of every other avenue of action, in the end, my dear comrades, you will make a rational decision,'' said Anna Chutesov. "And in the end, that decision has to be to use me. You have no one else readily available.''

A general from the armies in the East rose, pounding the table.

"That is ruthless, deceitful, and despicable. Do you expect us to send you on one of the most crucial missions in the history of the Soviet Union after you have done something like that?''

"Absolutely. I use the incident of upstairs as my main credential. Until this moment, gentlemen, I have not shown that I could kill. There is a room awash in blood on the first level that will attest that I can do this very well.''

Most of the men shook their heads. But an older comrade, one who had been through the revolution of 1917 and through the years of Joseph Stalin himself, nodded slowly.

"She's right. Beyond a shadow of a doubt our beautiful Anna Chutesov has proved she is not only the best person for this task, but possibly the only one. Good for you, Anna,'' he said.

"But what if she decides to use Rabinowitz for her own ends?'' said the other woman in the room, the one with the biggest biceps.

"Do you really think I would be so stupid as to try to control something that could convince me I was talking to my mother or father whenever it wished? Are you mad, or just acting that way because you are a woman in a room surrounded by men?'' asked Anna.

"I am every bit as good as the men,'' said the woman.

"Yes,'' said Anna without sarcasm. "You certainly

function at that level. Now, is there anyone here who remotely thinks I would wish to keep something like a Vassily Rabinowitz alive?''

There as no answer.

''My first job is to stop him before he gets his hands on the nuclear trigger or an army. This I may not be able to do. But you should be aware of what he can do, because a missile fired at our country may well not be the beginning of an atomic war. It could be some silly thing a frightened man would do, hoping to prove to us he is not as weak as he feels. Do you understand?''

''You mean to say we are to take an atomic explosion and do nothing?'' asked the commander of Russia's western missile station.

''No. I want you to end the entire world in a nuclear holocaust to teach a lesson to an already frightened man. Good day, gentlemen. I don't have time for any more of this.''

''What can we do to help you, Anna?'' asked the oldest man.

''If you believe in praying, pray Vassily Rabinowitz does not get hold of an army. I have read his psychological profile. I would say that defecating in one's pants at this moment would be an appropriate response to the situation.''

Vassily Rabinowitz liked the tanks. He liked the way they could line up and fire at a ridge and the ridge would explode as the shells hit. He liked the way the ground trembled as the tanks rolled by in review. He liked the way infantry had to scatter when the tanks rolled into their positions. He liked tanks.

He also liked the howitzers.

''Almost like a real war, sir,'' said the colonel.

Vassily tried to brush the dust of Fort Pickens, Arkansas, off his suit. It was no use. Dust, when rubbed off, tended to grind itself in, and there was more than enough dust in Fort Pickens for all the suits ever woven in all the mills of mankind.

"It's very nice," yelled Vassily above the whak-boom of the howitzers. "Very nice."

"Better than Nam, sir; we can see what we're shooting at."

"Yes, a mountain ridge makes a good enemy. Have you ever thought about fighting the Russians?"

"Sir, I think about it every day. Isn't a day goes by I don't think about it. They're the ones we should be fighting."

"Let's say tomorrow morning?"

"All we need is a little warm-up," said the colonel.

"What's this warm-up business?" asked Vassily. "You're getting paid to be ready. You have a big budget, Colonel. What is this warm-up business?"

"You're never ready for a big war unless you have a little one first. Better than maneuvers. Gets the kinks out."

"I always thought you had to be ready for war to have peace, not make war in order to make war," said Vassily.

"Both," said the colonel. He wore a field helmet and had a pistol strapped to his side. "If you weren't my commanding officer in Nam I wouldn't even be talking to you about these things."

"I just want to show the Russians we have an army willing to fight. I don't want to have a major war with them. I have no desire to kill them."

"Can't have a war without killing, sir."

"A few battles. That's all I want. Maybe only one battle."

"Wouldn't we all want that, sir. But you can't have your battle without a war coming with it."

"I was afraid of that," said Vassily. "By the way, don't you think those tanks should be firing while moving instead of standing still? I mean, if you needed guns to be still, then you could use howitzers."

"Our mode of training doesn't call for that, sir," said the colonel.

"Do it," said Vassily.

"But, sir—"

"Do it," said Vassily. Something inside him told him that if these men were to get ready even for a preparatory war they had better be prepared right, because the worst thing that could happen was to fight and lose a small war. Then he could never impress the Russians. America had to win its next war.

Vassily wrote down in his notebook: "One regiment, with armor."

He needed more. He needed divisions. And he needed divisions that could fight. He would not have been here himself checking things out, making sure the guns fired and the soldiers were there to fire them, but for his second encounter with the American military establishment.

Having failed with the firing of one missile, which he could use as a warning to the Russians to leave him alone, he had decided to go to the top. And this, as everyone knew, was the Pentagon, a five-sided building of immense proportions. Here the general staffs of America plotted production of war goods, battle strategies, and the maintenance of the most sophisticated and complex wartime equipment in the world.

It was also the place Vassily had soon wanted to flee, knowing he had better get his own tanks and guns and men to use them or he would never be able to defend himself against the Russians. The people at the Pentagon certainly weren't.

Vassily had easily gotten through every pass clearance system by simply looking in the eyes of every guard and protecting himself as someone with a pass and a lot of stars on his shoulders.

He found himself an important-looking man with real stars on his shoulders and immediately became that man's closest scientific adviser.

"I'm looking for someone who can get an army together. Nothing special. An army that if it had to, could win a battle or so. To be brief, I'm looking for someone who knows how to fight a war."

The man thought about that a moment.

"Could you be more specific?"

"Soldiers. Guns. Tanks. Planes. Fighting a war."

"Whew, that's a tough one," said the man with stars. "I would say your best bet would be the Military Concepts Formulation Bureau. I think they're the ones who might be able to help you. I'm sort of lost when it comes to guns and soldiers and things. I've been at a desk in the Pentagon for the last ten years."

"You look like a military man. What can you do?"

"I'm very military. I'm a cost analyst overview establisher. I cost-rate concepts."

Vassily's face showed enough confusion for the general to answer on his own.

"I'm the one who estimates if we can afford a situation. Cost in lives, weapons, national productivity, et cetera. You must remember. You helped me. We were up at MIT when we came to the conclusion that America couldn't afford to survive. We should stop paying so much to exist anymore because it was just too damned costly. You helped me get my first star. We shattered the concept of survival. Absolutely mathematically reduced it to absurdity."

Military Concepts was a small office with computer terminals at five desks. No one under the rank of full colonel worked in this office. It provided the crucial thinking for how and when and under what circumstances America would fight its wars.

Vassily thought this had to be the one place where he could get all his information.

He left it an hour later understanding less than fifteen of the English words, despite having gone to the best Russian schools for English, despite having gotten along very well in America with his English, even becoming skilled enough in the language to be named a "cunning criminal mastermind" by the New York newspapers, perhaps the finest connoisseurs of the underworld.

In the concepts room, Vassily heard such words as "finalize," "syllogize," "conceptualize refractions," "coordination of synergistics," "coordination response modes," and "insurgent manifestation devices."

In all his time there, he never heard the word "kill." Or "attack." Or "retreat," or any of the words he recognized as war words.

He even had these officers believing he was the chairman of the Joint Chiefs of Staff at one point. That proved to be absolutely useless because one of the officers said:

"We don't have to tell you these things. You know them. And most of all, sir, you understand that the last place you would ever come looking for anyone to know how to fight a war is here in the Pentagon."

Vassily tried two more offices and then just asked for directions to where the tanks and guns were kept. He knew he was going to have to do it himself.

But what he didn't know, and what was evident to most of the higher officers at Camp Pickens, Arkansas, was that this man they all knew intimately as different people was showing a surprising ability to move tanks and men around the fields in maneuvers.

"Reminds me of General Patton," said one officer, who had been a second lieutenant in World War II and had signed up in time to join Patton's Third Army.

"Yeah, Old Blood 'n' Guts," said another.

"Seems to want to get into a war, just like old Patton. Hell, good to have someone like that back in the Army."

Yet this man was even better than General Patton in one crucial way. Old Blood 'n' Guts could inspire most American soldiers to fight. This one could make even the cooks want to kill.

9

It was a thing of such splendor it deserved an immediate place in the histories of the House of Sinanju. Harold W. Smith, exhausted and worried perhaps more now than at any time in the history of the organization, was stunned to see Chiun leave the living room of the Vistana Views condo as soon as the price was settled, not even waiting to hear what the assignment would be.

"Unpack the histories," cried Chiun, pointing to the lime-green steamer trunk.

Remo did not look away from the window of the bedroom, which also faced the fountain. He had been looking at water for the last twenty minutes, thinking that maybe in a while he would look at the sky. That was what he was going to do for the day.

"Unpack the histories. This day is momentous in the histories of the House of Sinanju. And you, my son, are a part of it."

"Trunk's on the bed," said Remo.

"Come, you must affix your name too. This is not mine alone. I would not dare encompass such glory all by myself. If it had not been for you and your brilliant understanding that when your job is done, it is done, then I never would have achieved these heights. I am sure you will look on me as the Great Chiun. The followers of the Great Wang so did."

Seeing Remo continue to stare at the water, Chiun

opened the trunk himself. He whisked out a scroll and a bottle of dark black ink, made from the shellfish found in the West Korea Bay. The scroll was special parchment used by a dynasty of China so old even the Ming and Tang had no record of it.

It was parchment of specially treated yak skin that could endure moisture, cold, and heat over centuries. He placed five delicate stars in the middle of the document.

"Remember the last time you saw five stars in a history of Sinanju, Remo?" said Chiun.

"Yeah. The big Great Wang. Rah, rah," said Remo. Maybe he would get tired of looking at the sky by nightfall. Then he could always stare at his hands for a few days. His body felt like lead, with sluggish blood that made its way through his body strictly on memory. The rest of him not only didn't seem to be working well, but didn't seem to want to.

"You have seen two stars many times, and sometimes three. And twice you saw a Master willing to place four stars. But only the Great Wang himself placed five stars. And why?"

"For the basis of breathing techniques," said Remo.

"It is our law of gravity, and the universe. Five stars. Come, you must be here to take part in this glory."

"The reason you want me there, little father, is so that I won't take away your five stars when you're dead. You want to sell me on your deserving five stars, so future generations can call you the Great Chiun. I know that. So let me tell you now. Your five stars are safe, because I don't think I am ever going to read those histories. Or teach a new Master. So put down a hundred stars. It doesn't matter. It never did. I know that now."

"Are you looking at the sky yet?" asked Chiun.

"Water. Looking at water," said Remo. "Maybe tomorrow I'll look at sky. Maybe the next day. I still have my fingernails to tour."

"Body feels terrible, doesn't it?" chuckled Chiun. "As the Lesser Gi said, a man cannot see himself, especially when he is in the process of greatness. One never does. I myself suffered doubts, thoughts that I might be egotistical, self-centered, childish. How ludicrous, yes?''

Remo saw the darkness in the water, and toyed with the edge of the possible idea of wondering what Chiun would decide to give himself five stars for. Only three other Masters had given themselves such accolades. Two of them were reduced to four and three stars respectively, by later Masters of Sinanju. The force blow, which at the time was thought to be a basic element of Sinanju, was discovered later only to be an essential variant of the basic breathing technique of the Great Wang. And so a star was removed, even though this blow established something that appeared even to the Masters of Sinanju to be unique.

The blow was not the result of force but created the force itself. You could move your hand through walls and the force would not be behind it like in some weak, imitative karate punch breaking bricks. Rather the force would pull the hand and shatter the wall. It was basic, but not quite as basic as the breath of life that attuned the Masters to the real forces of the universe.

It was no accident that the first thing a human baby did when cut from the umbilical cord was to breathe. Never did the infant seek food first, or even warmth in times so cold that the temperature would kill it. First was breath, and so too was it last in death.

The breath was the hello and good-bye of life as Sinanju called it, as Chiun had taught him so long ago in those basic lessons when Remo thought there was something worth learning in this world.

''Recorded this day in the Masterhood of Chiun, discoverer of America, teacher of Remo, devoted pupil, for the greater and continuous glory of the House of Sinanju. It was by the hand of Chiun, agreed this day with the mad emperor representing the rich country of America—see Chiun's discovery of a happy people—a negotiation that will be considered basic in the business of Sinanju.

''Faced with a client emperor in desperate need, for

whom a perfectly performed service, while adequate in itself, proved inadequate for the emperor's needs, Chiun first established for the Master of Sinanju and his pupil Remo, now a Master but yet to achieve final levels, that they were free to leave. This was most important because from this came the basic and perfect negotiation, performed by Chiun himself.

"Having thus established that Sinanju had performed perfectly and was now leaving, the Emperor Smith, who only at times could be considered mad, but at this time had to be considered as shrewd as any emperor ensuing generations might face, made this offer. He would outbid any rival for the services of Sinanju.

"While this was basically a perfect position, Chiun, in his keen sense of proportions, understood it was only the beginning. For the country was rich, the richest in its time. And Chiun understood there was much more where that came from, for Chiun had already made arrangements with the same emperor to replace the entire treasure of Sinanju. That is, in one Masterhood to earn the total of all other Masterhoods. (For reference to the treasure, look under 'not Chiun's fault.')

"At that point, Chiun established no fixed amount, but rather a percentage above any other offer, so that Chiun would be free to get any other nation, emperor, tyrant, or king to make an offer, which Emperor Smith would be bound to exceed by ten percent. Chiun himself, in this one deed, had established the first limitless fee."

Chiun stopped reading and stepped back from the scroll.

"What does Smitty want?" asked Remo.

"I'm not altogether sure. He's still out there. I'll ask him," said Chiun.

"That hypnotist fellow. He wants him, I think."

"Some silliness. We do not call him Mad Harold for nothing," said Chiun.

Chiun looked at the five stars he had dared to give himself and smiled. They would hold, he was sure, if future Masters really understood the greatness of his breakthrough.

He put the scroll back in the lime-green steamer trunk, making sure it was tied perfectly.

Remo did not look back.

"Say hello to him for me," said Chiun.

"Who?" asked Remo.

"The Great Wang. You're going to see him soon," said Chiun. "And it is I, Chiun, who have brought you to this point."

"What should I say to him?"

"Ask him about whatever bothers you. That is what he is there for."

"Since he's dead, he's got to be an apparition."

"No. Definitely not. Not alive, but definitely not an apparition. You will see the Great Wang's smile, and the gentle curves of his too-full stomach. You will even feel the strength of his eyes, and his presence will be a bounty unto you."

"Close the door on your way out," said Remo.

"Good-bye, my son. When we next meet, you will be at a level you do not even suspect now," said Chiun, feeling the joy again of the time he had met the Great Wang.

But now to business and fulfilling the wishes of Mad Harold. It was a typical white American assignment, full of contradictions and absurdity, with no clear goal in sight.

For this virtually limitless price, Mad Harold did not want the throne of America called the presidency. He did not wish a great personal enemy destroyed, nor did he wish control of any land. As usual, reasonable requests were out.

There was this man from Russia.

"Ah yes, the czars, powerful men whom we respect, but we must warn you, O wise Harold Smith, you have seen their danger only in part. We who have served the czars, and therefore do not speak ill of them, nevertheless respect your resolve to protect what is yours."

"It's not protecting any property rights. This man is dangerous. He has this tremendous ability to hypnotize."

"Ah yes, the mind players. We know them. They are of little importance usually, but of course this one is of great importance. Most great importance," said Chiun, who knew that an ancient Master who had worked in the Roman Empire was once paid with five of them, Greek slaves who could do mind tricks, as they were called. He was given five of them in lieu of one good field hand to carry his luggage. Chiun remembers the comments about how the Master had been swindled by a Lucius Cornelius Spena, a very rich businessman who wished that a senate seat be suddenly vacated. It was not honorable work, but supposedly it was to pay well. And of course, it didn't. Sinanju never used slaves well and didn't believe in them. Every man, Sinanju preached, should be free to make a fool of himself, therefore leaving more work for assassins.

These things Chiun thought about as Smith went on about the man called Vassily Rabinowitz, an immigrant in a nation of immigrants. Smith would provide the tracking, and Chiun would perform the elimination.

"Most dangerous. Most dangerous. But may I ask, how, if we kill him, can he entertain for you?"

"We don't want him for entertainment. He's dangerous. Perhaps the single most dangerous man who has ever entered this country."

Chiun overlooked the insult because of the tremendous fee Sinanju would be getting. What could one expect from a madman but to think a hypnotist was more dangerous than his House of Sinanju that Smith had paid for? Any sane emperor, if he really thought that, would keep the whole matter quiet lest his lords serve those who bought the services of the other one, the one who here and now Smith declared as most dangerous.

"We will struggle but win, as always," said Chiun, careful to play on the fact of an awesome opponent, but just as careful to remind Mad Harold that when he bought Sinanju, he had bought the best in assassins. In fact, Chiun was thinking of adopting a fine American practice. In every new appliance he saw a note informing the purchaser that he had bought the best of its kind in the world, congratulating him on his wisdom in doing so.

Chiun thought it might be nice to have a scroll prepared for every future tyrant, despot, and king Sinanju served, letting each one know how wise he was in employing the finest assassins in all history. Begin it with:

"Congratulations, you have employed the finest . . ." et cetera.

Chiun nodded again to some more nonsense and then squeezed a small box Mad Harold put in his hand.

"Not now, Chiun. When you have succeeded in eliminating Vassily Rabinowitz, then press that button. I will know he is dead."

"But you know he is dead already, now that your Magnificence, O Wise Harold, had decreed him so."

"Nevertheless, I'd like you to use that. We are paying an extraordinary tribute for this. We don't even know how much yet. And this is the way I want to do it."

"Of course. We always appreciate direction and help in this thing we have only been doing forty-eight hundred years before America was born," said Chiun, allowing himself a little sarcasm. But Smith did not respond.

"Death to the evil hypnotist," said Chiun. As was his strange custom, a scant time later the telephone rang and it was the voice of Harold W. Smith. They had tracked down a probable place for Vassily Rabinowitz, the poor little hypnotist whose life would be forfeited in the most splendid financial arrangement in the history of the House of Sinanju.

"O wise one, how is a person in a probable place? A place is or it is not."

As soon as he said it, Chiun realized he never should have mentioned it in the first place because the answer was ridiculous to the point of the absurd.

Smith's system was tracking incidents most probably done by the poor hypnotist, things that would be reported to the police and to intelligence agencies. Smith had a machine that could scan and analyze these reports, and from these reports Vassily Rabinowitz was probably in Fort Pickens, Arkansas.

When Smith was finished prattling, Chiun asked the important question.

"Do you want the head or not? I know you traditionally don't take the head for your palace walls, but we recommend it, especially for an important assassination. It can be done quite tastefully."

"No. Just make sure you do kill him. There was an incident in Russia where tough KGB troops thought they had him and they ended up shooting each other."

"And secret, too, I take it. The usual secrecy."

"Oh yes. Absolutely. Secret. Of course. We don't want anyone to know we exist."

"Yes. Of course. Make a great assassination seem like a head cold. Very subtle, O wise one."

"No. In this case I don't care whether it looks like an accident. I want him dead. I want to be sure he's dead. Use the box. He's already probably into our armed forces. We only missed a nuclear launch in Omaha by a hair's breadth. This man has got to die."

"With the speed of the winds of the Kalahari, O wise one," said Chiun, who made sure he took enough time to be properly dressed. Nothing loud, even though America tended to be loud. A basic pink would be good for the kimono to be used in this assassination, a basic pink, a simple blow, a quick death, and then perhaps wait a week or so before hitting the button on the box. For after all, if the assassination proved so easy, might not Mad Harold think of reneging on that awesome reward? Of course, speed would show the greatness of Sinanju, and Mad Harold paid for the strangest things.

Chiun thought about that and by the time he reached Ford Pickens, Arkansas, Chiun decided to risk informing Mad Harold immediately. Then he would whisk Remo away to a saner emperor, a new Remo, a Remo who had seen the beneficence of the Great Wang and asked the important question only to get the important answer.

At the gate, Chiun was told that people who dressed in pink had to be women, or they could not enter the base.

How typical of American whites that they would insist that entrance to a military base require a sex-change operation. No wonder they had lost their last war, and probably would lose the next.

The guard held out his palm to bar Chiun's entrance and then didn't bother Chiun anymore. Most people didn't who needed immediate treatment for multiple fractures of the hand.

Chiun glided into Fort Pickens. He saw the flags, the uniforms, the appearance of activity while people were generally doing nothing. He could come in at night and do unseen work, but killing a lowly hypnotist for a vast fortune was so bizarre to begin with, he wanted to do it in daylight to make sure it was really happening.

Chiun surveyed the camp. Nothing much had really changed since the Romans except this camp was not defended properly. Romans would always have a moat and a wall. Americans made do with fences. Perhaps that was because they had guns nowadays.

He saw dust in the distance, always a sign of cavalry.

He stopped an officer to ask if he had heard of a Vassily Rabinowitz around.

"You mean Old Blood 'n' Guts Rabinowitz?" asked the officer.

Horror struck Chiun. Had someone already filled this enormous contract on the hypnotist?

"He is only blood and guts now?" asked Chiun.

"Only? He's the toughest, smartest general since George S. Patton, Jr. We call him Old Blood 'n' Guts."

"Oh, he sheds other people's blood. Ah well, this is good," said Chiun. Not only was Rabinowitz alive, but he blessedly had a better reputation than just a lowly hypnotist, a man who could convince some souls that it was warm when it was cold, cool when it was hot, and that they were barking dogs.

Some people could even be made to not feel pain, although why anyone would want to do that to his body, Chiun never knew.

One could sense, like with any great conqueror, the presence of Rabinowitz far off. Soldiers and officers alike looked strained and angry. It meant they had been worked properly. Great commanders could do that. Good soldiers did not resent it, rather they respected it even though they might complain from time to time.

"Old Blood 'n' Guts is something today. I don't know if he'll scare our enemies, but he sure as hell scares me," Chiun heard one officer comment.

"First time we've ever really done real maneuvers. I'll be grateful for war just to stop this torture."

When Chiun got to a broad plain surrounded by foothills, he could make out clearly by the deference of the men who the commander was. Tanks were firing on moving targets with surprising accuracy. Rebel yells came from men in the armored vehicles. This definitely was an army preparing well for war.

It would be a noble assassination, to go along with the noble price.

Rabinowitz was waving his arm and yelling. He stood on a platform, pointing with a swagger stick. He could yell orders to two people at once.

He had been described as a sad-eyed man, but these eyes flashed with joy. It was a shame that Chiun would have to end his career at this moment, not later, after he had become as famous as Napoleon, Alexander, or Caesar. But a contract was a contract.

"Rabinowitz," cried out Chiun. "Vassily Rabinowitz."

The man now called Old Blood 'n' Guts turned around. Chiun saw by the movement even before the voice that this was a recognition of self. People could not help doing it. It was more a proof of identity than the face, or even the

Eastern magic of the fingerprint. This was the simple reflex of the person identifying himself.

And Rabinowitz had done it with his eyes. Chiun knew that all the soldiers were looking now at him because of the beauty of his pink robe in this drab setting. Mad Harold had ordered secrecy, not invisibility.

The platform was just over his head. Chiun moved to it with grace, less effort than a leap, more motion than a step, and now he was face-to-face with the most gloriously rewarded assassination in all history.

The center of the skull begged for a single penetration, quick to the point of invisibility. The simple, basic blow with the force of it working inside the cranium, not outside, not even needing to penetrate.

Rabinowitz wore a plain battle helmet and fatigues. A small pistol was strapped to his waist. The light dust in the noon sun made the air almost like clay in the mouth. The boards on the platform creaked ever so slightly, and a few soldiers started to move up to the platform to get between Chiun and Rabinowitz. And then Chiun stopped his blow, stopped his blow short of the high yellow forehead and laughing black eyes and the equally pink kimono. A jolly fat man, no taller than Chiun, but with thicker hands and forearms, and legs one could tell were chunky underneath his trunk, looked at him, laughing.

"What are you doing here? What's your name? How come no one could stop you at the gate? What is that silly pink dress?"

The questions came so quickly that Chiun could barely answer them, but answer he must.

"Great Wang, what are you doing here?"

"Look, I asked you first. If I wanted to answer I would have answered first already. So what's with you and that pink dress?"

Of course the Great Wang was joking, but Chiun would never presume to refuse an answer.

"O great one, it is I, Chiun, I am here on the most

wonderfully paid assassination in all history. A mere hypnotist named Rabinowitz, and the price I got—''

"Who wants to kill Rabinowitz?''

"The Mad Emperor Harold. He is nothing, but I did not expect to see you again, great one, in my lifetime. It is Remo's turn.''

"Why would anyone want to kill a nice person like Vassily Rabinowitz?'' asked the Great Wang. Soldiers who had been advancing on Chiun made it up to the platform. In order to be absolutely perfect before the Great Wang himself, Chiun used the simplest of breathing combined with the basic force stroke, taking off heads as a form of honor. Nothing special, single movements through the spinal column, leaving the heads for the dust. He could have popped them up, caught them, and done a presentation, but that was flamboyance for customers.

The soldiers, seeing jackhammers smash off heads, went for their weapons or for cover. No one watched the horror without doing something, except for Old Blood 'n' Guts and the strange killer in the pink dress.

The old Oriental was talking weird. One of the soldiers thought of getting up on the platform with them, but the prospect of a severed head made him think twice. Far off, tanks stopped their firing.

Men crowded around the wood platform to see what the man in pink would do to Old Blood 'n' Guts. Someone chased a head, trying to match it to a body. Not knowing what to do with it, he put it down on the ground and covered it with his own helmet. Graves Registration should take care of that, thought the soldier.

"Mad Harold has the strangest assignments, Great Wang. But why do I see you twice in this lifetime? Is it that I, perhaps, am the greatest Master after you?''

"Shut up already with the greatness, hazarei. Is this Mad Harold a communist sympathizer?''

"I betook myself too much greatness, didn't I? For that I am sorry. Mad Harold is a client.''

"What do you sell?'' asked the Great Wang.

"What you did, magnificent one. The services of the greatest house of assassins of all time."

"And you want to kill this nice fellow Rabinowitz?"

"You know him, Great Wang?"

"Know him? Man's a peach. Life should be defended at all costs. He's our main client."

"That's what you came to tell me?" asked Chiun.

"And that you shouldn't let anyone bother me, either. Either one will do. Hang around."

"What joy, to be in your presence again, great one."

"A little bit to the left. You're blocking my view of my army. We're planning big things. Big. Ever have a war? I think they're fun. Used to hate them. Wondered why they had such bad publicity. Damned well couldn't be from the generals who ran them."

Was this the Great Wang? Chiun looked again. No assassin approved of war where thousands of amateurs worked or where the professionals got paid. But there was the high forehead. There was the jolly smile. There was the somewhat full body, and of course, there was the unmistakable kimono of Sinanju.

Chiun bowed at the Great Wang and stepped aside. With contempt he broke the box with the button Mad Harold has asked him to press when the assassination was done.

To understand Sinanju was to understand that if the Great Wang seemed odd, it was the student who was odd. For the Great Wang had gone to the center of the universe, and anything that was not of that center was off balance. So had spoken the many Masters since the passing of the "joyful one," as the Great Wang was known.

It was not Chiun, but it was Sinanju. Remo knew that. He had been looking at the sky, feeling himself become all the darkness the sun was not, feeling the water in the little fountain of Vistana Views, feeling all that was alive in him succumb to the lethargy of what might be the last sleep, when he heard the movement.

It was a step, but not a step. Most people walked on the balls or the heels of their feet. Sinanju walked on the whole foot. It was a rustling of a glide, so quiet one had to hear it with one's mind.

But it was there.

"I have been waiting a long time to meet someone from outside the village," came the voice. It was Korean, the northwest dialect, like Chiun's, but it lacked the shrillness. It had a laugh to it.

Remo did not answer.

"You're white. I always knew a white could do it. Good for you, Remo. Good for you, Remo Williams. Good for you."

It felt strange to hear that dialect say something so positive. Remo did not turn around. It was not that he was afraid it might be a mirage. He was afraid it might not be. He was at the lowest point he could remember. He felt worn and useless, and incapable of anything. More important, he didn't want to do anything.

"Are you feeling sorry for yourself? Have you become like Chiun?"

Remo did not like anyone talking about Chiun like that. He had often thought that of Chiun, and worse. But he did not like to hear anyone else say it.

"If you have something against Chiun, why don't you tell him?" said Remo.

"I have. I told him he was childish and self-centered. I told him sometimes he was ludicrous with his pretensions about who we are."

"You may be in my mind. I've achieved realities through my mind. I'm not even going to look at you," said Remo. There was laughter behind him. He ignored it.

"Of course I am only in your mind. So is the world. So is the universe, a mind inside a mind inside a mind, Remo. Ah, you are most certainly Chiun's pupil. He loves you, you know. He had a son who died, who did not survive training."

Remo turned around. A short, somewhat fat man with a

high forehead and a perfect smile sat on the bed, with his hands resting on his knees. He looked as though all the world was a joke.

"The Great Wang," said Remo.

This the figure dismissed. "Your Brother Wang, Master Remo. You are become a Master."

"So?" said Remo.

"Better than kissing a litchi nut. Why are you moderns so serious? You and Chiun. Both of you. You think you're saving the world. Chiun thinks he is saving the House of Sinanju, and between you both, neither of you has stopped one second to smell a flower or watch a sunset. What are you on earth for? To speed the population to its graves?"

"You weren't an assassin?"

"Of course, but not like you two. Are you getting paid by the head? What is the matter with both of you? Chiun kills at the slightest disappointment, you kill as though you personally can bring justice to the world, and both of you need a good night out. When was the last time you loved a woman?"

"A while ago. It didn't work out. It never does. I didn't know Chiun lost a son."

"Yes, he failed to be aware of his son's shortcomings, and in attempting a high climb the boy died. He doesn't want to lose you. He doesn't admit it, but he loves you, more than his son."

"He always rags me about being white."

"Chiun is a snob. The best thing he ever did was bring a white into the family. Remo, you're home. America is not your home anymore. It is your roots. But your home is Sinanju. And you are sad now because for the first time you are really leaving your home."

"Am I coming to a new level?" asked Remo.

"You have been there a while," said the Great Wang. "That is what hurts. From this moment on you begin to die."

"Why is that?" asked Remo.

"Because that is what happens to one who has reached his peak," said the Great Wang. And Remo knew it was true.

10

At five hundred yards Gusev Balbek could put a bullet through a person's eye during a windstorm. At a thousand yards he could bisect a chest. At fifteen hundred yards he could guarantee hitting a running man and stopping him.

That was with a sniper rifle. With a pistol he could shoot the beaks off low-flying birds. He would do these things for two hours every morning, partly to keep in practice, partly to keep the smiling commissars happy.

They would come, sometimes in the company of generals, and they would say most politely:

"Don't let us disturb you. We just wish to watch."

And then Gusev would put on the special performance. The honored guests would sit on a wooden stand made to look like a replica of an American inauguration platform. A dummy in a formal suit was made to move its arms by means of a small motor.

Gusev Balbek would walk fifteen hundred yards away, slowly, to impress upon them all how great a distance it was. Fifteen hundred yards was outside the cordon of protection of a head of state. All high officials knew that. Anything beyond a thousand yards just merited a cursory inspection to make sure no large band of men or a howitzer was lurking out there. A single person was not something security men would worry about at that distance. Everyone knew that.

And then just for drama, in the stands that represented

an American inauguration, the American presidential song, "Hail to the Chief," would play. And speakers would blare the noise of crowds applauding.

Then from the motorized dummy would come the recorded words of the inaugural speech. When this first was used, Gusev would fire on the lines "Ask not what your country can do for you, but what you can do for your country." The later speeches lacked that sort of dramatic high point. In fact, none of them were very good at all.

At the proper moment, Gusev, barely a speck in the distance, would fire. He always hit the dummy. Military men were always the most impressed.

Then Gusev would come in to a thousand yards, and while the spectators' eyes could barely make him out, Gusev would put a bullet right into the heart of the dummy, or a second, replacement dummy if the first was badly damaged.

And then at five hundred yards, where security men were unafraid of simple handguns, Gusev provided the pièce de résistance.

A photograph of the current President of the United States was taped to the head of the statue, and faster than they could follow, Gusev would whip out a handgun and shoot out the photograph's eyes, two quick shots. Then the exact scale photograph of the head would be passed around to the important visitors. They would look at the eyes and nod. Some smiled. Others said:

"If we have to. If we have to."

There were other demonstrations. Shots gotten off in a crowded room, a press conference, and the ultimate display. Firing three bullets in succession at the same spot on a sheet of bullet-proof glass, so that the first weakened the glass, the second penetrated, and the third went singing through the hole—all into a car moving 12.8 miles an hour, the speed of a presidential limousine touring an American city.

Gusev knew he was good, but he never entertained airs of being anything special. He came from a remote Tatar village in Kazakhstan, where everyone was an extraordinary shot. Throughout Russia there were enclaves of very special people who never dealt with the outside world and consequently inbred their weaknesses and strengths. Almost all Tatars were crack shots, as good with guns now as they had been with bows and arrows in the days of Tamerlane.

Gusev was just a little bit better than the rest of the townsmen. To the Russians in Moscow, he was magnificent.

And he noticed that during a time of crisis with America he would be called on more often to show what he could do. He would hear the important people say things like, "If worse comes to worst, we can always use Gusev."

But the shooting was only one small part of his training, just two hours a day. The other ten hours of training went into speaking and living as an American, quite a feat for a young Tatar who had since birth spoken only a dialect peculiar to the Mongolian archers of the Russian steppe from A.D. 1200 to 1400.

At first he learned words for food, but after twenty-five years of speaking English every day and being corrected every day, working at it ten hours a day, Gusev Balbek could pass on the telephone for an American, and from almost any part of the country to boot.

Unfortunately, four-foot-eight-inch-tall men with slanted eyes and skin that looked as though it had been stretched taut over tent poles for a dozen Mongolian winters tended to have difficulty passing themselves off as Alabama sharecroppers or Boston policemen.

Learning from the Americans the fine art of excusing deficiencies, the Russians merely used the famous American trick of labeling.

"Yes, we acknowledge certain visual complications," said the commander of the program.

"Everyone in America is going to notice this man."

"America is multiracial. There should be no problem."

"But once he shoots the President, how will he escape? Everyone will remember a four-foot-eight-inch man with skin like yak hide. They'll catch him. He'll kill many, but then they'll catch him and they'll know he's Russian. We want to be able to assassinate the American President; we don't want to pay for it. Otherwise we'd start a war right away.''

''We'll save him for situations so crucial that we are willing to be caught. We'll save him for crisis management. A crisis-management tool.''

And thus Gusev Balbek was kept practicing for twenty-five years, a tool that probably would never be used.

Until the morning he was shown a picture of a very round-eyed, sad-looking man.

''This is Vassily Rabinowitz. Kill him.''

''But he's not the President,'' said Gusev.

''No. He's more dangerous.''

''But I thought I was going to kill a president. I have been waiting twenty-five years to kill an American president, practicing two hours a day on marksmanship and ten on American language and customs, and now when I finally am told to do what I have prepared more than a score of years to do, my target is named Rabinowitz. Vassily Rabinowitz. Is he some dissident?''

''He's your target. Don't think because you have been learning to live like an American you are an American. You're a Russian.''

''When one starts to think for oneself it is hard to stop, comrade,'' said Gusev, who in every American election performed a practice vote, making decisions just like Americans.

''When one is Gusev Balbek from a Tatar town in Kazakhstan, one shoots Vassily Rabinowitz from fifteen hundred yards. At that distance you won't have to look into his eyes.''

Anna Chutesov was furious. She almost swept the contents of the ambassador's desk into the ambassador's face. Who had made this decision? What moron had made this decision?

"We had worked out that you would take everything we know to the proper Americans and together we would work toward eliminating the danger of this man. How could you decide on your own to kill him? I was in charge."

"It was decided we couldn't let America get hold of him. We have to kill him."

"What would they do with him? Why on earth would the Americans want him? What did he ever do for us except cure the headaches and sexual problems of the Politburo?"

Anna's face flamed. She knew how this dolt had gotten the ambassadorship. He was the only ranking member of the Foreign Bureau who could remember names, or wanted to. He was the one who could wake up in the morning not having drunk himself to sleep the night before.

When the Foreign Bureau found someone who didn't drink himself to sleep every night, that man had a job for life. Ambassador Nomowitz had been in the job a quarter of a century and was now dean of all ambassadors in Washington.

"Comrade Chutesov, I understand you have the highest authority here in America. But the highest levels ordered Rabinowitz assassinated before America got him."

"But don't they understand no one has him? That's the problem. He has them. No government can control him. He controls them. How can you control a man who makes you believe he is the most important person in your life? How? How is this done?"

"We have an extraordinary marksman. I was privileged to see him once. He is now near Fort Pickens, Arkansas, where we have located Rabinowitz. And we have made brilliant arrangements for smuggling him into position. I must say it is our proudest moment."

"Enjoy it until it blows up in your face. At best it won't work. That is at best."

"I won't even ask why," said Nomowitz to the beautiful, angry woman. He had heard she hated men, but that was from a notorious womanizer. Any woman who would not sleep with that man the very hour they first met was considered a man hater. But he could see why any man would wish to sleep with this beautiful woman. "But I will ask if you really do hate men, as they say."

"What would you think of a gender that doesn't care if the world blows up tomorrow but does wonder who I spread my legs for?"

"You do hate men."

"I just despise idiots."

"Oh, then you don't hate men," said Nomowitz, and didn't know why Anna Chutesov left his office laughing softly. She left word with the secretary for the ambassador to phone her when his solution failed.

Any fool would have figured out what was dangerous about operating alone in this situation. For if the sniper should kill Rabinowitz, who did the ambassador think the Americans would believe was dead? A Russian Jewish immigrant? No, Russia would be held responsible for killing the most important person in the lives of hundreds of Americans, whoever that most important person was.

What a wonderful way to start a purposeless war. The only way both countries had a real chance to stop this was to put their cards on the table, realize this man's powers were a danger to them both, and then, eliminating the chance of a war, eliminate Rabinowitz. If they really understood what was going on, they might be able to enlist Rabinowitz in a cause for good. However, that was too risky for the intelligence levels of two governments overwhelmingly staffed by men.

All Anna Chutesov could possibly hope for was that her side of the idiot equation was not using an assassin who could be traced back to Russia.

Gusev Balbek arrived at Fort Pickens on a stretcher. Horizontal, no one could tell this soldier was four-foot-eight and therefore below the minimum height for service.

"Legs were shot off in Nam," he said. He said it with a

Western twang. Having been wounded and not wanting to talk about it sounded so much better in Western American.

If he were a New York American, he would have to talk about it as the central fact of the universe, his and everyone else's.

If he were a California American he would have to show how he boogied on his stumps because he was too drugged out to know they were gone, and if he were from Boston he would have to go around contending the world was filled with giant freaks.

A Westerner could just keep his mouth shut after a few terse words.

He was amazed at how thoroughly his Russia had penetrated America. Customs agents whisked his phony passport through. He got special service on planes. He was used to American luxury. He had practiced living with it ten hours a day for the last twenty-five years. So when the sort of meal any Russian would give his eyeteeth for came to him in his first-class cabin, he sent it back because it was not hot enough.

In such a way did a four-foot-eight-inch sharpshooter with skin like a yak-skin tent make his way into Fort Pickens, Arkansas, where, on a high hill overlooking a maneuver area beneath him, his own private weapons were waiting for him.

They had assured him they would be here. They had come to America separately. Even with the great penetration of America by Russian forces they had wanted to make sure he would not be stopped with weapons. Because in America, more and more states were enacting gun laws, and who knew what one zealous policeman might try?

It had made Gusev Balbek nervous not to have his blessed guns with him, but in the heat of the Arkansas day when he saw the familiar gleaming blue barrels and the worn shoulder stocks of the balanced and delicately precise friends that had enabled him to practice on targets farther away than most men could even see, he felt a sense of relief. After all these years, he was here, and he was going to do the job of his life.

"Rabinowitz comes to that platform every day to lecture the troops," said the sergeant who had been waiting with the guns. "He has an Oriental in a pink robe follow him around. If the Oriental gets in your line of fire, take him out first, and then Rabinowitz. Good luck."

"I don't need to take out anyone but my target," said Gusev.

"This Oriental guy is weird. Wears a sissy robe but can outdo anyone in the division at anything."

"Not now he can't," said Gusev, getting off the stretcher and preparing his old friends for the day's work.

When the sun was at its highest, Balbek could see a jeep speed through the units of tanks toward the raised platform fifteen hundred yards away, down below the little hill where Balbek had loaded his guns.

He saw a robe flutter in the wind, but it was not pink but rather golden. Beside the robed one was the sad face of the first man he would kill.

At this distance those eyes could not see Balbek, but Balbek, because of the extraordinary sight of all Tatar villagers, could see Rabinowitz. No one ever saw as far or as well as a Tatar from Kazakhstan. In fact, the eye charts from the Ministry of Health were considered a joke.

As the villagers told each other, "That extra foot or two of height all went into our wonderful eyes."

Balbek saw Rabinowitz wave to his troops. He heard the troops yell back. He did not know what was being said below him, but he did recognize a harangue and he saw the anger build up in the face of the troops. He could tell a general whipping up his men for a fight.

The gun barrel felt cool in Balbek's hand. The sights had been filed off long ago. They only helped people who couldn't aim. And they were always off. He had yet to meet a Tatar who couldn't pick up a gun and tell just by the feel how far the sights were off.

What one aimed was the path of the bullet. Not the

sights. One used all the perceptions, not just eyesight, to aim. One sensed the wind on one's flesh, the dampness or dryness of the air, the way dust moved near the target. Taking all of these things into consideration, one allowed the course of the bullet to establish itself as one fired.

On the platform, Chiun saw the most curious thing. The Great Wang totally ignored a very obvious sniper in the surrounding hills. Why was he doing this?

He ignored the man as he aimed and fired, and he even ignored the bullet as it sped on its way toward his head.

This Chiun could not understand. He would have mentioned it, but voices took too long to travel at these times. And then he realized the Great Wang must be testing him. But with such a simple test?

Of course, it was clear. The Great Wang wanted to see variations on strokes, perhaps a lotus deflection of one bullet, and a windstorm of the next, and the wide-handed fat raisin of the next.

Up on the hill, Gusev Balbek fired eight shots right at the head and heart of Vassily Rabinowitz, and eight shots went off target every time they got near. Soldiers were lying wounded around the platform, some ten feet away, some a hundred feet away, but no one on the platform was scathed as the sun-bright kimono danced in the afternoon heat, reflecting the sun like its most glorious star.

Balbek released the trigger and steadied his rifle. He fired again, and again the golden kimono blazed in the sun, and again someone away from the platform fell down.

"Great Wang," said Chiun on the platform, "how many deflections do you want?"

"Who's shooting at the soldiers?" asked Rabinowitz, who to Chiun looked and sounded like his revered Great Wang.

"The sniper, of course," said Chiun.

"Well, finish him already," said Rabinowitz, and by that Chiun knew the Great Wang had approved of Chiun's variations of strokes deflecting objects.

As the division was still digging in, Chiun made his way

up the far hill, where he saw an obvious Tatar villager behind the rifle and asked him:

"What are you doing here?"

It was the first time in twenty-five years that Gusev had heard his native Raco Stidovian.

"I am here to kill Vassily Rabinowitz," said the stunned Balbek, also in the language he had not spoken since youth.

"You've developed a terrible accent," said the man in the golden kimono.

"How do you know Raco Stidovian?" asked Balbek.

"I am a Master of Sinanju. We work everywhere. How did a nice Tatar archer like you get involved with guns in America?"

"The Russians took me at an early age and forced me to do horrible things for them. They threatened my poor sick mother. They threatened to rape my sister and murder our entire village if I did not do their evil deeds for them," said Balbek.

"Good reasons to take up the gun," said Chiun. "A fine reason for you. Unfortunately, my fine Tatar, it is not really any sort of reason for me not to kill you," said Chiun. "Doesn't even warrant a second stanza."

The gun fired again from an arm's length away, and this shot was blocked even more easily than those fired from fifteen hundred yards. Gusev Balbek went into his last sleep before he could blink. He could not see that the killing blow was a swan's overlay variant of the basic thrust. When Chiun looked back toward the platform, he saw his Great Wang did not see it either. He was nowhere around. On the platform was Wang's friend Vassily Rabinowitz, good guy.

He was yelling:

"We have to get them before they get us. We can't put off the war any longer."

In the end, as a last resort, and only as a last resort, Ambassador Nomowitz gave in to reason. As instructed by

Anna Chutesov, he arranged for a time and a place where Russia would bare its soul to the American defense establishment. He saw Anna open a large briefcase with page upon page of top-secret documents. He saw her give them to an American second lieutenant to pass out to American colonels and generals and admirals.

He heard secrets told openly. He heard her detail the purpose of the parapsychology village, even its defenses. And then he heard what he was sure had to be treason.

She told them about Matesev and Balbek.

"Those are state secrets," whispered Nomowitz.

"You think they don't know about it?" said Anna coolly.

And then to the American officers in the little conference room built like an operating theater with rows and rows of seats set one above the other, she said:

"Under the foolish assumption that we should have him and you should not, we attempted to get him back for ourselves. I am sure you all see how ridiculous that is, when you consider that the man can make anyone believe anything."

"Damned right, Russky, he's ours now. Thanks for telling us he's at Fort Pickens posing as a brigadier general. Hell, we'll make him a four-star general."

The American officers applauded loudly.

When the applause died down, Anna asked:

"And do what with him?"

"Keep him in case we need him against you."

"For what?"

"To blind your minds as you would have blinded ours."

"Have you ever been to a general staff conference of Russian officers?" asked Anna.

"We know what you do," said the general.

"Then you would realize there is not much there to blind. Essentially we are dealing with someone who cannot be controlled, and ordinarily that would be no problem. The man would go through his life getting pretty much what he wanted. Unfortunately, we made a mistake and tried to harness him. Which we couldn't do.''

''Just because you couldn't, doesn't mean we can't,'' said the American general.

Anna smiled. ''I guess I am the fool. I didn't see that you should be no different from us. Well, let me tell you I can get a hundred and fifty more just as good as Vassily Rabinowitz, and I won't. He's not a weapon. He's a direction, and it won't be your direction, at least I hope it won't. This man, because of crimes we committed against him, has been terrified into making an army. And frankly, he's going to make a damned good one.''

''No problem for us,'' said the American. ''Problem for you.''

''Really, do you want a war with us because one man has nightmares about what we did to him?''

''No comment,'' said the American general, and the others applauded.

Anna Chutesov shrugged.

''Well, I hoped you would be smarter. Nevertheless, I wish you luck in getting control of him. And if you ever figure out what you're going to use him for, please let me know.''

Back at the Russian embassy, Nomowitz was furious.

''You gave away Russian secrets to their officers.''

''That is not the mistake I made,'' she said. ''The mistake I made was telling them where they can find him. Now they will go down there to Fort Pickens and everyone who goes down will join his army. He's only getting stronger.''

''A sworn enemy gets stronger and you don't worry.''

''Of course not. I know what to do. I know his profile. He will win his war, we will be duly impressed, and then we will give him what he wants.''

''What's that?''

''We'll leave him alone and let him play with the American army as he would have played with ours. I told them the truth.''

Of course, she hadn't. She just didn't want any more interference from back home, as she now worked on how she might be able to destroy Rabinowitz. For she was sure once this man had a taste of war, he would never want to give it up. She had read his profile back in Russia. Which made her even angrier that anyone would have been so stupid as to take him from his sleepy village of Dulsk to the parasychology clinic in the first place. She wished she could meet one man who used his mind. Apparently, in the last few days Rabinowitz had become assassin-proof. And that was just what she was afraid might happen if they sent their best people against him. But in this case, knowing who they had, and knowing what they didn't have, she was sure it was someone else who had tried to kill the hypnotist. If she knew who, she just might be able to give him something to help. But who in America was there? And who also understood what had to be done?

Harold W. Smith knew the moment Chiun's box had been destroyed. The worst had happened. And when he tried one slim hope of a chance of begging Remo into the mission, he got the strangest response from Remo.

Remo couldn't care less. He was talking to someone dead for forty-two hundred years.

Smith went home and from an upstairs closet removed his old army .45. He had not personally killed anyone since the Second World War. He knew he could not kill Chiun, but he also understood that Chiun thought him a sort of fool, and Chiun had never known Smith to lie.

He just might be able to lie this one time, first to Chiun, then to Rabinowitz, and then with one bullet do what the greatest assassins in the world had failed to do. He set the computers to self-destruct if he did not return.

The incredibly sensitive information in CURE computers could not be allowed to survive him. The organization had done its work over the decades, and now, rather than harm the country he loved, he would make sure his work would disappear with him.

Before he left he made one last phone call to the President.

"Sir, as you know, the Russians were after this man. Precisely because of that, we enlisted, as you know, our special people to stop the Russians. Second, now we have a danger in this one extremely talented man. He is incredibly dangerous. He has taken over at least a division as far as I know, and maybe more. I think he is going to start a war. I don't know why, but we have lost one man already, and the other is inoperative at this time. I am going myself. If I fail, you will not have the organization to serve this country anymore, but then again, no one will get hold of our vast store of information either. It will be secure."

"Good luck, Smith. I know you'll do what's right," said the President.

At Vistana Views, Wang, sitting on a stool out in the kitchen while Remo prepared rice, asked him if the phone call had been from the American employer.

"Yeah. He's going to play cowboy with this hypnotist."

"And you're going to let him go alone?"

"Sure," said Remo. "It's his life. It's his country."

"Think you're pretty tough, don't you, Remo? You and Chiun. You're so much alike. You both have an infinite ability to lie to yourselves."

"I'm not lying, and I'm not like Chiun."

"Oh, but you are. That's your great secret. That's why you fight and that's why you love each other. What is the matter with you two?"

"I thought when I got to see the Great Wang I would get answers to my questions. That's what Chiun promised. Did he lie?"

"No. You're just getting the answers you don't like. You're just like him, you know, but slick enough to cover it, so that most people think you're sane. You're a lunatic, Remo. Name me one thing you like that you give yourself."

"I like to be left alone," said Remo.

"That's the biggest lie you've told me so far," said Wang, bouncing from the seat to the rug.

Wang assumed a simple stance, feet flat, arms at his sides, appearing defenseless.

"All right, Remo is not like Chiun. Let's see what you can do. Let's have it."

"I'm not going to fight you," said Remo.

"You won't hurt me. I've been dead thousands of years."

"For someone who's been dead so long, you certainly made the floor bounce with your body."

"You and Chiun have an obsession with weight. You don't have to be skinny, you know. C'mon, paleface, let's see what you can do."

Remo threw a desultory blow at the stomach, but carefully enough that he was not off balance. The air swished as he brought back his hand.

"Just like Chiun. If it isn't your way, you don't want to play."

Remo wanted to see just how solid the Great Wang was, and he knew that he could at least get a hand on the man. He might not be able to defeat him, but he certainly could touch that flabby belly.

And he did, without Wang making one move to stop him. Remo's arm went right through into the coldest center of the universe and he screamed with pain, as Wang laughingly told him Chiun had tried that too when they had met, when Chiun achieved his highest level.

"Got to say this for you two. You and Chiun have got the cleanest blows of all the Masters of Sinanju. Like father, like son."

11

On the morning of May 11 three American columns under the command of a general some believed to be a reincarnation of General George Patton and others believed was their favorite commander, or father, or mother, or anyone close, invaded the newly liberated country of Sornica in Central America.

Sornica was newly liberated because after forty years of living under one-family rule, which was modestly oppressive with an army no larger than a police department, it was now ruled by a People's Council which had built a major army with major weapons, and was totally oppressive.

In the old regime, if one did not like the dictator, one could say it, but do little more. One could make a living, change jobs, marry whom one wanted, and if one didn't like it, one could leave.

The basic difference with the new Sornica was that no one was allowed to not like it. The newspapers which had published negative stories against the old oppressive regime, were now allowed the same freedoms. They could publish negative stories about the old regimes. When they published negative stories about the new People's Democratic Socialist Republic of Sornica, the enraged people shut it down.

The people were General Umberto Omerta, who was of the people, for the people, with the people. Anyone against Omerta was an enemy of the people. Therefore when he sent his newly expanded police force to close down the newspaper and beat up the editors, something that never happened under the old oppressive regime, it was the people responding to the outrage.

The people made sure anyone speaking against the regime changed their minds. They stopped people speaking openly against the regime within the borders. They also stopped people leaving, as was a tradition in liberated countries.

No one dared ask if it were the people doing the arresting, executing, and spying on reactionary elements, traitors, and running dogs of America. No one asked if they, too, were not people. That would have been treason and brought up the ugly answer that if it was the people these reactionaries were against, they had to be something else. And that something else was untermenschen, a system used by Nazi Germany to categorize some people as less than human, a system which used gas ovens to take care of those who were deemed subhuman.

But the reason Sornica was invaded this May morning was not because it murdered its own nonpeople or kept them imprisoned and had its children spy on their parents. It was not because Sornica ran several training camps to help other like-minded folk liberate their neighbors from mildly oppressive regimes.

Sornica had eighteen companies of Russian soldiers and technicians stationed on their soil. And it was these companies that the reincarnation of George Patton, everyone's favorite commander or parent, the man who sometimes walked around cleverly disguised as a Russian immigrant, wanted to destroy.

Rabinowitz understood that if he could demolish the best troops Russia sent abroad, they would respect him. It made no difference if he killed them or treated them as prisoners. What the Russians understood was power. If he could show he was powerful they would leave him alone. It was not by accident that the only treaty the Russian communists ever kept with scrupulous precision was that with Nazi Germany. It only ended when the Nazis invaded them first instead of Great Britain, which the Russians were hoping for.

Hearing the guns fire, feeling the power of his tanks churn through the mud that was called a road in Sornica, Rabinowitz felt a strange sensation. While he desperately minded being killed by people personally putting their hands on him, and despised being chased, gunfire set off a special thrill within him. He dashed to the front of his columns. He cheered on his best commanders. He stood in open fields with shells falling around him to curse those who did not keep up with the rest of the column.

By midday the best Russian armor lay smoldering in the plains and jungles of Sornica. The ever-deadly Russian helicopter gunship, the Hinds, had been lured into attacking what appeared like light armor vehicles and infantry, only to be demolished by the hand-held rocket launchers he had refused to let his troops use on the first gunships in the area. When the Hinds saw no rockets beneath them, Generalissimo Omerta threw in his entire fleet to enjoy the carnage. And at that time, and only at that time, were Rabinowitz' troops allowed to use their rockets, a perfect defense against the gunships. The Hinds were caught strafing en masse and went up like firecrackers above the battlefields of Sornica.

"I fear only one thing, Chiun, and that's to be killed by hand. I never want someone's hands on me again," said Rabinowitz, turning to his bodyguard, who was dressed in the black battle kimono used by the Masters of Sinanju when standing near an emperor who had taken the field.

"But how, Great Wang, could you be killed by anyone's hand?" asked Chiun.

"You never know," Chiun heard the Great Wang say. "But it's your job to see that it doesn't happen."

"But have I not passed every earlier test to reach my highest level?"

"This is another one."

"What kind?" asked Chiun.

"The most important one," said Vassily.

"Why?" asked Chiun.

"Because I say so."

"But is it not the function of the Great Wang on his visit to a Master of Sinanju to answer the most important questions the other Master has? Is not your very name the answer to all?"

"Will you get off my back already with this answer mishigas?" Chiun heard the Great Wang say. And Wang would not even answer in Korean, but insisted on using English, a sign of disdain for Chiun, who could not figure out what he had done wrong, but was vowing to change it, whatever it was.

Following an army was not hard. No army ever moved without everyone around it knowing it moved, and Smith arrived in Sornica with credentials he had prepared for himself as a member of the Defense Department. He found the air oppressive and humid. His breathing was labored, and he could not stand for long periods of time. A sergeant got him a glass of water and helped him find what could pass for shade in Sornica: humid moss under a tree that attracted mosquitoes and large flying bugs as yet unidentified by science. Both of them bit, and Smith knew he was back in a war zone again. Except in the last war, he had been a young man who did not have to rest in the middle of the day.

His .45 felt heavier than he ever remembered it, and some of the soldiers who passed by him thought that because he wore it in a shoulder holster, he was some sort of secret agent. Smith didn't want to look this way when he approached Rabinowitz and Chiun. Chiun would not be all that surprised, but the great hypnotist, seeing a possible agent, might react immediately, and Smith's only chance was to surprise Rabinowitz about his intentions. And of course deceive Chiun.

No normal person could even see the Master's hands move, much less stop them.

"Sergeant," Smith asked, "do you think it would be possible to get me some fatigues? I feel awkward carrying this gun like some agent. I'm Defense Department and I don't think I should look like CIA, do you?"

"Yessir. Can do, sir," said the sergeant. He was an old top kick and Smith knew that if anyone in any army could get what he asked for, it was this sort of man. But the sergeant came back before nightfall, shrugging his shoulders, his palms open in helplessness.

"No extra anything, sir. Bottleneck back there."

"You mean to tell me there are no extra uniforms in the supply columns?"

"Not a one, sir. This is a tightly planned operation. Old Blood 'n' Guts has counted every bullet."

"What?" asked Smith. He couldn't believe the good news. Rabinowitz was nearby.

"Old Blood 'n' Guts counted every bullet. He knows just what and when and where. We'd better get moving now, sir, if we want to get up to the front to see him. We've already wasted a lot of time looking for a uniform for you."

"I don't think there's any worry about catching up to Rabinowitz. I'll just wait for him here."

"But he says he won't stop until he takes the capital of Sornica."

"I doubt that's a possibility at this point."

"But, sir, he's outfought everything the commies threw at him, even their gunships. Good Old Blood 'n' Guts has defeated the Hinds gunship."

"Could you possibly pitch some sort of tent for me here to spend the night?" asked Smith. "That is, if you can find one."

"I don't know, sir. Supplies are pretty tightly accounted for."

"Good," said Smith. "I guess I'll just have to freeze in one of the cold nights of Sornica. Wake me if Rabinowitz should be back by morning, or Old Blood 'n' Guts— whatever you call him."

*   *   *

Wang was laughing.

"I'm not serious," said Remo. "I joke around a hell of a lot. I think the world is peculiar and I'm not afraid to say so."

"You never stop saying so. You take yourself so seriously, Remo."

"Hah," said Remo. He knew his anger was rising because his breathing told him so. Anger was the worst emotion to have, next to fear. It took away the other senses. "You know, here it is. I wait two decades to meet the Great Wang, thinking I will never achieve it, and now I finally meet you and you bust my chops more than Chiun. Chiun is the one who's serious. He thinks if we don't do this or that, the whole history of Sinanju is going to go up. He's been trying to get me married off to a Korean girl just to make sure the line will continue. Yeah. He's become a friggin' dating service."

"Why are you angry?"

"Because I'm disappointed in you," said Remo. "Frankly, I expected more. And I got less than Chiun."

"The whole world is less than Chiun to you, Remo. You didn't learn his stroke style so perfectly without loving him. Nobody communicates that perfectly without love."

"I respect Chiun, and yeah, I love him. All right. Does that make you happy, you giggling bean pot?" said Remo to the round, smiling face of Wang. "But I don't think he's perfection. We have a term in this civilization called neurotic. I think it would eminently apply to our Master Chiun."

"Would it also apply to someone saving the world, Remo?"

"Not the world. I tried to save my country, if you don't mind."

"How many is that? Two hundred and twenty million people?"

"About," said Remo. He was getting tired of this condominium, with its modern kitchen and living room and

Jacuzzi and televisions in every room, and most of all the fat, happy Wang with a belly as cold as the center of the universe.

All Wang had wanted out of that was to see Remo's stroke. Any Master could tell from one stroke what sort of powers a man had. Remo walked outside, and Wang followed.

"You know, in our day the whole world had two hundred million people. America is your world."

"Not anymore," said Remo. He noticed groundskeepers look at Wang. So they could see him too, Remo realized.

"Then tell me. Who is the more neurotic, a man who tries to save a line of assassins or a man who tries to save a country? Who?"

"Look, you've had your visit. Thank you and good-bye."

"You haven't asked your question yet," said Wang.

"All right, when are you getting out of here?"

"When you ask the right question."

"That could take forever," said Remo.

"You don't have forever. But it could take until your dying day."

"You don't mean that, do you?"

"Do you think I want to hang around you for fifty or a hundred years?" laughed Wang. "Chiun was bad enough, but you are worse. Every time you open your mouth I hear Chiun."

"No. No. Chiun's a racist who despises everyone else who isn't Korean. I am not a racist. The one thing I'm not is a racist."

And Wang tumbled along the sidewalk in gales of laughter, rolling himself like a hoop, entertaining some children playing on the lawns of the Vistana Views condominums.

"What's so funny?" asked Remo.

"That's just what Chiun would say. He would say all whites are racist and they're not even the best race."

"I don't say that about Koreans. I know Chiun's skills even though you knock him unfairly in spite of the fact that even you admit he's got the best strokes in the history of Sinanju.''

"I said cleanest strokes. And he would think that, too. Cleanest is not best, Remo. I never said you were the best."

"I have nothing I want to ask you," said Remo. "Case closed."

"Every time you wish something were so, you say 'case closed,' and I think it's because if they opened it up again you would find out you're wrong. Case closed?"

Remo suddenly spun and walked directly back to the condo.

"Chiun did the same thing. I said he was like his father. Do you know what he said to me? Told me he couldn't be like his father because his father acted childish and was self-centered and had difficulty admitting he loved someone. Came very hard. Do you think I'm lying to you, Remo?"

"Don't care," said Remo, slamming the door in Wang's face, which did not work, for while it ripped the door off its hinges with the force of the movement, it met Wang's fingertips and settled into the jamb with all the softness of a feather.

"People who don't care always slam doors like that," said Wang.

"I have a question for you. I never knew who my real mother and father were. I was found in an orphanage and raised there by nuns. The organization recruited me because they knew I had no family I would have to run back and see. Who are my real mother and father?"

"What a silly question."

"You know the answer?"

"Of course, but it doesn't even warrant breath. They're not your parents. Your parents are one person now and he is in danger and needs your help."

"Are you lying to me?"

"Only about the danger. He's only somewhat in danger.

Everyone is in danger when he doesn't know who he's talking to.''

Anna Chutesov heard about the initial successes of the three American columns secondhand from the buzz of gossip in the Washington embassy. The headquarters for Russian intelligence in the hemisphere was in Cuba, but Washington was still considered the main diplomatic foothold, even if militarily the important outposts were Cuba and Sornica.

Anna was trying to explain that even if they lost Sornica, they still had Cuba. And what good would Sornica do them that Cuba couldn't?

"From Sornica we can help liberate Honduras, Costa Rica, Panama, Mexico."

"What will you do in Mexico? Close off the border to stop people from escaping? America has been trying to do that for ten years now without success. You'll do it for them. But I'll tell you something. They're not smart enough to know that either. You'll have your big war then."

"We don't want the big war. We are not planning on the big war."

"Right, you want to stumble blindly into it like every other man. But don't worry, Rabinowitz is going to save you from all that. And then you will go down and surrender to him, and once you do that, hopefully we will get him relaxed enough to kill him, so that no idiot is going to try to use him again."

When the news that Russia's vaunted Hinds gunship had been made useless in the skies over Sornica, the Russian embassy fell into a morbid silence. Except for one happy voice of a woman singing Russian ballads her mother had taught her.

In a writers' conference in Washington, the Sornica minister of culture, Colonel Padril Ostonso, was called away from a panel discussion because of an emergency. He was excused to the thundering applause of many of the other writers.

"We sit here ashamed of America," said one novelist who had written a book whose heroes had stolen atomic secrets from America. "We are ashamed of our guns, ashamed of our tanks, and most of all, ashamed of the people who use them. What we can do to overcome this shame to all mankind that is happening today, I do not know. All we can do is to offer our brother Colonel Padril Ostonso our prayers, our support, and our applause."

Colonel Ostonso thanked them on behalf of the struggling writers of Sornica. Then he answered the phone. As minister of culture he was in charge of the writers. This meant two maximum-security jails for those who disagreed with the People's Council.

Those writers who supported the people were supported by them, and therefore they had homes. Those who were against the people had to support themselves, and if they managed to do so, the minister of culture wanted to know who was helping them. And since they couldn't support themselves without the government's permission, they were parasites and had to be put in jails.

At this very moment one of the American columns was nearing one of the jails, threatening to release the dangerous poets, novelists, and a photographer who dared take a picture of someone trying to hide from the people's draft, when everyone knew a photographer was supposed to photograph people volunteering, not evading.

"We cannot move them, Colonel," came the voice. "They're your responsibility. What do you want?"

"Do you have dynamite? Blow them up."

"We don't have dynamite. That's considered a building material and we haven't seen any of that since reconstruction of our homeland."

"Shoot them."

"All the bullets are being used for the front."

"What do you have?"

"They're old wooden buildings and I know my mother has an extra match left over from the bad old days of the dictator."

"Burn them," said Colonel Padril Ostonso.

"That's a bit cruel, sir."

"They're my writers. I'm the minister of culture. I can do anything I want with them. If I say burn them, burn them."

Colonel Ostonso hung up and returned to the conference, where he was greeted by more applause.

One novelist suggested that Colonel Ostonso should not even be on the panel because he was a policeman and not a writer, but that writer was declared a fascist, and the floor given over to Colonel Ostonso, who moved that anyone from the United States government be denied the right to speak. It was greeted by applause, except for the women writers, who thought that there were not enough women on the panel voting for the motion.

Of course there were protests, writers being writers, some pointing out that perhaps a conference on the freedom of writers should deal with the freedom of writers instead of how many writers on the panel were women.

One even was so bold as to suggest that communist countries were more oppressive to writers and that they, too, should be condemned. The final resolution, therefore, condemned the United States of America for oppression of masses of writers, and decried oppression anywhere of writers. Since anywhere might also include communist countries, it was considered a balanced document.

The tanks had not advanced more than a hundred yards in the last hour. Rabinowitz raced to the lead column.

"Get outta there, you lazy yellow dog," Rabinowitz yelled to the tank commander. He was only three miles from the capital of Sornica. He wasn't going to be deprived of victory now. The heat of the battle had driven him mad and now he didn't care if he died. Of course this was improbable with the Oriental in the black kimono around him. Chiun seemed to be able to catch flak with grace, even thanking Rabinowitz for the opportunity.

"I appreciate that you trust me with your life, knowing

that you yourself refuse to dodge death, giving me the honor of protecting you, Great Wang.''

"Just don't get in the way of the gun sights," said Rabinowitz to Chiun as he closed the hatch on the lead tank.

Chiun wondered why the Great Wang would use something as unreliable as a cannon. Perhaps he wanted to see how it worked like a toy.

One did not question the Great Wang.

Rabinowitz jammed his foot on the accelerator and nothing happened. The treads did not roll. The engine did not bark. All he could hear was the squeak of a pedal that needed grease.

"What's wrong with this damned tank?"

"Out of gas, sir. All the lead tanks are out of gas," came a voice from outside the tank. "We had an extra level of fighting and we used it up. A small battle we didn't count on. That's war, sir. A whole bunch of things you don't count on."

"I didn't count on that," screamed Rabinowitz. "We can't go forward without gas. In fact, we can't retreat without it either."

Remembering the tales of emperors past, Chiun asked the Great Wang whom he wished killed for the failure. Rabinowitz, now shrewd enough to know his assault was in trouble, tried to call for resupply, but almost instantly realized this would be impossible.

Before morning, the bulk of the struggling army was within fifteen miles of its furthest advance.

Rabinowitz even heard Russian voices a few times from the once again advancing enemy. He thought momentarily of using his special powers, but then he would have to abandon his army. And he liked his army. He liked his army better than he liked the village bicycle back in Dulsk. He had to share the bicycle.

An old man in a suit resting under a tree was shaken awake.

"That's him, sir."

Harold W. Smith blinked open his eyes. His bones were cold, and it was difficult getting up. He could barely make out Chiun in the darkness.

"Chiun, Chiun, I come in peace. Peace. I am your former emperor."

"Ah, most wise Emperor Harold Smith. There has been an enhancement to the contract I was to perform."

"What is it? I would have thought that if the Great Chiun were to eliminate someone he would be dead by now."

"Yes, and he would have been. But following the strictest of orders, I absolutely would not press that button if I had not killed him."

"I believe the orders were somewhat different, Chiun. But that doesn't matter, because I've come to make peace with Mr. Rabinowitz. I think he is just fine, and it was a mistake on my part."

Smith opened his jacket, showing the gun. He made it a gesture of openness and honesty. He really wasn't giving anything away. He was aware that Chiun and Remo knew if any man carried a weapon around them. They could tell it from his walk.

"I'd like to give Mr. Rabinowitz our support. I was wrong, Chiun. Totally wrong."

Vassily heard the Oriental speak a language he didn't know, and therefore did not understand that he had just been introduced to the man who had ordered Chiun to kill him.

"My name is Smith. I think you're doing a wonderful job, Mr. Rabinowitz, but I think you have supply problems, and I can help."

"We need everything," yelled Rabinowitz, turning to another colonel to tell him they had to hold now or it would turn into a rout.

"Sure, but we've got to get to the place to order the supplies. You are doing it wrong. You're doing it through the army."

"Where else do you get howitzer shells from?" boomed

Rabinowitz, while being shown the disposition of another column that had run out of gas.

"Just over the hill. Come with me. Chiun had better go on ahead to make sure no one has cut the phone link there."

When Chiun was too far away for even a Master of Sinanju to be instantly between Smith and Rabinowitz, Smith pointed to a tank down the road, as an example of where the gas really was. Vassily turned his head to look, and with the other hand Smith eased the .45 out of his holster. Closing his eyes so he would not lock on his gaze, Smith fired at the head right in front of him. Fortunately the shot was deflected, because he would have killed his own first-grade teacher, Miss Ashford, the woman who was practically his mother when his own mother died.

"I'm sorry, Miss Ashford. I didn't know. We have a problem here with a dangerous man. Get out of the way so I can remove him."

"Harold. He's not dangerous," said Miss Ashford in the warm New England sounds Harold Smith remembered so well. "You've been misinformed," she said.

"No. I haven't. He's dangerous. He's a hypnotist."

"All he wants, Harold, is to be left alone and to get at least two more weeks of heavy ammunition. He's all right with small-arms ammunition but he needs gas like he needs his own balls."

"Miss Ashford, I never heard you use words like that."

"These are hard times, Harold. We all have to work together. And I wish you would help the nice Mr. Rabinowitz."

Smith tried to explain all the things he had done since the Putney Day School, how he worked for CURE now, how he was saving the nation. But he knew in his very soul that he had been wrong, really wrong.

He learned one thing from Miss Ashford, whom he trusted above all people: to serve America best, he would have to help this invasion. Join with Chiun, who knew what was best. Respect his elders. Be God-fearing and honest. Tell no lies, except, of course, if it helped this invasion.

Harold Smith went to work with a joy and an enthusiasm he hadn't felt since high school. He knew he was doing right. He had never been so certain of it in all his life. It was a certainty that was welcome after all the years of toil in the gray years of America's survival.

The first thing he did was make sure the CURE network was not destroyed. He got to a long-distance phone closer to the shore, and put in the proper coded instructions that would save all the incriminating evidence of two decades. And once saved, he now turned it all over to the one person he could trust more than himself. Miss Ashford. But it was not just any Miss Ashford. It was a Miss Ashford in all the best things she represented.

She had the sort of probity Harold Smith had sought to emulate. She had an integrity and honesty he had clasped to his bosom and that still lived within him. So the conscious mind that might have told him Miss Ashford had to be a hundred years old by now did not let him know anything was wrong when he saw her as she was back in Putney, forty years old.

Nothing was wrong. She from whom he had learned and by whose ideals he lived his life was just as alive on the tank-clogged roads of Sornica as she had been sixty years before in Putney, Vermont.

It was who he was that had been unleashed. And so he talked to her, and every time he described access to this part of government or that part of government through the network he had set up, Miss Ashford said:

"Good. Good. That's wonderful."

And thus, step by step, the entire CURE network was handed over to a man in the midst of a battle against his Russian enemies.

"You mean to say you are able to draw on any American government organization's computer files without them knowing it?" asked Miss Ashford.

"Have you been for years," said Harold proudly.

"All right, maybe we can do something with that after this war. Right now, get me gas. Gas, My kingdom for gas," said Miss Ashford.

12

Wang handed Remo the telephone.

"It's for you," he said.

Remo waved the phone away.

"I'm leaving," he said.

"You can't leave. You don't know where you're leaving from or going to. You're in your time of transition, the last transition you will ever make. Speak to the man. It is your current contact, Harold Smith."

"Tell him I no longer work for him. I've done the last meaningless hit of my life."

"Ah, you think every assassination has a purpose, Remo? There you go again. Savior of the world. Chiun saves the House of Sinanju and you save the world. What a pair of dullards you two are."

Remo took the phone that seemed to leap from Wang's pudgy hand into the sweep of Remo's arm, so that while Remo was trying to snatch something, he couldn't help but look as though he was really in a sort of cooperative dance with Wang, who was still smiling.

"I told you I'm through, Smitty," said Remo.

"And you quit for good reason, Remo," said Smith. Remo could hear artillery fire in the background. Smith sounded happy. That was strange. He never sounded happy.

"Look, Remo. For all these years we have been fighting what seems to be a case of creeping national rot. We've gotten bigger and better, and the country gets weaker and worse. But I have found something down here, something very special. The sort of spirit that made America great.''

"Then enjoy it," said Remo, and hung up.

"That's the way you treat a client?" asked Wang, shaking his head in amusement.

"I'm not going to lie to him like Chiun. Chiun tells him all sorts of nonsense, and then does what he wants. That's how we differ. I tell him flat out. Good-bye. When I say good-bye it doesn't sound like three hundred verses of praise for the pope."

Remo nodded on that one. He was right.

"So serious," said Wang. "How you both treat clients amazes me. So serious. Chiun odorizes the atmosphere, and you, Remo, grimly announce the absolute truth. The two of you are so alike."

"If truth and lying are alike, then you can call anything the same. I got you there, Wang. Unless you're like Chiun and can't admit when you've been defeated. Maybe that's part of the Sinanju heritage. I don't know. Your ball game. Case closed."

"Then if it's closed, I can't tell you that someone who thinks a client is so important as to tell the absolute truth to him all the time is the same as someone who thinks a client is so important as to be lied to all the time. I guess they both don't think the client is important, eh?"

"Twist the truth any way you want, fat man," said Remo. "I'm gone."

"No you're not. You're right here," said Wang. "What you want to run from is the truth. And you'll run forever and never get away."

"Do we live forever?" asked Remo. "How long does a Master of Sinanju live? I mean, I'm twenty years older than when I began, and I look a year or two younger. I don't know how old Chiun is, but he moves perfectly."

"Ah, Remo, do you really want to say that last part? Do you really think Chiun moves perfectly? Have you not been listening to what I said about the Masters?"

"You said Chiun and I had the cleanest strokes in the

history of Sinanju. And what the hell do you mean, we treat clients with too much importance?''

"I can mention only one country that exists today that existed in my day, and that's Egypt. And believe me, it's not the same country. I can mention no dynasty that existed in my day that exists now. No border that men died and killed for is today what it was then. They all go, Remo. Your America will go. Everything goes.''

"Except Sinanju. That's what Chiun said.''

"No, I think he said the techniques. And why has that remained the same? Because people are the same. The Sinanju techniques have not only stayed the same, they have gotten better.''

The phone rang again.

"Remo, just hear me out,'' said Smith. "Please, I'm asking for whatever the last two decades has meant to you.''

"Shoot,'' said Remo.

Wang laughed. "How grim,'' he said. "Chiun would be effusing his head off. But you tell the truth. So important. So different, you two.''

Remo covered the receiver with his hand.

"Let me get this over with before you start the needles again,'' said Remo.

"So personal. You and Chiun. Everything is personal.''

"Yeah, Smitty,'' said Remo into the receiver.

"You probably have heard of the war going on in Sornica here in Central America,'' said Smith.

"No,'' said Remo. He signaled for Wang to throw him one of the wonderful fresh Florida oranges. Wang's fat hand dropped on a pile set in a pink bowl. He nicked the top one with his thumb and then sent it spinning to Remo. The force of the spin tore the white underbelly of the orange skin away from the meat in a single strand as though a careful cook had removed it. The peel landed on the rugged floor, and the orange dropped into Remo's hand.

"How did you do that?'' asked Remo.

"Chiun didn't teach you?"

"No. He doesn't know."

"We must have lost it in the Middle Ages. Works better with the old hard oranges. Less skin. Tighter meat. With the old oranges of Paku you could land both the peel and the orange just where you wanted. No picking up off the rug," said Wang.

"Never heard of Paku."

"See?" said Wang. "Biggest trading center of its age. Only good thing it ever did was produce the tight small orange that could be spun out of its skin better. Go back to your client with that in mind."

Remo uncovered the receiver again.

"Yeah, Smitty."

"Is someone there?"

"Yeah."

"We still have to maintain secrecy, if nothing else. Remo, today there is a battle going on that will decide the future of mankind. We are struggling here in Sornica against an evil that must be eradicated. And for the first time in years, I see a light at the end of the tunnel. I see a real chance to save America once and for all."

"Paku," said Remo.

"What's Paku?" asked Smith.

"Another center of the universe," said Remo.

"I don't understand. But look. Chiun is here, and he'll tell you for himself how important this is."

Remo waited, whistling.

"You're hurt and angry, aren't you?" asked Wang.

"Get off my back," said Remo.

Chiun's squeaky voice rattled the telephone.

"Remo. Wonderful news. Wonderful news. We have found the right emperor to serve, and guess who serves him also?"

"I can't imagine you happy, little father," said Remo. "What's going on?"

"See?" said Wang. "Both of you walk around all the time in a state of unhappiness. Identical."

"I'm happy, asshole," said Remo.

Wang laughed at the curse.

"Remo, even the Great Wang is here serving Vassily Rabinowitz, a wonderful guy. And do you know what? Mad Harold was wise after all. We're all here, Remo."

Instead of covering the speaker, Remo created a vibration in the plastic. The hand never could cloud a voice to someone who had been trained to hear.

"Can there be two Great Wangs, one in one place and one in the other?"

Wang saw what Remo was doing and understood the problem.

"No."

"How do I know I have the right one?"

"Are you happy?"

"Not really," said Remo.

"Then that's who you are. Is Chiun happy?"

"Yes."

"How many times do you remember him happy?"

"Well, you know, he can get happy at times. Not too long. He likes bitching better, but I've seen him happy."

"You know you have the right one."

"So, does he?"

"Ask him, ask him about any problems. Chiun is always collecting injustices. He talks about them and you pretend they don't exist. You're a wonderful pair."

Remo stopped masquerading the sound vibrations on the receiver.

"Things are pretty good down there, huh?" he asked.

"Perfect. We have finally found the right emperor. And Smith understands too. I tell you, Remo, everything about everyone down here is perfect."

"Thanks, Chiun. I'll be right down," said Remo, getting the coordinates in Sornica where Chiun, Smith, and Rabinowitz expected to be at the end of the next day's advance.

"Wherever you are, I'll find you," said Remo. And he hung up.

"Chiun's in trouble," said Remo. "I don't know if I can save him. That hypnotist has got Smith. I remember Smitty couldn't be hypnotized. Did you know that? He was telling me once. He tried to get hypnotized to relax, and it wouldn't work. He had no imagination. He'd look at a Rorschach ink blot and see an ink blot. True."

"What's a Rorschach ink blot?" asked Wang.

"It's something new. People who are supposed to heal the mind make up random cards with ink blots, and the person is supposed to say what it looks like to him. It really says what's going on in the person's mind. If he sees violence he has violence on the mind. Happiness, he has happiness on the mind."

"Oh, the Tow Dung. It's done with mud on a white plate. Same thing. How can you rescue Chiun now if the man who has him can turn your mind against yourself?"

"I don't know," said Remo. "I'd like that to be my question you've got to answer. How can I save Chiun? How can I save Smith? I'm helpless."

"People are helpless in order to get others to help them. You're not helpless. But I must admit this sounds like the greatest challenge ever to the House of Sinanju. What are you going to do, Remo?"

"I don't know."

"Are you frightened?"

"A little. I hate to think of Chiun with his mind scrambled."

"And what if he thinks you are some enemy who is to be killed? What will you do when you have to fight him to the death? Have you thought of that?"

"Hey, I'm supposed to ask the questions. You're supposed to give me the answers."

"Fine. Here is an answer. Since you cannot figure out a way to rescue Chiun and this client for whom you have developed an attachment even though you claim to hate him, find someone else who can reason. Someone who can think brilliantly."

"I don't need help."

"You just said you were helpless," said Wang, laughing at how much Remo and Chiun were alike.

"Just give me the answer to the big question and get out of here," said Remo.

"Ask me the question," chuckled Wang.

"Never mind the question. Give me the damned answer, and stop playing games. Give me the answer," said Remo.

"Yes," said Wang, and Remo found himself staring at the blueness of the sky over Vistana Views, and he knew the Great Wang was gone. He had come in the last transition of Remo Williams, and he was supposed to answer the one great question Remo had.

And truly Wang had. The answer was yes.

But Remo still didn't know what the question was. Remo did not pack to leave America for good, but walked out of the condo into the Florida sunshine, headed for Sornica and the war that was supposed to be going on there.

Anna Chutesov felt elation at the defeat of the Russian forces stationed in Sornica, then despair as Rabinowitz' columns retreated, then elation again as they seemed to be getting all the gas and ammunition they needed.

"Good, now let's get someone down there to surrender to Vassily Rabinowitz before he fouls up this campaign."

"But we don't want to lose Sornica to the Americans. They're reinforcing."

"Have you noticed how they're reinforcing? Have you ever seen supplies move that well and quickly with the Americans?" asked Anna. "Have you been actually reading the reports instead of looking at colored lines on maps that tell you nothing except where some people surmise other people were at the time the ink was wet?"

"The Americans are getting behind this war on a grand scale. We must support our Sornican brothers," said Ambassador Nomowitz.

Wearily Anna Chutesov brought the ambassador to a

large map of the world. What so depressed her was that she was sure the Russian high command was thinking just like Nomowitz. And why shouldn't they? They all had the same testosterone levels. Wasn't a woman in there? She knew now that she herself had to go down to Sornica. There was no alternative. But on the flimsy hope that this might be one of the occasions that the male mind could see light, she drew a line from America to Sornica and had Nomowitz count the inches. Men were good at counting inches, possibly because that's how they judged themselves in so many ways.

Then she drew a line from Russia's munitions factories in the dead center of all the Soviet republics, farthest away from any invasion.

The line went from the middle of Russia to Murmansk and then began a water route. With every inch she drew she described which hostile nations they had to pass— Norway, Holland, France, England—and finally out into the Atlantic, where the greatest navy the world had ever seen now patrolled, the navy of the United States.

The line kept going. It finally arrived at Sornica. And Nomowitz had to move the ruler many times to count the inches.

"Every bullet, every shell, every missile we want to have there, has to travel that far. If we reinforce we will have to supply those men with bullets, and gas and tanks and guns, and toilet paper and food, and cigarettes and hats, and clothes and boots and shoelaces, along all those inches. Every man we put there will be a burden on our economy. The bigger it gets, who do you think is more likely to win? Look at the short hop the Americans have to take."

"When the going gets tough, the tough get going," said Nomowitz.

"You're a real man," said Anna Chutesov.

"Thank you," said Ambassador Nomowitz.

She said no more but headed right out of the Russian embassy toward a plane for Sornica. She would have to figure out a plan there. Her Russia was going to be of no help. And she had heard that stupid phrase used by American football coaches who had a pathological interest in the outcome of a football game which, fortunately, no one's life depended on.

But in real life, if the going gets tough, a person should stop and figure out why. Then he should calculate whether he should pay the price. In other words, think what one is doing, rather than blindly use the last ounce of one's strength.

It was not reassuring that these were the minds that controlled nuclear weapons on both sides.

Should Vassily Rabinowitz fail at this, Anna was sure he would stop at nothing to get control of America's nuclear arsenal. The Russian intelligence reports had indicated a very Rabinowitz-type situation had occurred near a base in Omaha. There he had failed, apparently because he had not reached the high command. But what would prevent him in a panic from reaching America's President?

Then there might be more than just hostile words out of America. Then there might be some force behind their threats. And Russians, being real men, would respond in kind.

Anna lit up a cigarette in the smoking section of the airplane bound for Sornica. As the sulfur flamed intensely at the end of the match, she thought, the world will go like that. No one is going to be a coward.

The flight was filled with American journalists on their way to the war. Only one reporter hadn't decided who was in the right and who was in the wrong. The others didn't have much respect for him. They said he had the mentality of a police reporter.

This was a new breed of journalist who added his interpretations to stories. To show he wasn't prejudiced, he was almost uniformly prejudiced against his country. This group was already determined not to believe anything an American officer told them.

Actually that was a good career move. If the stories

were politically correct they won great press awards given out by other journalists who also thought with political correctness. And with enough politically correct stories they would get prestigious columns with bylines and no longer have to hide their prejudices.

It was no accident that an entirely fabricated news story had recently won the top award. Anna's only surprise was that the newspaper actually admitted falsehood and returned the prize. That was different. The story was, of course, politically correct, reestablishing what a hard lot blacks had in America and how little whites cared.

The real problem that none of them seemed to know was that intelligence agencies were just as bad as the supposed free news organizations. The male mind could view nothing without prejudice. In America women were fighting to be just like men, and sadly, they were succeeding.

The plane stopped in Tampa, and a thin man with dark eyes and high cheekbones got on, taking the only seat available, next to Anna. Several other men had attempted to sit down, and Anna, wishing to be left alone, cut their egos in half.

She could still hear mumbling up front about how much she needed a really good act of fornication. What that really meant was that they wanted her to go to bed with them and tell them they had provided such, reestablishing their egos at the level they had enjoyed before they dared to try to sit down next to her.

The man eased his way past her legs to the window seat.

He did not buckle up on takeoff.

In a crash that meant he would go flying around. He could fly around into her.

"The sign says buckle up," said Anna. She knew men could read. That was how they passed along their worst misinformation.

"I don't need to be strapped in."

"I suppose you are going to be held in place by your big wonderful male organ?" said Anna.

"No. I have better balance than the plane. But you go ahead," said the man.

"I have. Now you."

"Lady, I've had a lot of trouble today. Let me give you the best advice you have ever had. Leave me alone."

The man turned away from her. Anna gave him one of those smiles she knew could melt men.

"Be a good fellow and buckle up. Won't you? For me." The smile promised a bed with her in it. Men would do anything for that.

"What's the matter with you, lady? You crazy? Didn't you hear me?"

"I am trying to help us both," she said. She gave him the wanting eyes.

"Lady, I'm not going to put on a belt just because you're faking sexual interest. Go play with the reporters in the front of the plane. I have problems and you can't help me."

"What makes you think I'm faking?"

"I dunno. I know. Like I know balance. Good-bye. Case closed," said the man.

He did not look at her again, but over the Gulf of Mexico some turbulence threw the plane around and even knocked a flight attendant off her feet. Even those buckled into their seats screamed as they were tossed around. Anna gripped her seat with whitened knuckles, and she caught a glimpse of the man to her right.

He was not moving. There was no strain. No being thrown back and forth, held only by a strand of cloth called a seat belt. He was simply seated as he had been since the plane took off.

When the turbulence subsided, she looked closer. His chest was not moving. The man was not breathing. Was he dead? She poked his shoulder.

"Yeah?" he said.

"Oh," she said. "You're alive."

"Been that way since birth," said Remo.

"I'm sorry. You weren't breathing."

" 'Course not. I don't need your nicotine sloshing around in my lungs."

"But we've been in the air a half-hour."

"Hard part is keeping the skin from breathing."

"So my smoke bothers you?"

"Any smoke, lady. Not just your smoke."

"Yes, yes. That's what I meant," she said. "Of course I meant that."

"Don't smoke and I'll breathe," said Remo.

"How do you do that?"

"You got twenty years, I'll teach you. In the meanwhile leave me alone. I've got problems."

"I'm good at problems. I'm very good at problems," said Anna. Who was this man? And if he had special powers, might they not be used against Rabinowitz? She wondered these things even as she realized her sexual wiles would not work.

"Yeah, well, figure this one out. Take the most perfect machine and mess it up because it doesn't know who is who anymore, and then try to save it when it might kill you."

"You going to the war?"

"Sort of."

"Is this messed-up mind hypnotized, by any chance?"

"I didn't say it was a person," said Remo.

"Machines don't forget who is who. People who are hypnotized do. That can be very dangerous."

"I don't know who you are," said Remo.

"I am Anna Chutesov, and I am probably the highest-ranking Russian official you are ever going to meet. I am on the other side that doesn't have to be the other side. I know your country has not even ordered this war. I know you are facing the most dangerous man who ever lived. I think you need me."

" 'Anna' would have been enough," said Remo, and went back to the window. But he could not shut this cold, beautiful woman out of his mind.

What he couldn't shut out was her remorseless logic.

"Let me guess. We realized Vassily could be dangerous and therefore we panicked and tried to capture him with a special force. General Boris Matesev."

"Never heard of him," said Remo, who had killed Matesev when saving Vassily Rabinowitz, an act he now regretted enormously. How could he have known how dangerous Vassily was?

"Perhaps," said Anna. "But you see, Russia, knowing how dangerous Vassily was, tried to get him back. If you know someone is dangerous, logic dictates 'leave him alone.' If everyone had left poor Vassily alone, he would have bothered no one. But we panicked. We attacked him. That's what men do when they are afraid of something. If they're not running from it, they're killing it. Or trying to. They will do anything but think."

Remo turned from the window.

"Yeah, how would they handle Vassily now? He's not the same man he was when I rescued him."

"Exactly. Now you're thinking."

"I'm thinking I don't know what the hell to do. That is what I'm thinking," said Remo.

"Excellent. You know you don't know. That's the first step in knowing. The reason you feel bad and depressed is that you are under some absurd impression that, without the facts, you should know right now."

"You're on the other side," said Remo.

"Of what?" asked Anna.

"Whoever is fighting each other nowadays. Won't matter a thousand years from now."

"You think brilliantly. What's your name?"

"My name's Remo. And no one ever said to me I was smart before. And I never claimed to be. I just try to do what's right. That's all. Case closed."

"You're right. That is stupid, if you think you can close a case just by saying it. I have got the same interests as you. Let me take a guess. Are you part of that group that stopped Matesev and that ridiculous attempt at the sniper assassination?"

"Wouldn't you like to know," said Remo.

"Yes, that's why I'm asking. Why do you think I'm asking? You really are a man. A man's man," said Anna, shaking her head. "I thought you had some intelligence."

"I did Matesev. Chiun probably did the sniper. He's working for Rabinowitz now. So is Smith."

"And so is your whole organization. Never before have we seen supplies move so smoothly in your military."

"They have everything, then."

"Not quite. They don't have you, and they don't have me. But we have got to make sure they don't."

"I can't kill without closing in."

"We can think first. We can go down there and see just what's going on, and understanding that we don't know now means that we do know we have to figure out something else."

"But I don't know what it is."

"Neither do I. But the difference is, Remo, all my life I didn't know what things were until I figured them out. We'll be all right," said Anna.

"You're kinda cute," said Remo.

"No. I'm gorgeous. You're cute," said Anna. And Remo remembered what the Great Wang had told him about finding a mind that could think things through. Was this an accident? Or was this Wang in some disguise? It didn't look like a disguise. Remo touched the back of her hand, seeking out the nerves that could arouse a woman. Slowly he began, and slowly he saw her eyes light with sexual fire. It wasn't Wang.

"Is that it?" asked Anna.

"I was just finding out who you are."

"Are you going to leave me like this?"

"Do you want to make love?" asked Remo.

"Not necessarily," said Anna. "I just want an orgasm. Finish what you start, or don't start."

When Remo was done, Anna gave him a big smile. "That was wonderful," she said.

"I'm pretty good," said Remo. "You should see what I can do working the rest of the body besides the wrist."

"I was talking about having an orgasm without having to take off my clothes or get intimate with a man," she said.

"Oh," said Remo. He sort of liked taking off his clothes. It did help the mood. He also liked taking off a woman's clothes at the appropriate time.

"I suppose," he said, "we're going to have a sexually active, noninvolved relationship."

"Only if you keep your hands on my wrist," she said. "Where did you ever figure out that the wrist had an erogenous zone?"

"The whole body is an erogenous zone if you know how to use it," said Remo.

"Could you teach me that trick on the wrist?"

"You have to know balance and things."

"Do you ever need women?"

"I don't need women. I like women. Say, what are we going to look for down in Sornica? Once you lock eyes with this guy you're done. And I'm sure Smith knew that, too."

"Good point. Then we know now Vassily can seize your mind even if you are not looking at him. We'll have to plan on working on his hypnotism. The point is that we may figure out how to succumb while still being able to operate. That may be a solution," said Anna.

By the time the plane landed they were the only ones on the press plane who were not sure what they were going to find.

13

The defenses around one small area were incredible. The Sornicans had dug themselves a network of concrete trenching and underground tunnels. Vast, flat, open fields—deadly target ranges for the defenders—surrounded these hills.

The most modern weapons in the Eastern-bloc arsenal sprouted from more hidden bunkers per foot than any site outside Russia.

Every patrol ran into this, and Rabinowitz had shrewdly bypassed it in the opening days, in order to get at the main Sornican force. Besides, all interceptions of communications from those hills revealed Russians talking.

He wanted to save them for last. But now was last. The Sornican army, supplied by Russia, trained by Russia, filled with recruits from the land drafted under protest, now had returned to its villages in peace. Only its high-ranking officers with their American goods wanted to continue the fight. They had never lived so well before this supposed people's revolution, and in their Gucci loafers and eyeglasses they were telling their favorite columnists about American oppression, aggression, racism, and poisonous minds.

No one could deny America had sent three columns of troops into the heartland of Sornica.

"Why does America hate us? We feed the poor. We lift the shackles of oppression. So they must destroy us. America is the enemy of all mankind,'' said the chairman of the Revolutionary Council, Umberto Omerta.

An aide ran into his mountain villa with the grim news about the revolutionary struggle.

The People's Democratic Revolutionary Council of Sornica was down to its last case of Dom Perignon. The beluga caviar was still in good supply, but all of Comrade Omerta's designer eyeglasses, fifteen thousand dollars' worth kept securely in his five estates, were gone. His suicidal revolutionary commandos had not been able to save them because they were defending their compact-disc players and Zenith stereos. They had lost no men, but they were executing those Sornican peasants who were refusing to die for the revolution—or to guide Western reporters to sites of American atrocities.

Any body would do. The more mangled the better. The nice thing about these modern reporters was that most of them were interpretive journalists.

Some few would ask how this body or that body got to the side of the road, and where the proof was of who killed it. Then the revolutionary suicide commandos would accuse the reporter of being an American agent, a fascist, or a Jew. The latter was especially useful in front of Arab groups, but generally anti-Semitism, after a half-century of disuse by the left, was now considered not only acceptable, but a sign of being progressive. Once this was the province of only the radical right, but it now suited the revolution perfectly, especially since the monster-maniac-fascist-Zionist heading the American invasion was named Rabinowitz.

President Omerta used the name extensively. He knew it would be instantly identifiable. He knew the columnists he was talking to would also use it extensively.

''Only a Rabinowitz would seek to suck the blood of poor peasants trying to be free,'' said President Omerta. ''They're all no good. Bloodsuckers. Why would anyone want to attack a peaceful, freedom-loving people, other

than to suck the blood through their evil fangs sharpened
on Passover wine.''

In previous years, statements like these would have
been considered racist, but now the columnists couldn't
wait to get down the words ''courageous opinions, strong
convictions.''

Omerta signaled that the last bottles of Dom Perignon
were to be opened. This was an emergency. This was a
fight to the death.

And then someone yelled.

''The Americans have got the hill fortress surrounded.''

''Excuse me,'' said Omerta. ''I must attend to the struggle immediately.''

He ran to the man who had just screamed out the bad
news. He cornered him in a closet. He wrung his neck so
hard, his own designer glasses almost fell off, and this
during wartime, when President Omerta had no idea when
he would be able to get back to America or Europe to do
more shopping.

''Listen, stupid. The next time you mention the hill
fortress in front of Americans I will have you shot. Have
they taken it yet?''

''No. But they have it surrounded.''

''What are the Russians doing?''

''Fighting to the death, sir.''

''Good. Now Russia must reinforce. They can never let
the hill fortress be taken. We're saved. We may have a
world war.''

''What if we lose it?''

''If it goes on long enough, we can't lose. We have
friends in America. Go in there and feed them the party
line. And don't get it wrong. Remember, this stuff is
going to be taught in the classrooms in America.''

President Omerta dashed out of his mountain villa,
screaming for a command car.

''You want to get to the Russian ambassador?'' asked
the driver. He knew about the hill fortress being surrounded.

"No. I want to get away from the Russian ambassador. We were supposed to defend that with our lives."

"And we didn't?"

"If you had a choice of Louis Vuitton luggage or five hundred smelly Russians with equipment, which would you take?" said General Omerta.

Rabinowitz looked at the map. Chiun stood behind him. Everyone was covered by the hot dust of Sornica, caked onto their faces by the sweat of battle.

Everyone except Chiun. Somehow he managed to bathe twice a day, keep his steamer trunks with him, and maintain a happy appearance.

Several times Rabinowitz had heard him say:

"This is too much like a war. We must stop wars, with all these amateurs doing the killing."

"They're not amateurs. It's a great army. When the Americans get down to fighting, no one can beat them. No one."

"Still an army. After all, how good could hundreds of thousands of people be, Great Wang? Let us face it. These are soldiers."

"Right. I'm doing something with them. Leave me alone."

Now the situation on the map looked grim. The massive amounts of weapons, the way they were used showing virtually limitless ammunition, made the cost of taking the hill too great.

"We could keep it surrounded, and starve them out," said one colonel who felt he was talking to an old instructor from West Point. He had always thought this man he had learned to love with more respect than any other, had been denied battlefield command. But he was glad to see he was a general now.

"The problem is," said his old instructor, "that may be just what they prepared for."

"I don't follow, sir," said the colonel.

"Look. If they are firing their ammunition with abandon, and they're not raw troops as we know they're not, then they have an almost limitless supply of ammunition. Therefore, we've got to assume they have the same in food and water, at least for a half-year. But that's not what worries me." Rabinowitz felt the men crowd around him.

He was in this thing now. Thousands of people depended on him for their lives; any move he made affected them. And therefore any problems they had were his problems. For a moment he realized that in his quest to be left alone, he now had eighty thousand people who could not leave him alone because their lives depended on him. And they were the ones on his side. Then there was the enemy. Which understandably wanted to kill him. And of course the Oriental who kept him alive.

And Harold W. Smith of America's secret organization, who could get him supplies while no one in America could stop him. Of course, Smith in his brilliant calculating mind had figured out that in the question of supply transfers, it was only marginally more helpful to have the American bureaucracy on your side than against you.

"Something special is hidden in that hill. There has been nothing else defended like it in the entire country," said Rabinowitz. He could not worry about being left alone. He was in a war. But why was he in this war?

He didn't have time to answer that. He had a military problem. Something was up there that could possibly be incredibly dangerous. How would they attack it without suffering enormous losses, losses so staggering they could make the whole campaign a failure?

He could address the attacking troops, work on their minds, making them believe they could not be hit by bullets. The few survivors might take the hill. So he could get them to do it if he wanted. That was not the problem.

He turned to his officers. Every suggestion that came back had to do with waiting for long-range bombers that would take at least a day to employ if Smith could get them employed. He had been having trouble with the air force because they had special command frequencies not available to the rest of the military. This was to prevent an accidental nuclear war, he said.

He turned to Smith.

"I know of only two men who could get through that crossfire alive. And one of them is working for us now," said Smith.

"One man. There's a division in those bunkers. I know it. One man can't do it all. I don't care how wonderful he is," said Rabinowitz.

"For every weakness, O Great Wang, there is a strength. For every strength there is a weakness," said the peculiar Oriental with the incredibly fast hands.

The firing continued from the hill at an ear-numbing rate.

And then Rabinowitz understood what the weakness had to be.

"The ammunition. Of course. It's the ammunition. If they can fire like that, they must have an incredible storage facility for ammunition. We get one in there with a delayed explosive timer, and set off the whole thing. Attack just at the moment of explosion. The timing has to be great, but it can work."

"Who can get through that field of fire alone?" asked a colonel.

And then Chiun got a strange order from the Great Wang.

"Look, schlep yourself over to those bunkers in the hills, and lay this delayed explosive. Use your tricks and stuff. Don't worry about me. I'll be safe."

"I would never worry about you, Great Wang. You are Sinanju. To worry about you would be to insult you. But to sneak explosives into place is not the work of Sinanju. Who do we wish to kill? What great man is there?"

"What who? Just do it. C'mon. The whole attack is delayed. Something's in there and we have to get it," said Rabinowitz.

"An explosive. An explosive will kill just anyone. A

soldier would use an explosive. He would use it like a gun. He doesn't care who he kills. He does not have the aesthetic sense of an assassin. Would you ask me to be a common soldier, Great Wang?''

''Not only am I asking, but I'll tell you something else. You'll love it. It is a new taste sensation to blow up people instead of taking off their heads with your bare hands. God forbid you should offend your aesthetics. Okay? Do it.''

And so Chiun, who had never defiled the teachings of Sinanju, was shown explosives to kill whoever happened to be near them when they went off. And sadder still was the fact that he believed now that he was enjoying this.

He did not need darkness to move unseen upon those in the fortified hills. He needed only their fear and the tiredness of their eyes, and the deflection of the heat rays. For in the midday, the human eye contracted and in so doing lost an almost imperceptible portion of its field of vision. And in these portions did Chiun move that day with the explosives in his hands.

''I can't believe they're not firing at him,'' said one colonel.

''They can't see him,'' said Harold W. Smith, peering at the open field with binoculars. He was getting computer terminals rigged for the front because that was where Rabinowitz usually was, Miss Ashford's best friend and the salvation of America.

''He's visible to us,'' said the colonel.

''Right, because we're looking at him from this angle. But in the hills they have the wrong angle.''

''Man would make a tremendous ranger,'' said the colonel.

''He'd never do that sort of work,'' said Smith.

''Well, what does he call that?''

''A new taste sensation, I think. Don't know,'' said Smith. ''Got to get back to the terminals. You people could use more reserve ammunition down here.''

Like even the ancient forts, there was an entrance to the fortress, and this entrance was the most heavily defended.

And just like Sinanju had always gotten into ancient forts, Chiun avoided the door but worked his way into the earth. Dissolving the fresh concrete and iron-rod reinforcements with one hand, he carried the explosive device in the other hand. Entering the tunnel, he saw a surprised Russian soldier, and even though he was no one important, Chiun sent him instantly to the fastest possible death.

First the soldier had seen the wall of the bunker dissolve. Then an Oriental in a black kimono came through it. Then the soldier was out of pain forever.

In classical Russian, Chiun asked the whereabouts of the ammunition stores, and at first those he met did not wish to reveal this information, especially to a non-Russian with a time bomb. But after just a moment's reasoning, when the pain became tolerable, they were able to express themselves better.

Chiun set the timer, placed the device well into a rack of artillery shells, worked his way through the first outside wall he came to, and left the hills safely because at this angle some of the defenders could see him.

Why, he wondered, did the Great Wang want him to do a soldierly duty, and why, more important, didn't he mind more? These were serious questions, and even the massive explosion of the hill behind him did not distract him from them. Was something wrong? Why had he enjoyed that dastardly deed, of killing people he did not even know or respect? And what about Mad Smith? Why did he think he was now wise? The man was white from the day he was born.

Chiun did not care about the excitement of the attack. Amateurs attacking amateurs. Not a decent, clean stroke among them. American troops poured into the Russian defenses, and a lead column stopped and called for the general himself. Rabinowitz.

They had found what the Russians had defended so thoroughly. They had found why the Russians had not let the Sornicans man these positions.

In deep, reinforced silos, so well secured even the explosions did not damage them, were intermediate-range nuclear missiles, so deadly accurate they could zero in on the desk in the Oval Office at the White House.

Russia had violated the latest arms treaty by sneaking missiles right into these Sornican hills. They could have launched a first strike from a direction in which America had not prepared to defend.

The news was wired to Washington immediately, and just as immediately, the great debate on the wrongness of invading Sornica now disappeared. It was apparent these three columns had saved the nation.

And the missiles were there, right in the ground where even a television reporter couldn't miss them. Only the columnists held out.

"Doesn't matter," said one woman who had managed to blame Arab terrorism on the President. "Do what we did in Kampuchea where the Khmer Rouge were forcing children to murder other children. If you think this is bad, Cambodia was worse. It was like the Nazi holocaust. Millions rounded up, worked to death, slaughtered. Entire cities emptied of people."

"I remember, I welcomed the Khmer Rouge," said the columnist for the New York newspaper.

"Blame the Americans," said the columnist for the Washington newspaper.

"How can we do that? These are Russian missiles aimed at our population centers."

"When the atrocities of the Khmer Rouge came out, I blamed America because America had been bombing Cambodia. Therefore, American bombs made those people mad."

"But lots of people have been bombed without ending up slaughtering each other. Look at the British in World War II. They were bombed much worse than the Cambodians. It didn't make them savage animals."

"Don't bring in facts. Just say it. We'll be fine. When I'm really cooking I say I'm facing harsh truths. Goes over beautifully in Boston with all those colleges there. The harsher the truth, the better.''

"So the harsh truth is, we're responsible for these missiles, and they are there because we are invading.''

"That's facing the truth,'' said the Washington columnist who had faced the harshest of truths in Iran before the Ayatollah Khomeini, Cambodia before the Khmer Rouge, and Vietnam before people were willing to risk their lives by the thousands in flimsy boats to escape their liberation.

In Washington, two things became blatantly apparent. One, America had been fortunate to detect the missiles, and two, no one could quite figure out the command structure that had ordered it, other than that it had something to do with that strange situation in Fort Pickens, Arkansas.

Alone, the President reached out for Harold Smith, the last, best, desperate hope of America. He had been looking into that thing.

It was good that the missiles were discovered and removed. But who knew what would happen next time? Who knew where this force would be taken? And if it could invade Sornica without authorization, what would stop it from invading Washington? Every man the President had sent down to the field to find out what was happening kept coming back with stories of a great commander. And invariably that great commander was different for each person.

Eerily, this force seemed to have better access to the American government than the President himself. It was the sort of access held by only CURE itself, and Smith, the lone man America trusted with this.

If anything happened to Smith, these computer networks were to self-destruct. And the President knew this would be in effect because when he dialed that one number that so many presidents had come to rely on, it would, for the first time in two decades, give a simple little response so many numbers got, that the number was out of service.

It would work automatically like so many disconnects

did, as CURE had worked so successfully by relying on people doing things automatically without thinking of why or how they did them. And it would be over.

Or there would be Harold Smith on the line, putting this "salvation network," as the President had come to think of it, into action tracking down the new force.

The President dialed and he got the one response he never thought he would get. A busy signal.

CURE was on line and working, but he couldn't get through to it.

Remo and Anna Chutesov saw the explosion in the distance. They had arrived at the Sornica airport while it was still under control of the Sornican forces.

"The first thing we have to do is find out where Rabinowitz is so that we can stay away from him. Then if you see the most important person in your life, turn away and run. I will do the same. Because then it will mean we have seen Rabinowitz."

"I got another problem."

"What's that?"

"The most important person in my life really is here. He was my teacher and the only real father I ever knew."

"That's a problem, because what we want to do, must do, is find out more about Rabinowitz, and the people who can tell us are your friends from that secret organization you belong to."

"I can't believe I told a Russian about that," said Remo.

"You didn't have any choice. You can't rescue them without me and I can't help you without knowing who they are. So you made a correct decision."

"I dunno," said Remo.

"We know now that Rabinowitz is more dangerous than ever on one hand because of his access to those special sources of information and on the other because a Master of Sinanju serves him. You did the only thing that could possibly help save them. And why?"

"The last answer I got on a major question was yes. All right, yes. My answer to why is yes."

"I don't understand you, Remo, and since my specialty is not pathological mental disorders, I will not attempt to try. The reason you have helped us is that we must have as much information, especially precise information on Rabinowitz, as possible. Why?"

"No," said Remo.

Anna Chutesov had sighed. In breathing she filled out her blouse delightfully, nothing overbearing in her figure, just pure sexiness in a blouse now made more sexy by her perspiration in the Sornica sun.

"We must know everything about Vassily Rabinowitz because the first time we come within eyesight of him we are going to have to know precisely how to kill him."

"That's what I said, yes," said Remo.

Anna had been impressed by the way Remo smoothly guided them through the lines. He knew where people were before she saw them. He knew their moves without thinking. A few times he explained that people with weapons had to move certain ways, it was in their nature. They were small things, but a house of assassins working through millennia picked them up along with other techniques and compiled them, each new Master building on what the other knew. Sinanju was the name of the town from which the assassins came, although Remo was Caucasian. Chiun, his trainer, knew the same sexual techniques as Remo.

"He must have taught you everything but how to breathe."

"Breathing's the most important thing he taught me," Remo said. By the time they heard the major explosion far off, Anna Chutesov knew Remo loved this Chiun, and he kept repeating that they were very different. Although some people who liked to bust chops thought otherwise, according to Remo.

"What other people?"

"You wouldn't understand. But he was the one who gave me the answer 'yes.' "

"What was it 'yes' to?"

"The most important question I could ask."

"Which was?"

"I don't know. I didn't ask it. I couldn't figure out the question. So I got an answer without a question."

"Is Sinanju like Zen Buddhism?" asked Anna.

"No," said Remo. "It's Sinanju."

He guided her to lie down in a soft, leafy bank. In a short while a patrol came by, Indian faces in Soviet uniforms.

A young girl with a Kalishnikov stared directly at Anna but kept walking. She was no more than fifteen feet away.

"Why didn't she see us?"

"People don't see things they're not looking for. Patrols look for movement. They don't see. They're looking for mines under their feet. Snipers somewhere. People don't see what they're not prepared to see."

"And what do you see?"

"What's there."

"Is it hard?"

"I don't know of anyone outside of Sinanju who sees what's there. Some think we're some kind of super thing, but that's not so," said Remo. "It's just that nobody else uses their bodies properly. Or minds, to be more precise. Most of the body, like the brain, is unused."

It was startling, but true. Anna Chutesov knew that less than eight percent of the human brain was ever used. These people from Sinanju apparently used much, much more.

This Sinanju, not Rabinowitz, was a weapon she could use. Safer than a nuclear warhead, and absolutely precise. If they got out of this alive, she was going to get this man for Russia. And if he happened to stay around for her, well, she could live with that too, she thought, as a most contented smile crossed her face.

Then came the explosion and the rush of American troops. Remo commandeered a jeep and driver. It was amazing how he could touch one nerve and make a person do what he wanted. Including Anna, Anna thought with another broad grin.

"Remo, I want to really get you with your clothes off," she said.

"I got work," said Remo.

"What you need, Remo, is a good mind-bending screw," she said.

And from the side of the road came a wail like a siren. But no siren ever made that noise. An angry-faced Oriental in a black robe was staring at Remo and Anna, pointing at their jeep. Remo made the driver stop.

"Slut. Don't you dare talk like that to Remo. Remo, what are you doing with that white girl? Come, we must pay our respects to the Great Wang."

"I think that's Chiun," said Remo. "Do you see an Oriental?"

"With a wisp of a beard?"

"Yes," said Remo.

"Yes, I see him," said Anna.

"That's Chiun. Don't talk dirty in front of him. He doesn't like it."

"Killing is noble, sex is wrong?"

"You got it," said Remo.

"Who is she? How can I bring you to the Great Wang when you have a disgrace of a white girl with you?" Chiun asked.

"I'm white," said Remo.

"Great Wang doesn't have to know that. He could think a grandparent was Korean."

"He knows. He knows I'm white. He liked the idea."

"Liar," said Chiun.

"Who's the Great Wang?" asked Anna.

"Who is this slut with the mouth of a sailor?" asked Chiun.

"Great Wang is the one who answered the question without waiting for the question," said Remo.

"Is he from Sinanju?" asked Anna.

"The most," said Remo.

"Answer her before me. Has that wanton so crazed your mind with lust that you do not answer me before her?"

"Her name is Anna Chutesov. She is here to help."

"Have you had relations?" asked Chiun.

"I don't think so," said Anna. "Tell me about this Great Wang you so admire. Is he the one who gives you orders now?"

"The Great Wang does not have to give orders. A Master of Sinanju follows his wishes before the orders are given."

Anna saw the strange floating movement of Chiun and it reminded her of something. That was how Remo moved through the jungles.

"Does the Great Wang move like you and Remo?" asked Anna, and suddenly Chiun was no longer speaking English but conversing in Korean.

Remo answered in the same language.

"What is he saying?" asked Anna.

"He's saying why did you ask that question in particular?"

"So he knows something is wrong. He is aware of that."

"Little father," said Remo. "How much is wrong?"

"Nothing is wrong," said Chiun. "Everything is better than it has ever been. Even Emperor Smith thinks so."

That name, too, sounded familiar to Anna Chutesov. But she was about to see something coming down the road that would tell her the problem was no longer in Sornica, but in Russia itself. And she had to get Remo out of here, otherwise there might not be much of a world to save, even for a Master of Sinanju.

14

Anna saw it coming down the road.

"Oh, no," said Anna. "Those idiots."

Large trucks trundled slowly along the dirt and pitted Sornica's Route 1. On their beds were fat tubes like giant sewer pipes. In the front were cones. In back were afterburners. On the side were big red stars with Russian lettering, and even American television couldn't miss it.

They were medium-range Russian nuclear missiles, far more accurate this close to America. Far more deadly. And there was absolutely no military reason for it.

The advantage was negligible because with the number of nuclear warheads in stock, no one needed accuracy. Did they think someone would fire three nuclear missiles, wipe out three cities, and then sit down to talk?

But worse, far worse, the Americans would make a great display of this. The Russian generals would be humiliated by such a great loss; after all, this was not just a client state that had fallen, but Russian soldiers. Then, just like after the Cuban missile crisis, they would launch a new round of face-saving experiments. The last one had bankrupted the weak Russian economy, and the next might well mean war. There was no more money for a new generation of weapons. That was why Russia was pushing so hard lately for a freeze. Which was also why America was pushing for new weapons.

Of course there was no advantage. But men thought so.

In this case there was less advantage than in urinating up a
wall to see who could go higher. That was a useless boys'
contest. This one was suicide.

"She's a Russian agent of sorts," said Remo. "Looks
like we got your missiles."

"You have. They have. We have," said Anna, throwing up her hands. "Men. What are you going to do with
them? They have no more purpose in your hands than they
did in ours. Where is Rabinowitz?"

"Your heart wishes him no good. You may not come
near," said Chiun.

And to Remo, in Korean he said:

"Rabinowitz is a friend of the Great Wang. If this slut
gets close to Rabinowitz, kill her."

"Sure, sure, little father. Will do."

"You didn't say it like you meant it."

"Tell me more about Wang. Could you point him out to
me?"

"Haven't you seen him yourself?"

"I did. He gave me the answer."

"So you know now," said Chiun, his eyes sparkling,
his face crinkling into a smile.

"Yeah. I know the answer is yes."

"That was my answer, too," said Chiun. "The first
time I saw him before Fort Pickens, and when I saw him
again."

"What was your question?"

"It is very personal. I don't wish to say," said Chiun.
"What was yours?"

"Nothing much," said Remo.

Anna, hearing the two babble in Korean, asked what
they were talking about.

"Nothing," they both said in unison.

"We should find this wonderful Mr. Rabinowitz," said
Anna. "But look, Mr. Chiun. You obviously feel I am a
sort of danger to him."

"How can you be a danger? Both I and the Great Wang
protect him."

"Then let's find him. And I will make you this promise. We won't come within five hundred yards of him. We just want to ask a few questions. And perhaps you can take those questions to him, and bring back the answers."

"I'm not a messenger," said Chiun. "Remo can ask the questions of him."

"No," said Anna. "Definitely not. Tell Mr. Rabinowitz we have a message for him from his mother in Dulsk. Tell him I bring peace from the Soviet Union. Tell him he has won, and that we respect his strength and his power, and now we wish to sign a treaty with him personally. To assure him of his safety. Russia will assure him of his safety."

"I assure him of his safety. Who are you to assure him of his safety? You can't keep your hands off innocent young men."

Remo looked around. He hadn't seen Anna touch anyone else. She had her hand on his arm. Chiun stared at it with hostility. Remo knew that, for Chiun, this was too much affection for a woman to show in public.

A simple bow from ten feet away was considered proper by Chiun. Touching was obscene. America had once been described in his histories as a land so degenerate that people kissed strangers to say hello. Italy was beyond the pale. Saudi Arabia was all right, except they were a little lax in enforcement.

They only cut off hands. Why cut off hands, reasoned Chiun, when it was the mind, not the hand, that committed the crime? Chiun had hands and never once had they committed a crime on their own. Nor, did he think, did anyone else's.

And so Chiun not only saw this blond woman with the beautiful, high cheekbones and devastating smile touching Remo, but Remo allowing it. Standing there, allowing, as though nothing was wrong. Degenerate whiteness coming through again, and just before he was to meet the Great Wang again.

"You are not going to walk like that toward the Great Wang," said Chiun.

"Tell me," said Remo, keeping Anna's hand just where it had been placed, "did you ever learn, little father, how to be in two places at once?"

Chiun did not answer, but stared at the hands. Finally he said:

"You're keeping that obscene slut's touch on you just to bother me."

Anna removed her hand.

"Let's hope he doesn't get pregnant by this," she said, with a sharp smile.

"I never learned to be in two places at once. One place at a time is enough," said Chiun. "More than enough. In fact, essentially wonderful."

"I wonder why the Great Wang wouldn't have taught us that trick, because while he was with you, he was with me also."

"You didn't see the Great Wang, then," said Chiun. "How disappointing."

"He has a belly like the cold center of the universe, like all that is not of this earth. Perhaps you might want to test this Great Wang."

"He's not 'this' Great Wang. He's *the* Great Wang," said Chiun.

"Right," said Remo. But he knew Chiun was bothered. Chiun agreed to take them near Wang's friend Rabinowitz if the white slut could control herself.

"You're such a man, Chiun," said Anna. "You're the quintessential man, Chiun."

"Thank you," said Chiun.

"I thought you'd respond like that," said Anna.

Near the headquarters, several Russian prisoners were being herded into trucks. They looked frightened, and Anna assured them they would not be shot. She was angry that any fool would send them in here so close to America for no purpose whatsoever.

Well, she could make them have a purpose. She could

quiet down this man. She might just be able to stop him from going further.

It was a tremendous defeat to Russia that he had won.

"Remo, I've changed my mind," said Anna.

"Just like a woman," said Chiun. "Changing your mind. Watch out for this one, Remo. She's no good."

"And would it be just like a man not to change even if new facts came in?" asked Anna. She gave him one of her smiles again. He was the sort of man who would be tolerant of amusement, she felt.

"A proper man would know all the facts beforehand," said Chiun. "Where did you fall into this thing, Remo?"

"We met on a plane. She's all right."

"I am going to speak to Rabinowitz. I am going to assure him he is safe, and he can believe it now. If I come back in any strange way, try to get me out of it. If you can't, please kill me quickly," she said.

"Just like that?" asked Chiun. "You want an assassination, for nothing? Free? Remo, don't you see what she's doing now? She's getting away with being murdered."

"If he gets you, what am I going to do?" asked Remo.

"Try to figure out what hasn't been tried yet and try it. But one thing you can't do is go directly in. Stay back and think. I don't know what the hell they're going to do back in Moscow. This is too much of a defeat. I only wanted a little one to make Rabinowitz comfortable."

"Good luck," said Remo, and gave her a light kiss on the lips.

"You're doing that because it bothers me," said Chiun.

"I'm doing that because she's beautiful and courageous."

"I'm supposed to believe that?" said Chiun.

"I don't know what you believe. I never know what you believe."

"For two decades I have given the best of my life to you, and you remember nothing. I have given you my thinking, and this thinking you now throw away to indulge in public obscenities."

Anna laughed.

"You two sound so much alike," she said.

Off on a hill, Rabinowitz was meeting with his commanders. Anna headed toward the hill as Remo and Chiun stayed back watching her. Chiun wanted to know what the experience was like with the Great Wang, Remo's first experience.

"The second is not nearly as good, I can tell you, Remo."

"He said you and I have the cleanest strokes in the history of Sinanju."

"He said that?"

"Yeah. I think I told you before. He said we have the best strokes. Identical, he said. Said he could be looking at you when he saw me deliver a blow."

"I teach well," said Chiun.

"Not everyone can learn," said Remo. He did not mention Wang had told him that Chiun had a son who had died.

"The teacher is first."

"To pour water into a glass, one needs the glass, even though the water is first. Otherwise it splashes in uselessness," said Remo.

"Where did you learn to talk like that?"

"Who do you think I've been palling around with for the last twenty years?"

"I don't like it."

"Neither did I."

"You sound like a fortune cookie," said Chiun. He folded his hands within his black kimono, and Remo stuffed his hands in his pockets.

"Wang said something so silly I don't know if I should repeat it," said Remo.

"Wang never says anything silly," said Chiun.

"He said we were really just alike under it all. That our differences were illusions."

"The Great Wang never said anything silly. Until now."

"Absurd," said Remo.

"I am ashamed that you were the first one he showed his great flaw to."

"What great flaw?"

"He cannot judge people as well as we thought," said Chiun.

"He certainly does know when someone is ready to be a great Master," said Remo. "I mean, he appears."

"He can judge quality, true. I may be the only Master to be at the great level whose student was also at that level. Two for me. That is a record."

"But not enough to be called the Great Chiun. That must be done by succeeding generations in the histories."

"You still have to learn about negotiations. I hope in your passage you have learned to appreciate that."

"He called us dullards. Said we're too serious. Me about America. You about the House of Sinanju."

"Wang was fat," said Chiun.

"I thought so too," said Remo.

"Lacked control of his eating," said Chiun.

"I thought we had no fat on our bodies," said Remo.

"We don't," said Chiun.

"He does," said Remo.

"We're not alike at all," said Chiun.

"Not at all," said Remo, and both of them could not remember a time when they had agreed on something so thoroughly, which was another proof they were not alike. And for a second time they agreed thoroughly.

Anna Chutesov saw him on the high hill. She wished Remo were with her, because he had a way of moving through defenses that was astounding. She thought she might be stopped, but ironically at a headquarters position itself there was more confusion than at some outpost where people might fire.

Rabinowitz had staff aides, of course, and when she said what she wanted, she made a crucial mistake, one that anyone who ever tried to deal with an institution or corporation would have known was an error.

One she should have known. But she had no choice. She had to speak to the aide.

And as in all organizations, the aide was more difficult to deal with than the leader.

"I have come to surrender to Mr. Rabinowitz and offer him anything he wants," said Anna.

"Who are you?"

"I represent Russia in this situation."

"Then how come you're not with the prisoners?" said the aide.

"Because I never surrendered. I am here to speak with Mr. Rabinowitz," she said, hoping he saw Rabinowitz as Rabinowitz and not some love-authority figure from his past.

"You haven't surrendered to anyone yet, right?" said the aide, a young captain.

"That's right."

"Then you're my prisoner," he said.

As Anna passed Remo in a truck crowded with Russian missile technicians, she waved. Remo was on board with hardly a leap, separating her from the men and helping her off the truck.

"I'll have to take you up there myself," he said.

"No. I don't want you near him. You're the world's last chance, Remo. I'll go with Chiun."

"He doesn't like you."

"Spoken like a man. What on earth makes you think that with a possible world disaster, I would care whether he likes me or not? All I want him to do is go with me. You can get him to do that, can't you? And just maybe I'll be able to see something neither of us have. Right now we have to get Vassily defused from his anxiety."

Chiun agreed to take Anna Chutesov to see the Great Wang's friend Vassily Rabinowitz, provided she kept her hands to herself, made no lascivious moves, and gave up any designs on Remo.

"Done. Absolutely. The easiest promise I ever made," said Anna.

"Don't trust her. She's Russian," said Chiun.

"I'll be all right. You two go ahead," said Remo. He remembered his days long ago from Vietnam when he was a marine and he thought fighting was done with a rifle against people you didn't know. How different it was, he thought, watching the columns of American soldiers slogging along the roads.

Now he understood that to kill another properly you really had to know him, know his moves, his essence, what he was. It was the knowing that made Sinanju different.

Would that mean that Vassily Rabinowitz might be the one man he and Chiun could never kill because he was the one man they could not know?

It was a good question. He would have to ask Anna that when she returned.

Anna thought walking up the hill toward the headquarters with the old Oriental was like walking with Remo, except the older man expressed his hostility, which in a way wasn't all that hostile. It was more like intense peeve. Both he and Remo had extraordinary powers and demanded that the world conform to their realities. For the most part they could effect bits of that, but the world was too big even for those like Chiun.

She had crucial questions about Rabinowitz. And the answers were interesting.

Chiun had been planning to kill Vassily until a legend of Sinanju stepped in to tell him Vassily was a good man.

"What were you thinking at the time just before your legend stepped into your path?"

"I wasn't thinking anything. I was working."

"Killing?" asked Anna.

"If you must be so crude. But then why should I expect anything but crudity from another Remo pickup? He's had hundreds of women, you know. You won't be any different. So don't even try."

"You have my promise," said Anna.

"Do you know what the historical worth of a Russian promise is?" asked Chiun. "Your revolution didn't change anything. Czar Ivan, of course, was the wonderful exception. But otherwise, I would never work in Russia without payment in advance. None of us did. And you have only yourselves to blame. We could have saved you from the Mongols, but you wanted credit. Never again.''

''I take it past czars did not pay their bills.''

''Ivan the Good did. There was always work and he paid promptly.''

''Some people call him Ivan the Terrible.''

''Russians are always good at propaganda.''

''This Great Wang could not appear to both you and Remo at the same time, could he?''

''I don't discuss work with women.''

''Think of me as a Russian.''

''Worse yet.''

''Think of me as the woman who will not touch your precious Remo again.''

''Wang does many things, but not appearing in two different places simultaneously. He doesn't do that.''

''And you know Remo saw Wang because he has made this transition you spoke of.''

''Yes,'' said Chiun.

''Then do you ever wonder that this might not be the Great Wang you talk to?''

''My wonderings are my own.''

''If you threw a blow at Wang, of course you would kill him.''

''No. He has been dead for centuries.''

''So then it would not matter.''

''Correct. One can throw a blow at the Great Wang. Our strokes, mine and the one that I taught Remo, are the cleanest, if you didn't know. In all history.''

''That's wonderful,'' said Anna. ''Could I see you throw one of them at the Great Wang?''

''No. You wouldn't see it.''

''Could I see the results?''

''Can you see this?'' said Chiun, and Anna only saw a rustle of the dark kimono.

"I didn't see your hand move."

"Too fast. You'd never see it."

"I have a sister more beautiful than me. And she lip-kisses in public. I wouldn't tell her about how cute Remo is if you'd show me you did that."

"I don't make deals with harlots, especially concerning the family heritage."

"But you are worried about the Wang you see, aren't you?" said Anna. And Chiun fell silent.

And so by the time she reached Vassily Rabinowitz she understood that his powers were even more than convincing someone they saw someone else. Rabinowitz had been able to reach a core of thinking that would transcend a person's normal logic. She also knew that the moment Rabinowitz even suspected danger, her mind would not be her own. Even worse, she would not know something was wrong; she would not be able to understand that anything but something wonderful was happening.

The happy faces of the American officers coming out of the meeting with Rabinowitz did not make Anna feel any better. Rabinowitz might be broadcasting his powers now toward anyone who came to him.

This had not been the case at the parapsychology village. She had checked this out carefully. Cleaning people, and those around Vassily who were not in authority and not a threat, were never affected by him.

According to his dossier, occasionally he would perform tricks for them.

If they didn't like the weather he would change it, and they would return to their homes soaked to the skin, claiming the day was sunny.

He made things disappear easily, because all a person had to believe was that they were gone to stop seeing them. But other than these random tricks he did not practice his powers on those who were not a danger.

"Old Blood 'n' Guts will see you now," said a sergeant.

"Sometimes they call the Great Wang that. It is an American term of endearment," said Chiun.

Anna's mouth felt dry. She smoothed out her skirt. She told herself that she was going to feel good things for Vassily. She was not going to let off any vibrations of hostility. She would show servility from the beginning.

"All right," she said. "I'm ready."

Several colonels left, laughing. They gave Anna lascivious looks. She lowered her eyes.

Be subservient she told herself again. Think subservient.

"You can come in now. But make it fast," said another guard. He nodded to Chiun.

Chiun led the way.

Inside, Rabinowitz sat on a lounge chair. A gaunt lemon-faced man worked a computer keyboard. He did it with such skill and speed, Anna was surprised he was not younger. More important, he seemed to be able to access things with a smooth precision most computer operators lacked. They always seemed to be trying things that had to be tried again. This man just did things. Anna glanced at the computer terminal and saw the coordinates for the entire southwest railway system. Apparently this man, whoever he was, had jumped the communications for four independent railroads and was now operating them in the service of moving supplies south toward debarkation points, appearing on the screen now as Sornica.

"O great one, here is a woman whose virtue I cannot vouch for," said Chiun.

"I've come to surrender," said Anna.

"Don't have time for that," said Vassily. She still saw him as Vassily. Good. He didn't need her for anything.

"Russia wishes to surrender. You have won. We have an apology for sending General Matesev and the sniper. Russia guarantees the safety of your family. Of your loved ones. Of your return if you wish. Russia is no enemy of yours." This Anna said in Russian so Vassily would understand he was speaking to another Russian.

"Because I beat you, right?"

"Doesn't it make sense?" said Anna, praying he couldn't

read minds too. Because she knew while it made sense, those who ran the Russian military did not make sense.

"I don't care. You can't hurt me now. No one can hurt me now," said Rabinowitz. "And you'd get my parents out of Dulsk if I asked and if they wanted, you know why?"

"No," said Anna.

"It doesn't matter now. That's why."

"I don't understand."

"I don't need an army. I've got better than an army, and I beat you."

"Yes, Vassily. You beat us," said Anna. Were all men like this? Did they have to crow about these things? Apparently that was what parades were for.

"You can't touch me now. Tell that to the Politburo."

"I'll be happy to, Vassily."

"You can tell them I don't care about them either. I don't have to beat them anymore."

"That's very good, Vassily."

"I don't have to beat them anymore because I am getting myself a whole country for myself. That's why."

"Good, Vassily."

"And he's getting it for me, Harold. Show me all the males making over two million dollars a year who are under twenty-five years old. I want their names and private lives."

The computer operator punched a few keys, and faces, mostly black ones in basketball uniforms, appeared.

"All right, give me State Department officials who have made embarrassing mistakes in the past that we know about."

Another list came up, but this time with white faces.

"Okay, now give me stockbrokerage houses which haven't lived up to SEC regulations."

The screen turned into a blur of names and faces and did not stop.

"Miss Ashford, this will take all day," said the lemon-faced man.

"All right, that's enough. Now, you go back and you tell your friends I am in the process of getting a country and if they want to cut a deal I have nothing against them. But also tell them I'm Russian too. So I know their word isn't worth anything."

"I understand that."

"All I want is to be left alone. Now send me Remo."

"I've been with him. I'll get him."

"He is the only friend I found in this country. Hell of a guy."

"Yes, Great Wang," said Chiun.

"He has his good points, Miss Ashford," said the man Anna was sure was Smith.

"He's a fine fellow, and I'll get him now," said Anna, turning her eyes toward the door.

"You have a nice ass," said Rabinowitz.

"Thank you," said Anna, very careful to control any hostility in her voice. No man who ever said that understood what he was saying. Nice ass for what? Sitting? Fornicating? It hardly played much role in the act. No, what they meant was that the round softness appealed to them. As though a woman's body was an art object.

Well, her object was to get out of the headquarters right away without looking back.

"I will escort her, Great Wang."

"That's all right, I'll do it myself. Fine. We'll be back in a shake of a lamb's tail," she said.

"Perhaps you'd better go, Chiun. Someone may shoot her because she's Russian."

"I've heard them say the same thing about you, Great Wang, which is not true."

"Yes, I've heard that said of you, too, Miss Ashford," said the man who had to be Smith.

"No problem. I'm gone," said Anna, holding her breath. She was out of the headquarters and in the hot Sornica sun, hoping with all her body and soul that Chiun would not come along. She had to reach Remo first. She had to reach Remo now. Remo had to know. He was the only one who could save civilization, and if Chiun got to him first, he might be no better than the slaves in that headquarters.

She forced herself not to run. She also knew that she had to look as though she was in charge of something, otherwise some MP would arrest her and it would be back into the trucks.

She almost twisted an ankle on a loose rock going down the hill. Somewhere off to the left she heard small-arms fire. The Americans were mopping up. Someone said that the Sornican forces were trying to escape with their Gucci eyeglasses, Louis Vuitton luggage, and Bally shoes.

She didn't want to look around, but she knew both Remo and Chiun moved so quickly and silently she would never know they were there until they were there.

A soldier offered to give her a hand. She slapped it away. Where was Remo? She didn't see him. Had he attempted to sneak up on Rabinowitz and try an execution? If he had, he was a fool. This was not the place to kill Rabinowitz. She knew that now from what she saw. And she was not the one to do it. It had to be Remo. But he couldn't do it here.

Suddenly she felt a grip on her arms like a giant vise. It was Remo.

"Where are you going?"

"To find you. Where were you? You didn't go up to Rabinowitz. You didn't risk him, did you?"

"You mean the greatest guy in the world?" said Remo, smiling.

"Just joking," said Remo.

"You bastard," screamed Anna, swinging at Remo's head. It looked like she hit, but she hadn't. She had only touched his face with her blow. "How could you scare me like that? How could you do something so insensitive and stupid and useless?"

Remo thought her anger was even funnier.

"You're such a man. You're such a real man," screamed Anna. "What a stupid, stupid joke."

"I thought it was good, too," said Remo.

"Do you know that if you are lost, everyone is lost? Do you know what's going on? Do you know what I found out?"

"How should I know? You haven't told me yet," said Remo. He looked up toward the command post. He saw Chiun leave, and by his very first step, Remo understood there was trouble now worse than anything Anna Chutesov might have uncovered.

"Rabinowitz is in the process of taking over your country. He's not frightened anymore. The world has become a game to him. He might start some war somewhere now just for the fun of it, and there's nothing we can do here. We're helpless."

"We might be more than helpless," said Remo. "We might be dead. We've got to get out of here."

Anna glanced up to where Remo was looking. Chiun,

his friend, had just left the headquarters. He was walking slowly.

"He's coming after us."

Anna looked closer. Chiun seemed to be strolling.

"How can you tell?"

"Look at his walk," said Remo.

"I can't tell any difference."

"You're not supposed to," said Remo. "He's ready to kill. And it may be me."

"Why?"

"Dunno. Maybe Rabinowitz figured out why we're here. Maybe he's after you, not me."

"We can't do any good here anyhow. Let's run."

Remo saw the eyes of Chiun. Did the little father know? Was this some other mind that was coming to do battle? Did Chiun perhaps think Remo was just some other target? There was no anger in the face. Remo had been taught that anger robbed one of power. Anger was usually a result of weakness, not strength. And it caused such damage to the nervous system. To relax was the efficient way to use the powers of the human body.

"There is a way to finish off Rabinowitz," said Anna. "But it's not here. It's in Russia."

"Why didn't you think of it there?" asked Remo.

"Because I didn't have time and I didn't think I'd need it. I had to get here right away. I thought I could defuse Rabinowitz. I thought maybe we could even destroy him if we had to. I see now, we can't. I saw it in that command post."

"What are we going to find in Russia?"

"The secret to his powers. I am sure they are in Dulsk. I found something that men always miss."

"There are no women in Russia? They didn't miss?" asked Remo. He took her arm and guided her out into the road.

The staff car with officers and a driver didn't stop until the driver was pulled out of the window as the car passed Remo's grip. The car stopped. One of the officers declared Remo under military arrest, and another officer helped that officer regain his feet after Remo and Anna were off in the car.

Remo did not look forward but kept his eye on the rearview mirror.

"We can outrun him, right?" asked Anna.

Remo laughed.

"Is that another joke?" she asked.

"No. No, we can't outrun him in this car on these roads."

"Then why are we driving?"

"It's hell trying to bring you through a jungle."

"I thought you enjoyed it. You were touching me tenderly."

"I was holding you up and moving you forward and I was touching you that way so you wouldn't break," said Remo.

The man in the black kimono reached the road, and there he placed two feet wide apart and then, so all the world could see, slowly like two sedate windmills, brought his long fingernails out from his sleeves and in a wide arc swung them above his head and then down sedately into a folded-arms position.

"Damn," said Remo, and Anna saw his face pale and his lips tighten.

"What's wrong?" she said.

"I hope he doesn't think it's me here."

"Why?"

"Chiun just gave me the Master's Challenge to the Death if I ever come back."

"But you've got to come back. We're not going to Russia not to come back. We're going to Dulsk to get hold of the mechanism that will destroy Vassily and his powers once and for all."

"I'm not going to kill Chiun to do it. If I could."

"You have to. It's for the world."

"That is my world back there, telling me he'll kill me if he ever sees me again," said Remo.

"Maybe we can break Vassily's hold on him," said Anna.

"You don't think so," said Remo.

"How do you know?"

"You didn't say it like you meant it. Well, let's get on with it."

Getting into Russia was not nearly as difficult as getting out. Nobody ever tried to break in, least of all from its surrounding countries. Anna insisted they not go through formal channels on the entrance even though she had the highest clearance. They reached Dulsk in a day.

"It would have taken us a week, if the Russian government authorized speedy entrance," she said. "I don't know why your intellectuals find communism so attractive. Couldn't they imagine everything run by your post office?"

The road leading to Dulsk was like a strip of asphalt through Kansas, a rutted strip of asphalt. Anna kept looking at the road and then at the map and then saying, "Good, I thought so."

"You mean it's a big deal to find someplace here?"

"No, no. I came from a village not unlike Dulsk. And yet, I think it was very much unlike Dulsk. I am hoping it was unlike Dulsk."

She looked up ahead.

"How far can you see, Remo?"

"Farther than you."

"What do you see ahead on the road?"

"Road," said Remo.

"What kind of road?"

"Like the one we're on. Asphalt."

"Wonderful. I thought so. I thought so."

"What's wonderful?"

"The answer to Vassily Rabinowitz' powers. They just may not be so exceptional. I want to warn you now, threaten no one in the village, and absolutely do not let anyone know I am an official of the Russian government. We will say we are friends of Vassily Rabinowitz, who has sent us. That is the only reason we are entering Dulsk. Do you understand?''

''Not a word,'' said Remo. What could a road have to do with an answer to extraordinary hypnotic powers?

On the side of the road, Remo stopped at what looked like a farm stand. He didn't know they had them in Russia. Several tractors sat in the fields, with men sleeping on them. In one small dark patch of earth several people labored with perspiration dripping off them.

''Those are private lots. The tractors are part of the collective. We send them new tractors every year because the old ones rust.''

''Don't they oil them?''

''Sometimes, but basically they just drive them out into the middle of the field to look as though they are busy, and if a government official comes along they start them up again. Many of those tractors have never been in first or second gear since they drove them there.''

''It looked automated,'' said Remo.

''It is. Some genius of a man came up with a report that automation does not improve farming. He should have said that it does not improve farming in Russia.''

At the roadside stand, Anna bought some potatoes and bread and a piece of meat wrapped in an old used slab of wax paper.

She smelled the meat.

''Almost fresh,'' she said. ''Good meat.''

''Why are you buying that?''

''You want to eat dinner, don't you?''

''They don't have restaurants?''

''Certainly they do. Do you want to drive to Moscow?''

The roadside stand was actually a converted tiller which someone had found could hold vegetables if all the blades were flattened. It also prevented it from rolling around and made it quite steady.

Remo looked at the meat. He shook his head. He didn't want to eat dinner.

With every asphalted mile of road passing underneath

their car, Anna became happier. She even sang Remo some of the songs from her childhood. He could see she loved her country, even though it was populated by fifty percent men. The male population did not bother her. It was the way it ran things that bothered her.

"What is so important about an asphalt road?" Remo asked.

"Ah," said Anna. "You would not see it because you're an American, precisely because you're an American."

"Right. I don't see it. A road is a road."

"In America, Remo. But in Russia, a dirt strip is a road. A muddy length of roughly flattened area without trees is a road. A bumpy asphalt strip here is a major highway."

"So? So there's a major highway to Dulsk," said Remo.

"That is where I have you at a special disadvantage. Do you know what Dulsk produces?"

"Sure, every American studies the economy of Dulsk in grade school," said Remo. The car they were using was a rackety oil-leaking imitation of an American 1949 Nash, a car that had not survived the competition. It was communism's claim that they were more efficient because they didn't produce a hundred different kinds of things when one product would do.

In a way they were right. It did make sense. But the reality was that there were very few cars in Russia and they all stank. As Sinanju always maintained, logic was not the greatest strength of the human mind.

"Even if you lived in Russia, Remo, you would know of no major thing that ever came out of Dulsk. Dulsk is one of our many backward little villages, without electricity, without paved roads, and which tourists are never allowed to visit."

"But we are on a paved road," said Remo.

"Exactly. How did Dulsk manage to get one? More important, on this major road, why was there no major battle fought between us and the Germans in World War II?

The front moved back and forth here many times, Remo, but I have yet to read a report of a major battle.''

"So?"

"So use your brain, Remo, even if male hormones are flowing through it," said Anna. "Think. Think. What are we here for? Why do we come to Dulsk to find a way to stop Vassily Rabinowitz? Why have I been saying the answer is here?"

"Yes," said Remo.

"What sort of an answer is this 'yes'?"

"It's the one I got."

"It doesn't fit the question."

"I didn't even get a chance at my question," said Remo.

There was no radio in the car, but he was sure there was nothing worth listening to in Russia, anyway. Then again, maybe there was. What else did they have?

"The answer to our problem is that everyone in Dulsk has this ability. I am sure of it now. Everyone is born with it.''

"Great, out of the frying pan into the frying-pan factory," said Remo.

"Not necessarily," said Anna. "They would be just the ones to tell us how to stop their Vassily. That's why we are coming as his friends. Do you see?"

"I see we are going to a village where we are going to see a hundred Chiuns and a hundred of whoever is important to you. That's what I see."

"Hah," said Anna, slapping Remo on the shoulder. "We will see what we will see."

She ran a smooth hand over his leg.

"Where is your erogenous zone, Remo?"

"In my mind."

"Can I get to it?"

"No."

Slowly she unbuttoned her skirt. She couldn't catch his eye. She buttoned it back up.

"Perhaps I should go in first," she said.

"I don't speak Russian," said Remo. "What'll I do if they put you under?"

"You could come in after me."

"Let's go together."

"Why?"

"I want to be there. We win or we lose. I can't do much around here without you," he said. "Then again, I might not want to do much around here without you."

Dulsk itself looked like an awfully poor Midwest town. But Anna explained that for Russia it was unusually rich for a town that offered so little to the state. There was no iron foundry or electronics plant. No major defense establishment. Just a peaceful little village with churches, a synagogue, and a mosque. And there was no KGB office anywhere.

"I knew there wouldn't be. I knew it," said Anna.

Across the street a man in a white blouse, high boots, and dark pants glanced at Remo.

"You, stranger, come here," he said.

"Yes, little father," said Remo. It was a good thing Chiun was here too, because Remo didn't really speak Russian. Of course he could get by if he had to. Chiun was always working on him to improve his language.

"Sir, sir," called out Anna in Russian to the man whom Remo was calling Chiun. "We're friends of Vassily Rabinowitz. Please. Please. We mean you no harm."

"That one is very dangerous," said the man.

"Can you release him?"

"I am afraid."

"You can always do that to him again, can't you?"

"Oh yes, whenever I am afraid again."

"You mean it works automatically when you are afraid."

"Yes, pretty miss. And I cannot turn it off."

"Chiun," said Remo to the man, "why the Master's death challenge?"

"What is he talking about?" asked the man. "I don't speak English."

"A Master never challenges his son," said Remo in English.

"He sounds dangerous. I know he is dangerous," said the villager.

"Do you know what he's talking about?" asked Anna. The man shrugged.

"I won't fight you. Of course I won't fight you," said Remo in English.

And then turning to Anna, he asked:

"Where'd Chiun go?"

"He was never here, Remo. You have been talking to this man, and we've learned a lot. They transmit whatever they need to survive into your mind."

"Okay," said Remo. "But where's Chiun?"

"He was never here, Remo."

"I know he was here. He was more here than he's ever been."

"No. This man needs you to believe that for his survival. It's automatic. It's the greatest survival mechanism I've ever seen in a human being."

"If you have come to help Vassily, let me take you to his mother. The poor woman has been grief-stricken since he left."

Mrs. Rabinowitz lived in a thatched cottage with a small garden in front. She was visiting with some other women. They sat around a pot of tea. Anna wiped her feet on a brush mat at the entrance. The door looked as though it had been hand-carved.

"I still feel it was Chiun," said Remo.

"That's what makes the whole situation so dangerous. And yet you might be the first who has come out of this. You understand it wasn't Chiun?"

"I have to tell myself that," said Remo.

The two were invited in and now Anna said:

"Hi, Mama." But Remo didn't understand it. It was in Russian.

"Remo, I'd like you to meet my mother," said Anna.

"You've threatened one or two of those women," said Remo. "I doubt your mother is here."

"She's visiting," said Anna.

"Don't you remember what we were here for?"

"Well, maybe my mother can help," said Anna.

"Ask your mother or mothers if any of them speak English."

Anna spoke in Russian again and three women nodded.

"Look," said Remo. "There's a big danger to the world, and one of your boys is causing it."

"Vassily," said one woman, round-faced as the rest. "What has he done now?" she said in English.

"He's gone to America, and he's taking it over," said Remo. "He's already started one war."

"What does he want with a war?"

"I dunno. He wanted a war. Anna understands him better. She's all right. She's Russian. She wants to help."

"There are Russians and Russians," said all the women. "What kind of Russian?"

Remo shrugged.

"Is she from the government?"

"She thinks they're all idiots," said Remo.

"Did you see where my mother went?" asked Anna in English.

"She was never here," said Remo.

"Now I know how powerful this thing is," said Anna. "She was more real than my own mother."

"So you think the government is run by idiots," said one of the women.

"They're men, aren't they? Look. We have a real problem going on here. Vassily Rabinowitz, who went to the parapsychology village, has gone on to make lots of trouble. America and Russia are about to go to war. I don't know what the idiots are going to do in Moscow but I suspect now that there is going to be another arms buildup or something even more useless. And in America, Vassily is in the process now of taking it over."

"That's Vassily's problem. We never get harmed by wars," said Vassily's mother.

"You will by this one. You can't convince an atomic weapon you are close relatives or teachers," said Anna.

"You mean those bombs that blow up countries?" asked another woman.

"The very kind," said Anna.

"Vassily was always a troublemaker," said his mother.

"Not meaning to be insulting, Mrs. Rabinowitz, Vassily was everyone's problem."

"That's why he left," said another woman.

"He was different," said another.

"Maybe you could tell me something about these powers," said Anna. "I suspected everyone had them when there were no histories of battles around here. Every patrol must have thought they had stumbled onto their home towns."

"Something like that," said one of the women.

"And when I saw the asphalt road coming in here I assumed the commissar for the district thought he had relatives here as well as the production leaders."

"Something like that," said another woman.

"Everyone in this village has these powers, don't they?" said Anna.

"Something like that," said another woman.

"I guess it's a natural survival attribute of Dulsk," said Anna.

"Nothing like that," said one of the women.

"It's a miracle," said another.

"It's a blessing. It's kept us all safe, and if Vassily hadn't left, we'd still all be safe."

"What I meant was that this miracle is a natural phenomenon of the people of this village. As you know, certain species have survival attributes which enable them to be around longer than these species that don't. Apparently you—"

"Shut up with your scientific nonsense, pretty little girl.

What we have here is a miracle. A downright genuine miracle.''

"A wonderful miracle. But if you're a communist you wouldn't understand it.''

"I am willing to listen," said Anna. They poured her a cup of tea, and several of the women insisted she eat something because she could use some meat on her bones. Didn't Remo think so? Remo didn't think so. Remo was too skinny too, they said.

Anna ate the delicious ginger cookies while Remo sipped water. They were the first outsiders to hear the story of the miracle of Dulsk.

In the twelfth century there were many wars around Dulsk, and sometimes holy men started them and other times holy men were victims of them.

But it came to pass that one especially battered holy man made it to their village in very bad shape. His head was bleeding, his eyes were puffed closed, and both his arms were severely broken.

The villagers could not tell if he were a Ruthenian-rite Catholic, a Russian Orthodox Christian, a Muslim, or a Jew. His mouth was so battered that he could barely speak. But they knew he was a holy man because he mumbled prayers constantly.

As he recovered he realized that the villagers did not know of which faith he was. Which group would the holy man favor? All of them had taken good care of him.

Now, in Russia, special holy men all had special powers. Some could see in the dark. Others, like Rasputin, could heal the sick. Some could be in two places at once. And yet others could make objects fly from a distance.

And he most certainly was a holy man.

Which group would he be with? Each wanted him because these holy men could bestow special blessings. And each knew there would be many blessings for those who rescued a holy man.

When his mouth healed and he could speak, he refused to do so, because some people could tell a man's sect by his voice. He chose instead to write on paper. And what he wrote would change Dulsk forever.

"There is something beautiful in all of you. Look at how well you treat me, each of you thinking I am one of your own. I see for all of you arising out of my misfortune an even greater blessing. From this day forth, everyone who looks upon you will see the one closest to his heart. No one will come here but he will be of your group, or kind, because he will be like me, of your family."

The women repeated the note word for word.

"And so by our good deed, we were all blessed by this holy man and we never had any trouble until my son, thinking he could show off, went to that parapsychology village."

"They didn't think that there were others like Vassily where he came from, did they?"

"Oh, someone came, but his mother told him to leave the village alone," said one of the women, grinning.

"Would one of you come with us, and tell Vassily to stop what he is doing? Because with us it's like speaking to a mother. No, worse, I used to be able to disagree with my mother," said Anna.

All the women shook their heads.

"Vassily never listened to anyone," said one of the women. His mother sadly nodded agreement.

"He was a problem child," said the mother. "What I did to deserve that, I don't know. What did I do? I ask myself. And do you know what I tell myself? I tell myself, 'Nothing.' I did nothing. He's your problem now."

"And if he starts a war?" asked Remo.

"It would be just like Vassily to start a war if he felt he was being picked on."

"I'm talking about a war that could destroy the world," said Remo.

"He'd do that," said his mother.

The other women nodded. "Just like Vassily."

"Is there anything you can give us to help us?" said Anna. "How can we get through his defenses?"

"There is nothing you can do to him. He is not the problem. It's what happens in your head, young lady. That's the problem. Your problem is all in the mind. Your mind."

"That doesn't make it less of a problem," said Remo.

"We don't have our minds," said Anna. "That is the problem."

An old man in a green KGB uniform ran up the path to the Rabinowitz door. He banged heavily on the hand-crafted wood.

"Ma. Ma," he screamed.

"Do you want me to get it, Mrs. Rabinowitz?" asked one of the women.

"Yes, thank you," said Mrs. Rabinowitz.

The youngest woman answered the door, and the KGB man, who was at least ten years her senior, said:

"Ma, Ma. They've got the village surrounded. Someone spotted a high official returning to Russia without going through channels. And she's got enemies. Her name is Anna Chutesov, and she's gorgeous. She's with a man. Who are they?"

"Your brother and sister. Help them," said the woman who answered the door.

"C'mon, sis. We gotta run," said the officer. And it was just like that. Instantaneous.

"I'm not worried about the Russians," said Remo. "I'm worried about what we do when we get back to America. I still feel my little father is around here."

"I feel the same way about my mother," said Anna.

"Sis, will you hurry up? I can get you through the cordon but you have to move quickly."

Remo and Chiun thanked the ladies. It was a peaceful town, this Dulsk, and perhaps it was because of those powers that the people could be peaceful to themselves. Anna still thought it was heredity.

"Totally logical that it was an inherited characteristic of the people," said Anna. "And they made up a holy-man tale to explain it to themselves. That's how religions get going.''

''You communists will do anything to explain away a miracle.''

''And how do you explain it, Remo?''

''I don't,'' said Remo.

At the cordon, the Russian officer had to be restrained from explaining Remo and Anna were his sister and brother, because the others would not believe what he said.

''But, sis, you've dated a couple of the guys. They'll let you through.''

''You go up there and tell them that,'' said Remo. And when he was gone, Remo told Anna that there would be a time in a very short moment when she could drive right through the roadblock.

''All you have to do is wait for that time. I'm going up ahead.''

''What are you going to do?''

''A Sinanju miracle,'' said Remo.

''But there are no miracles in Sinanju. You're an accumulation of body techniques over millennia.''

''I wouldn't bet on that. I punched the belly of a dead man and found the center of a laughing universe,'' said Remo. ''I don't know we're not a miracle.''

''You're saying that to bother me, Remo.''

Remo smiled and leaned back into the car, kissing Anna long and softly, his body close to hers.

''That bothers me, too,'' she said. Remo didn't say anything but he was feeling it work both ways now.

At the guard post it became apparent that Remo was not the brother of the officer even though the officer swore it. Remo fit the description of the man with Anna Chutesov, a high party official who had reentered the country without clearance.

Remo was told to put his hands in the air and walk slowly back to the car with the guards. There, they would take Comrade Chutesov back to Moscow.

Remo lifted his arms. Unfortunately he had two throats

in his hands as he did so. This rapid movement broke vertebrae. A kick into a sternum transformed the heart muscle into goulash. The officer who thought Remo was his brother told him they both would never get away with it. Remo told him not to worry.

"Even though you're my brother, I'm going to have to take you in after this," said the officer, reaching for his gun. But he shook his head instead. "I can't do it. I can't do it. I could never do this to you. And what's so strange, I never liked you. In fact I used to arrest you all the time."

Remo waved for Anna to bring up the car.

"That was amazing. I never even saw your hands move," she said.

"What are you happy about? I've got to face the man who taught me," said Remo. "No one's better than him."

She could sense his eyes on her, and her body almost tore itself away from her will to throw itself at his feet. Thousands of men, perhaps millions of men, had loved her from afar, had seen her on the screen. She got hundreds of flattering letters a week from men and women, begging to be near her cool beauty. And never before had she responded.

But just minutes ago she had met a man at the most important party in New York. He was short with sad brown eyes, and spoke with a Russian accent that could stop your breathing if the onions he had just eaten didn't do it to you first. Everyone was saying he was the most important man in America. And no one knew why. He knew everything about everyone. Actress Berell Neek had been told not to cross him. Cross anyone in the room but him.

Berell had that perpetually sensitive face that was always playing sensitive roles. Directors gave her plenty of screen time to be silent with her warm sensitive eyes and her full sensitive lips, and sometimes they would have wind blow through her soft blond sensitive hair.

But Berell Neek had the soul of a calculator. She had been in front of audiences since she was five, and the only spontaneous orgasms she had in her life came during dreams about being raped by gold Oscars while reviewers tauntingly screamed how great an actress she was. Men held no appeal for her. Women held no appeal for her. Even fans held no real appeal for her. She preferred to be worshiped loudly, but from afar.

The only food for her soul was applause. And so when she met the man smelling of onions downstairs at the party, she endured his gross mannerisms, his onion smell, his too loud laugh, because he was important. She had decided to give him a whole fifteen seconds of her sensitive, nodding approval, then move her sensitive, caring face and body off toward other important people. She had never seen so many in one place before as at this party. It had truly lived up to its name. It was The Party. Not just the party of the year, or the party of the decade, but The Party.

Everyone who was anyone was here, and those who were not here would forever feel some shame if they thought themselves of any significance. All the cabinet members had attended, and the President was supposed to arrive later. The five biggest producers in Hollywood were here as well as a half-dozen scientists Neek had recognized, and if she recognized a scientist he had to be colossally important because she knew so few of them, even though her sensitive picture had appeared in scientific magazines.

She even recognized major industrialists. And they had to be major for her to recognize them, although Berell Neek's sensitive beautiful face had appeared in many business magazines.

Everyone talked of power, of a man who could do anything, knew everything. She had heard stories about this man who could tell if you cheated on your tax return fifteen years ago and what the soil was like on your Darien, Connecticut, estate. He knew everyone there was to know, and everything about them there was to know. And so the party was more than just electric. It was thunderous.

Like a storm, it fed on itself. The more important people

saw other important people, the more they felt their power and the power of others.

There were comments about the invitations too.

"I got mine at my winter hideaway which no one but me and my wife knew about and she died five years ago," said the inventor of a new generation of computer technology.

"I got mine on my own computer terminal that no one could get into," said another.

"I got mine from my banker, who said I had better go," said a Hollywood producer.

This party was for the powerful and by the powerful, thrown by someone who might be more powerful than all of them combined. The noise was incredible as people who could make decisions by themselves met others of the same stripe, and almost by the sheer impact of their ability to get things done by colliding in this room, began to change the world they lived in on their own.

It was in this exhilarating atmosphere that Berell Neek tried to get away from an onion-smelling sad-eyed man with a Russian accent, even though she knew he had thrown the party.

But at that moment, she couldn't get enough of him. She wanted him more than William Shakespeare telling her she was the greatest actress of all time (one of her most erotic dreams). She wanted him more than a Broadway smash in which applause for her lasted over ten minutes. She wanted him more than all the Oscars lined up end to end, even more than the three she kept in her bathrooms, kept there of course to be used in interesting ways.

And so she left with him for a private room upstairs where, slowly and tantalizingly, she unbuttoned her blouse and revealed her bosom, never shown on the screen because that would have ruined her sensitive image, when in fact she would have posed nude mounting a giraffe with an umbilical cord in her teeth if it would have furthered her career. As she exposed these wonderful breasts, Berell Neek was barely able to keep from leaping on the magnificent Vassily Rabinowitz. Even his onion breath was sexy.

"Get with it. I don't have all day, already," he said. And the passion of his voice sent rapturous vibrations through Berell's quivering body.

"You're going insane with lust for me," said Vassily as he felt her perfect body on his. "Hurry up," he said, while watching her smooth pink flanks work against him. "Whoopsa daisy. That's it," he said on his quick completion. "Okay, get off, and tell the world, especially that good-looking redhead downstairs, about the best sexual experience of your life."

"It was magnificent," gasped Berell Neek.

"You're going to kiss and tell about this all over Hollywood. Get my phone number from my assistant, Smith, and give him any details about anything or anyone he wants to know. He's the morose gaunt one."

"Everyone is morose and gaunt after you, darling." Berell Neek wept the first real tears she could remember. It had been such a strong experience, she could not stop her crying.

"And zip," said Vassily, picking up a magazine as he lay on the soft couch underneath the soft lights of brass and gold lamps.

"What?" she asked.

"Fly," said Vassily. "You unzipped while getting on. Now you're off. Zip back up."

"Oh, yes, dear. Yes, dear. Yes," she said, kissing him even as she delicately, and with the sensitivity only Berell Neek could show, pulled the metal zipper over his magnificent love organ.

"Don't make a production of it, already. It's a zipper. Zip it and get out."

Vassily Rabinowitz sighed as she left. He was really alone. At last he was alone. No one would dare come up to him, the man who had drawn the most powerful people of America to his Fifth Avenue duplex. The President would arrive soon and then he would control the presidency as well, doing whatever he wanted.

And so he would control America. Then what? Maybe

he would go for Russia too. Have a big summit meeting and get them in line also. And then what? China? He didn't want China. The truth was, the world was beginning to be boring.

Vassily Rabinowitz had discovered what the Romans found when they had conquered the world and organized it. What every businessman felt after he achieved a goal he had set for a lifetime, Vassily now felt.

Everything he wanted was his whenever he wanted it, and the human animal, designed to struggle for its existence, and now without that struggle, began to malfunction in massive gloom. He understood now why people stayed in Dulsk and warned him never to leave.

"You'll be unhappy, Vassily. None of us is ever happy outside. Here we work. We have to work. And it's good. We have peace, and we have winter, which is hard. But we have spring, which is sweet. And as the holy man said, a spring without winter lacks taste and joy, but is just the weary weather of our souls."

Vassily remembered these sayings from Dulsk, and understood now why it was important to have a woman able to say no, to make the yes worthwhile. He understood it was important to have someone actually be your friend instead of being tricked into friendship. He understood the importance of hard work to make play fun. He understood now, he thought, even the meaning of death, to make life so precious.

And so in his own pain, he understood that to make his days even bearable now, he would have to bring the world to the brink of destruction because then he might be destroyed also, and stepping toward this edge was the last excitement the world allowed a man who could instantly hypnotize anyone.

At first he only wanted to be left alone, but that was when he left Russia. Now he wanted excitement. And a nuclear war would actually do that. It was perhaps the last thing that would do that.

He called in Smith. He liked the man's mind, what was

left of it. Smith came in with his hair neatly combed, smiling as though he were back in Putney Day School.

Rabinowitz liked the way this genius who could get to the insides of every organization would often raise his hand for permission to go to the bathroom.

"Smith, I'd like a nuclear war. What do you think?"

"It would destroy everything, Miss Ashford. Do you really want that, ma'am?"

"No. Not destruction of everything. But how could we risk destruction of everything? You know. How many missiles would have to be fired in order to risk starting a nuclear war? Is it one nuclear warhead? Three? Fifteen? Ten fired at Moscow, what?"

"Could it be none of the above?" asked Smith.

"Might."

"I would say three would be a real risk, and two would be a minor risk. Everyone knows that one would not do it, although almost everyone who isn't aware of nuclear strategy thinks one would do it."

"Yes, one is a warning."

"No. One is an accident. Two is a warning."

"And I always thought one was a warning."

"No, Miss Ashford. I would estimate two was a warning. One could be an accident, and in a secret agreement made years ago between the Russian premier and an American president, each gave the other to understand that they were not going to go to nuclear war over a possible accident. I believe the Russian said: 'We're not going to destroy the Communist party for a few hundred thousand deaths.'"

"And the American president?"

"He said that while the loss of an American city would mean a staggering loss to America, he probably could explain it away to a nation numbed by fear, that it was an accident."

"Funny, I always thought that one would at least be a message," said Vassily, remembering what he had tried in Omaha. Now he saw he would have needed at least two.

"But three, aimed directly at nuclear installations, would be more than a message. It would be war."

"But what about three unimportant cities?" asked Vassily.

"That I would estimate would be the gray area of nuclear war."

"I'd like to use the submarines."

"We have an admiral here tonight, Miss Ashford, but as you know, firing America's missiles is not an easy thing. There are safeguards upon safeguards."

"Well, Harold, work it out," said Vassily.

"Can I go to the bathroom first?" was Harold W. Smith's last question before he set the enormous network of CURE to subverting the nuclear safeguards of his nation.

It was perhaps one of the great hotwires of all time that Smith performed that evening. He first tickled out the defenses at the Strategic Air Command, and at the Naval Nuclear Strike Force.

The tickling was really seeing the defenses come into action, those passwords around the country that had to be sent in order to arm the nuclear arsenal. As a backup there had to be people physically placing keys into triggers, but Harold Smith, always an ingenious boy as well as a good boy, figured out that these keys used the same electronic codes. In other words, the physical backups were ordered by another set of electronics.

Everywhere Smith's computer encountered a code word, it marked a block. The organized mind, which Smith acutely had, understood that the way to solve a problem was not to batter one's head at an obstacle. An obstacle was just that. An obstacle. So when he came to a password defense he labeled it and moved on. Within twenty-five minutes he had a network of obstacles laid before him on his computer screen, but they also told him exactly how America's nuclear defense system could be used.

There were always two codes, each requiring the other to kick on with a yes before it went further. And they followed two distinct paths, as clear as telephone poles. Two parallel poles that were required to work in unison or the missiles would not be fired. They were the President and the military. Both had to agree along their lines of command or there would be no launch.

There had to be one high-ranking officer on one line to start the command and the President on the other. All Smith had to do was break the top password along both these lines and the rest of the orders would follow like a switch on a lamp. Bingo. He was going to light up the world.

The news was so good, he had to run to tell Miss Ashford. He almost skipped into her office.

"Harold," he heard her say. "Don't be ashamed to boast. Boasting is fine. Lets me know what I have. I think you've done good work. But we don't have to break any code at all. We have the admiral we need right here, at the party, and the President is arriving soon."

Vassily waved the happy old man out of the room with the one reward Smith had asked for.

"Sure I'll give you an A. I'll give you an A-plus. But only when the first three bombs drop. Hey, can you change one of those targets to be outside Russia? Maybe we can do Paris. Nice cloud over the Eiffel Tower and everything. Make sure you don't come anywhere near Dulsk. Not within a hundred miles. And send in the admiral for a little talk."

The talk lasted less than fifty-two seconds, whereupon he got the password from an admiral who would not even tell it to his father but would tell it to his subordinate when he believed a nuclear war had started.

Vassily removed that idea from the admiral before sending him down to the party, and then sent the first code word for what Smith had called first parallel path.

"All we need now is the President's code word to launch," came back Smith's voice over the line to his computer room in the Fifth Avenue duplex that combined two entire floors of a building. It was down the street from where Vassily had started his weight-loss/quit-smoking/improve-your-sex-life clinic.

"In a few minutes," said Vassily.

"I wonder if I might go to the bathroom again," came the voice of his computer operator.

"You've been," said Vassily, reminding himself that just because he was the most powerful man in the world didn't mean he should be the easiest to get along with. He was going to reduce the old man to one BM a day and that was it.

He walked to the large picture window. He could feel the vibrations from the dancing below. It was a very loud party, but there wasn't a neighbor important enough to complain. He looked out over Central Park. All of this might be a nuclear cinder before morning. Risk. It was a wonderful stimulant.

It made life livable. Down on Fifth Avenue he saw the motorcycle policemen lead the long dark limousine. It was the President of the United States. He wondered if he could spit down from the window and hit him. But he knew too many Secret Servicemen might panic and he could be dead. They were all over the place protecting the President, but Vassily knew they were no match for him. He had the best protection in the world.

A man moved through the Secret Servicemen like a ballet dancer through a subway crowd. They couldn't stop him. He got to the President. He pointed up toward the party. The President looked up. The man looked up. It was Vassily's only friend he met in America, Remo, the one who saved him from the Russian commandos.

The President nodded. The President turned back to his car, almost pushing his beautiful wife ahead of him. The motorcade sped off with sirens blaring, and the other password was going with him.

"Chiun. Chiun," called Vassily. "Get up here."

Chiun was there so silently and so quickly, Vassily could have sworn he had been waiting all along.

"Get me the President. I want him here now. He's running away."

"Are we finally going to make Smith president, O Great Wang?"

"Just get him, and if you see Remo again, kill him. He's got to be killed. You must kill him. He's in my way. He has pushed friendship too far."

But something strange happened. The old Oriental with the great powers began to tremble, the beginning of the word "No" was coming out of his mouth, wrestled by his own mind back into his throat, and the very energy coming from the body began to vibrate the plaster off the ceiling.

"All right, all right already," yelled Vassily. "He's not Remo, but your worst enemy wanting to do battle. Is that easier? Do I have to go back to the stuff I used on you back at Sornica? All right, I've done it. I'm Mr. Easy. The guy who looks and acts like Remo is your archenemy. Now kill him in peace. Or he'll kill you. But on one condition, the same I gave you at Sornica."

Chiun listened and felt a relief of such sweetness as he had never felt before in his life. He did not know why he was relieved, but the world was now good again, devoid of the awful conflict that had racked his soul.

"Bring your great enemy before me and let me see a fight between you two. The kind of fight I would have seen if he didn't run from you back in Sornica. Okay? That kind of a fight. Could you give me that?"

"Great Wang, it shall be a fight to glorify you and Sinanju. It shall—"

"All right already," said the Great Wang, in the person of Vassily Rabinowitz. "Can we have it here right after you get the President?"

But the fight was not to be in the living room of the Great Wang on Fifth Avenue. In the elevator of the building, coming in as Chiun was going out, was his worst enemy.

He looked like Remo. He spoke like Remo, and that made it all the more onerous. Chiun felt a deadly hiss emerge from his throat. His entire body assumed its most acute form of power, as he had been trained since childhood. Total energy. Total concentration as the hands made wide circling arcs in the death challenge.

Anna Chutesov screamed and tried to press herself into the walls of the elevator. The light bulbs above them shattered from the force of a human being coming into its total power.

"Little father. Don't fight me. Don't fight me. I'm Remo," said Remo, even though he was not sure whether he was facing Chiun or Vassily Rabinowitz. Anna had warned him about that and he had practiced in his mind, going up against Chiun despite his own will. This was what he had to do. His mind had to conquer itself. It was like turning one's own intestines inside out.

And it was not working. Remo could not lift his hand against this man.

And then he knew his body would do it for him. The stroke was coming from Chiun. That perfect stroke of pure cleanliness made more powerful by its purity. He knew it and his little father knew it, as his little father had taught it so long ago, so often, over and over from those first days right after the breath training.

The stroke that Remo did not even think about making because it was more a part of him now than his most intimate ideas.

And the horrible thing about that stroke was never before in all his years had Remo in the training sessions been able to stop it. Chiun, by his own volition, had stopped himself. But this stroke was not going to stop until Remo was crushed by it, the one stroke made perfect by a lifetime of devotion. His body moved in what was the defense, trained into him over and over, and never before able to stop that blow. And the stroke went by him, deflected by the proper acceptance of it, fast enough and strong enough for the first time in Remo's life.

Remo had done it. He had transcended Chiun for the first time, and even as he drove into his beloved teacher's body with a stroke to destabilize but not harm Chiun, Remo understood why. It was the Great Wang's visit.

When Wang visited Remo it was at Remo's transition to his ultimate.

"You are at your peak," Wang had said.

When Wang had visited Chiun, Chiun was at his peak. And it was the law of the universe that that which was at its most powerful was beginning its decline. All these years Chiun had been declining, and now Remo had made that transformation to stand above him.

There was both sadness and relief as Remo laid the great Chiun, now stunned, in the corner of the elevator.

The lights came back on.

"What happened? The lights blinked off and now they're on. What happened to Chiun?" asked Anna.

"The greatest fight of my life," said Remo.

"But it happened so quickly. It was an instant," said Anna.

"What do you want, fifteen rounds of people punching at each other's bodies in padded gloves?"

"I wish I could have seen some of it, at least," said Anna.

"You wouldn't have been able to, even if the lights were on. Too fast for your eyes. But even if I slowed it down, you wouldn't know what was happening."

"That is Chiun," she said. "Unfortunately you have met the Chiun who is not the most Chiun. He's waiting for us somewhere in this building under the name of Vassily Rabinowitz. Good luck, Remo."

"Thanks, and when Chiun gathers himself together again, don't tell him he lost a fight, all right?"

"He'll remember, won't he?"

"I don't know what he'll remember," said Remo, and he took the elevator up to the floor where the big party was going on, and asked around for Vassily Rabinowitz.

Everyone knew Vassily. He was either a great guy or a person one should know. It was a room filled with people impressed by their own importance. The very fact of being with each other seemed to make these people turn on to themselves.

There were bankers and publishers and owners of networks. There were surgeons and scientists, and industrialists and politicians. There was the presidential cabinet. All the power brokers in America were here, and there was the only one person Remo cared much about and he was unconscious in an elevator. And another he cared about somewhat and that one's brains were fried. And the man who did it could do it to Remo.

Everyone knew Vassily but no one knew where he was. A television anchorwoman turned her charm on Remo. Remo turned it back to her.

"You don't have to be rude," she said.

"Yes I do," said Remo.

"Do you know who I am?"

"Another jerk in a roomful of jerks," said Remo. Suddenly in the vast length of the floor, there was silence. Someone had called this august assembly of personages "jerks."

A titter of laughter played through the crowd. Most of the important people dared not laugh lest someone think they were threatened.

"Jerks?" asked the anchorwoman. And she laughed quite loudly.

"Yeah. None of you or anything you do will be remembered a thousand years from now. Even your children, if they're twice as important as you are, won't be remembered. So who are you?"

"It's not a thousand years from now that matters, but now," said the woman.

"Now you always have," said Remo, and someone said that because he wore jeans and a T-shirt, he probably was never invited at all, and several of the many bodyguards were invited to throw Remo out, to loud applause.

They joined the art on the walls, some of them sticking, some of them not.

"Rabinowitz," bellowed Remo. "I want you. And I want you now."

The room was quiet. A door opened. The crowd parted.

A little man with sad eyes walked in quite confidently. Remo went for his head, but this time he did not harm Chiun. Chiun was more frail than he should have been. More worthy of love than usual.

"Are you all right, little father?" said Remo.

"Yes. But I'm your friend Vassily Rabinowitz and you do whatever I say."

"Good, Vassily. I'm glad to see you again. For a moment I thought you were Chiun."

"You're going to kill Chiun. He's no good."

Remo was nodding yes, when he thought of Chiun. All the being that was his said kill Chiun. Everything said kill Chiun. All breathing said kill Chiun. He would kill Chiun, except there was a thing coming up in his throat, and it was something far off in the cosmos that he was a part of. It required the answer "No." And the answer "No" came out of his mouth. No was the answer to that.

"I've got to have your total loyalty. You cannot resist. There is nothing left in you to resist," came the words, and even Remo's blood cried out: Kill Chiun.

Remo threw himself onto the floor and fought his blood. He fought his blood and his being and his knowledge and everything he felt and saw and understood. His hands and his heart would not lift against his little father, Master of Sinanju. If they reached for Chiun, Remo would crush them. If his legs carried him to Chiun, Remo would break them, and far off in a place without light, but of all light, Remo heard the word he needed to hear. It was the great answer to the greatest of all questions.

And the answer was "Yes." The Hebrews heard it in the words of Mount Sinai which said: "I Am Who Is."

And the Christians heard it on the third day, when the answer for all eternity was a yes to life.

"Yes," was the answer to all that was. All that was good was yes. All being was the great yes of the universe.

And Remo saw the Great Wang laughing at him, and in the cleanest strokes of the history of Sinanju, Remo did as his little father taught him, bringing the blow from the very breathing itself, and severed the head of the Great Wang laughing at him.

When Vassily Rabinowitz' head rolled on the ballroom floor people screamed in horror. Remo's eyes cleared. His body ached where he had hurled it down, shattering parquet flooring into splinters.

He had performed a perfect blow. There was not a drop of blood on his hand. It had been in and out of Rabinowitz' vertebrae at the precise speed to sever with both heat and force. In fact, it was only now that the heart muscle of the headless corpse on the floor finished its last pumping action, creating a dark red pool where the head containing the sad brown eyes had been.

"Who are you?" asked a stunned broadcaster.

Remo didn't answer questions. He went upstairs and following wire circuitry to its source found Smith behind a computer terminal.

Smith was tired and confused.

"Remo. Where are we?"

"Fifth Avenue. Rabinowitz' duplex."

"Strange. Last thing I remember is preparing to kill him. What's this on the computer screen?" Smith shook his head. "Oh no. Have they gone off yet?"

"Have what gone off?" asked Remo.

"You would have known if they did. I hot-wired our whole nuclear-defense establishment. Has the President been here?"

"No. I turned him back," said Remo.

"Good. I see. Yes. Right. Let me close this down before we all go up. Where's Rabinowitz?"

"Part of him is in the ballroom and another part, I think, has rolled into another room. I'm not sure."

"Thank you. We needed you and you did your job. You can go now, Remo."

"Here's as good as anywhere," said Remo. "I'm an American. I believe in this country."

"You mean you've veered away from Sinanju philosophy?"

"No. It is Sinanju philosophy. Here is good. I'm here. Yes. I'll stay."

"Did Rabinowitz find out about CURE?"

"You not only told him about it, you put it at his service."

Smith groaned. "Anyone else?" he asked.

"There's a Russian lady who knows."

"She's got to go."

"I think she's a good person."

"I'm not judging anyone. I'm trying to save the country."

"I don't think there'll be any harm to her knowing. Talk to her."

"Is she good-looking?"

"She's stunning, Smitty."

"I thought so," said Smith suspiciously.

"She's got brains."

"Even more reason to terminate her."

"Talk to her."

Anna Chutesov was still cradling Chiun's head in her hands when Remo helped them both out of the elevator, carrying Chiun in his arms.

He hated himself for the blow he had delivered to Chiun, and yet if he had not, he would have been in pieces like Rabinowitz.

"Remo says I should talk to you," said Smith to Anna. "I'm afraid you understand why we must terminate you. You know about us."

"Typical stupid male response. If you don't know what to do, kill. Gorilla."

"We can't be compromised," said Smith.

"Why would I want to compromise you?"

"To take over our country. Weaken America."

"Why on earth would I want to do that? Do you think we don't have enough troubles in Russia? Do you think we need two countries to mismanage instead of one?"

"That hasn't stopped you from taking Eastern Europe and trying to do the same thing in Afghanistan," said Smith.

"Men. We are lucky to have you as an enemy. Now we have someone to wage some kinds of war against. Do you know why we fight wars? Because that's what we've always done. Do you know why we have yet to build successful socialism?"

Smith shook his head.

"Because no one has done it. And I'll tell you what you have done, jerk. In defeating us so handily in Sornica, you now have all our idiot generals planning revenge just like after the Cuban missile crisis. Little boys' egos are now at work, bankrupting my country and endangering yours. If you wish to kill me, go ahead. I can't stop you. It's what morons do. You can kill someone, so go ahead and do it."

"But how can we be sure we will not be compromised?"

"Because I may want to call on you someday, jerk, and you may want to call on me. There, you have it. An ally for peace or a corpse. Take your choice. Since you are a man, I assume I am dead."

"No one has ever called me a moron," said Smith.

"I bet Miss Ashford did," said Anna.

"How do you know about her?" asked Smith.

"You were taking her orders down in Sornica."

Smith sighed.

"All right. We'll take a chance."

"No choice anyway, Smitty. I'm not doing it," said Remo. "And neither will Chiun. You want to kill Anna, you'll have to figure out a way yourself, and probably over my dead body. Which means you won't."

Remo smiled at Anna.

"I'm thinking of giving you a crack at more than a wrist," he said.

"If you didn't come to me, I think I'd start an atomic war to get you," said Anna. Her voice was soft and low.

"Really?" said Remo, and Anna threw back her head and laughed.

"Only a man would believe something so stupid," she said, blowing him a kiss. "What egos you all have. It's a wonder we haven't been blown up yet."

Remo took Chiun out into the fresh air of Central Park beneath the late Vassily Rabinowitz' apartment. The lights of the city glowed around them. Remo worked Chiun's spine to get the nervous system working toward healing itself.

"Where am I?" asked Chiun.

"Just came out of hypnotism. You locked eyes with the late Vassily Rabinowitz."

"Did I do anything embarrassing?" asked Chiun, rubbing his chest where Remo had stopped his blow from going further.

"No. Never, little father," said Remo.

"Did someone land a blow on me?" asked Chiun, horrified.

"No, little father. No one could do that," said Remo.

"Then how did I get this contusion?" asked Chiun.

"I think Vassily hypnotized you into fighting yourself, little father."

"Really?" asked Chiun. "And who won?"

"You, of course, little father. No one can beat you," said Remo, and he felt in the night all around them the great yes of the universe. It was love.

ABOUT THE AUTHORS

WARREN MURPHY has written eighty books in the last twelve years. His *Trace* series novel, *Pigs Get Fat*, received the 1985 Edgar Allan Poe award from The Mystery Writers of America. *Grandmaster*, co-written with his wife Molly Cochran, won the 1984 Edgar Award. He is a native and resident of New Jersey.

RICHARD SAPIR is a novelist with several major book club selections. He is a graduate of Columbia University and lives with his wife in New Hampshire.